FROM THE DIARY OF CONRAD STARGARD

vvvvvvvvvvvvvvvvvvvvvvvvvvvvvvv

I tried to get back to what I was doing, but other things were nagging me. I sent a message to Francine: MY DEAR WIFE, IF YOU DO NOT WISH TO JOIN ME AT THREE WALLS, WHAT WOULD YOU THINK OF BEING MY REPRESENTATIVE AT CIESZYN? CONRAD.

Francine answered back within the hour: MY DEAR HUSBAND, YOU ROB ME OF THE CROWN OF POLAND, AND NOW YOU WANT TO STUFF ME INTO A BACKWATER PLACE LIKE CIESZYN? MAY YOUR DEAR SOUL ROT IN HELL! FRANCINE.

I deduced by this that she was still unhappy.

By Leo Frankowski
Published by Ballantine Books

THE ADVENTURES OF CONRAD STARGARD

COPERNICK'S REBELLION

LORD CONRAD'S LADY

Book Five in the Adventures of

Conrad Stargard

Leo Frankowski

A Del Rey Book

BALLANTINE BOOKS ● NEW YORK

I would like to thank Phil Jennings, Tomasz Kamuzela, Bill Gillmore, and Debra S. Haberland for their kind help in proofreading this book and for their many valuable suggestions for improving it.

However, any overt sexism and male chauvinism noticed in this work is totally the fault of Bill Gillmore, and all complaints should be directed to him at the Dawn Treader Bookshop of Ann Arbor, Mich.

—Leo A. Frankowski

A Del Rey Book
Published by Ballantine Books

Library of Congress Catalog Card Number: 90-93037

ISBN 0-345-36849-5

Manufactured in the United States of America

First Edition: September 1990

Cover Art by Barclay Shaw

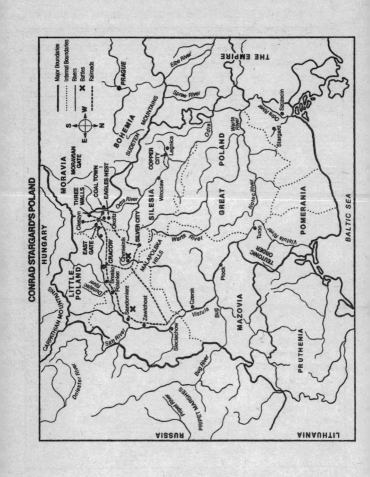

CONRAD STARGARD'S POLAND

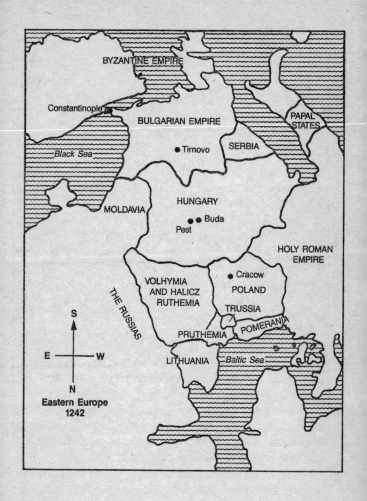

Eastern Europe
1242

PROLOGUE

ON THE lush African plain, at two and a half million years B.C., two small brown individuals were sitting naked on a small hill. To all outward appearances they were a pair of type twenty-seven proto-humans.

"There's blood on your leg," he said.

"I'm menstruating. The antifertility vaccine is wearing off. It's been a hundred and eighty years, and the shot was only supposed to last a century."

"Yeah. My shots are wearing out, too. My eyesight is going bad, and my joints hurt a lot in the mornings."

"We're getting old," she said. "Just like people used to grow old before technology."

"They'll never find us, you know. If they were looking, they would have been here by now."

"What did we ever do to deserve this?" she said.

"*I* didn't do anything. *You* dumped the boss's cousin into the thirteenth century when the guy didn't even know about time travel."

"Shut up! I don't want to talk about it again."

"Well, there's something we ought to talk about. We're getting old. Before too many more years, we won't be able to take care of ourselves anymore. If we stay with the protos, they'll treat us the same way they treat their own parents when they get too old to be useful. They'll just abandon us," he said.

"So?"

"So we have to do something about it! We have to make sure that there's somebody around to take care of us when we get really old. See, my antifertility shots have worn off, too. For the next few years you can still have children, and I'm still fit enough to take care of you and them. If we raise them right, they'll take care of us when it really gets bad."

"You're such an asshole. Do you think I'd have children and raise them to live in this environment? To be savages two million years before any other real people exist? No way."

"Will you say that when you are starving to death because you have no teeth to chew your food with? By then it'll be too late to do anything about it!"

"You're also a damn coward," she said.

Chapter One

▽▽▽▽▽▽▽▽▽▽▽▽▽▽

FROM THE JOURNAL OF COUNTESS FRANCINE

Everyone seems to be keeping diaries now, and I suppose I should do so, too, though mine will be written in French so that the maids can't read it. Perhaps writing will help me take my mind off the horror of my situation.

I sit here in my husband Conrad's city of Three Walls on the tenth of March, 1241, looking out from a tower window on the area that he calls his killing field. He named it thus because it was used yearly as a place to slaughter the surplus wild animals on his extensive lands here in southern Poland. It is a part of what he calls his game management program.

The field still earns its name, though in a far more gruesome way, for the beasts now concentrated on the field below are an *entire horde of besieging Mongols*!

My husband trained all his men into a mighty army and took them to the east to defend the land against the Tartar invaders. In so doing, he left the defense of his cities to the women, and we are less sure of our abilities than we pretend to be. Why he left our strong walls to fight hundreds of miles away is a matter of dispute among us. For mine own part, I think that if he wanted to find Mongols, he could have saved himself the trip.

We wait here, not knowing if our loves are alive and not knowing how long we ourselves may yet live.

My reader, if any there might chance to be, will therefore forgive me if I write on more pleasant times in more civilized places.

My childhood was a pleasant one, for my grandfather was a bishop, and to be a bishop in France means to be wealthy and powerful. This was all the more true because his diocese was centered on the wealthy city of Troyes, and it stands astride the major trade routes between Flanders, where the cloth is made, and Italy, where the world's cloth is dyed and finished. Two great fairs were held there every year, and Grandfather got his share of it.

My mother was his only child, and since my father held the very high post of Grandfather's privy secretary, we lived in the palace as part of Grandfather's household.

Grandfather's palace was a vast and beautiful place, as full of color and statues as the great Cathedral of St.-Pierre, which stood just across from our courtyard. Our palace was much larger and far more sumptuous than the palace of the Count of Troyes, though of course the count had other palaces and castles in the countryside.

Suffice it to say that until I was nine years old, I had four servants, and my mother had twice that number. My days were spent in pleasant amusements and in learning from my tutors the arts of reading and writing and sewing.

We were very happy until two great tragedies struck us within a year. The first was that the Church declared that all members of the clergy must be celibate. They may not marry, and further, they had *never been* married! This meant that both my mother and I were illegitimate, for my father was also an ordained priest. This ruling was none of my grandfather's doing, and for a time he was able to protect us from this calamity.

Then, within the year, my wonderful old grandfather died of a plague. Since my mother was no longer born in wedlock and my father was but a priest who was living in sin, there was no inheritance for us. The new bishop had no desire to associate himself with the sinful life of his predecessor, so my father was turned out of his job, and we all were turned out of the palace. We had neither friends nor influence, for although my father was a learned man, his family was of no great means or prominence. For a long time we were at great strife to get enough food to eat.

At long last my father secured a position as a professor at the University of Paris, so we made the long, hard journey to that city. Being a mere university professor was of course a position far below his previous one of secretary, and we had to subsist on whatever the students felt like donating after they heard his lectures. Somehow, my mother was able to make a sort of home for us in our single rented room above a tavern and across the street from a brothel. I was able to continue my education by attending free of charge my father's lectures and those of his fellow professors, for they made this arrangement with each other. Thus we lived until my fourteenth year, for my father considered our location to be convenient for him. He taught classes in a room that the university rented above the brothel.

Then my dear father died, and our situation became dire indeed. Many told me that I had become a great beauty, and I was much noticed by the students and the young guildsmen of the city. Yet being poor and without a dowry, I got no offers, or at least no offers that a virtuous young woman could accept. Indeed, the most persistent of my followers was the owner of the brothel, and his proposal was for a position that I did not desire. Such a life is sinful, dirty, and short!

Then I met a young student who had recently taken Holy

Orders and would soon be returning to his native land of
Poland. He asked my mother for my hand, and at first she
turned him down, for a priest could not possibly marry. It
was this fact that had caused all our difficulties in the first
place! But he persisted and proved to her that the Gregorian
reforms that forbade the marriage of the clergy had not yet
been ratified in Poland and, further, that they were not
likely to be. Thus, my mother blessed our marriage as the
best that I could do without any dowry at all. The very day
of our small wedding, she left us to join a convent, being
tired of this world and its pain.

As the rent was not paid on my mother's old room, I
spent my wedding night with my new husband in his bunk
in a student dormitory. Nothing took place that night, but I
put this down to his shyness, considering that there were
other students in the same room. And truthfully, I was not
precisely sure at that tender age just what should have taken
place, anyway.

It was early spring, and we left the next morning to go to
Poland on foot, for my young husband was almost as poor
as I was. We traveled all spring and summer across France,
over the many Germanies, through Bohemia, and into Silesia, that westernmost of Polish duchies. We made the trip
barefoot for lack of the price of shoes, and indeed we were
often hungry, yet as I look back on it, we had a good time.
We were young, we were in love, and we were traveling
through a world that was forever new.

Yet our love was not physical in the carnal sense of the
word. John did not seem to want to talk of it, and I decided
that he did not want to burden us with a child until such time
as he could properly support it. This made his actions seem
pure and noble to me, and of course I did not press him
further.

At length, in the fall, we got to the city of Wroclaw and

reported to the bishop there at his palace. Compared to that of my grandfather, it was an inferior place, yet for two ragged and barefoot travelers, it seemed sumptuous indeed!

The Bishop of Wroclaw was a pompous old man, with a character far different from that of my beloved grandfather. He acted not at all pleased with his two new ragged guests. Indeed, we seemed to embarrass him. He gave us each a new set of cheap clothes and sent my husband on to a new post within days.

This was at the new town of Okoitz, which Count Lambert was then just starting to build. When we arrived, there was nothing but a clearing in the woods with a half-finished wooden wall and a few huts built against it. And in this we had to survive a cold Polish winter!

My husband still did not properly consummate our marriage, yet it seemed to me that to endure pregnancy and childbirth in those difficult conditions would be dangerous indeed and that poor John was again sacrificing his pleasure for my own welfare. I loved him all the more for it.

Count Lambert, on the other hand, had no such inhibitions. His wife stayed on their other lands in Hungary while the count merrily swived every unmarried peasant girl in the village, and did this somehow without a bit of complaint from their parents! In truth, my husband never chastised him for his actions, either, in part because had we been sent away by the count, we might have had a hard time finding another parish that would take us in. Though the marriage of the clergy was legal in Poland, yet was there much prejudice against it.

And so the years went by at Okoitz. In time, a large wooden church was built adjoining the count's rustic palace, and we had a decent enough room adjoining the church. Our situation became comfortable and secure, and I began to yearn for a child. Also, the count's example with his eager peasant girls convinced me that physical lovemaking must be as enjoyable for the woman as for the man, and it was a pleasure that I still had not partaken of!

After many long, tear-drenched conversations, my "husband" finally admitted that his abstinence was not the result of the nobility of his mind. It was the result of the inability of his body! He couldn't properly play the man's part in the game!

There was no one with whom I could talk this problem over. Indeed, the women of the village all came to me with their difficulties, but as the wife of the priest, I wasn't supposed to have any troubles of my own. I had to be sweetness and light and wisdom, me, an aging virgin of seventeen! Slowly I decided that I was perhaps not a married woman at all, for by the laws of the Church and of the state, a marriage must be consummated to exist.

Then Sir Conrad came to Okoitz out of the east, burdened by some geise that he might not tell of his origins. All the town was buzzing about his prowess as a warrior, for he had single-handedly rid the county of an entire band of outlaws that had been murdering the people and stealing the cattle.

Yet when first I saw Sir Conrad, I thought that I was looking on a messenger of the Lord! He was incredibly tall and handsome, with a true hero's litheness of body, with fine, broad shoulders and — dare I write it? — the most lovely posterior I had ever seen! And there was about him such an astounding aura of wisdom and learning and kindness that my heart went out to him in that instant. In truth, I remember that I let out a little squeal of delight, despite the fact that my husband, John, was in the room with us.

In the months that followed, I tried to convey to Sir Conrad that I would be eager to do anything that he desired, but such was his sense of honor that he would not even think sexual thoughts about a woman that he thought to be married. And since Count Lambert let Sir Conrad make full use of his peasant girls, there was no need for Sir Conrad to look farther afield. Not to mention the fact that those girls were all years younger than I.

Sir Conrad had an almost magical horse that could run at an amazing pace for hours on end. It could answer questions by nodding or shaking its head, and it never soiled its stall but went out in the bailey like a well-trained dog. It was astoundingly gentle to all, even the smallest child, unless it felt its lord was in danger, at which time it became the most deadly of beasts! I greatly admired this animal and often visited its stall.

Sir Conrad was a great master of all the constructive arts, and he built for the count great windmills and an entire cloth factory. He brought with him hundreds of types of seeds that grew into vastly productive food plants and radiantly beautiful flowers. He knew a thousand songs, and I was sure that he thought them up on the spot, though he denied it. He could dance a dozen new steps, and I thrilled to be in his arms for his waltz, his mazurka, and his polka. He could tell a thousand wondrous stories of lands and times far, far away. Many were the nights that he talked until midnight of the adventures of nine-fingered Frodo or of Luke Sky-walker. He loved children and was always telling them some new story or teaching them some new game or making them some new toy. He was a master of the sword, the chessboard, and the pen. How could I help but love him?

For all this work, and to encourage him to continue it, Count Lambert gifted Sir Conrad with a vast tract of lands in the mountains to the south of Okoitz. Sir Conrad went to these lands with a half dozen of the count's peasant girls, and I feared at the time that he was leaving my life forever.

He returned monthly, but not to visit me. He did it in feudal duty to the count, to oversee all the new construction at Okoitz. I watched from a distance and hoped.

My relationship with John was steadily deteriorating, and it got so that I could hardly bear to be in the same room with him, let alone the same bed. Yet such was as it had to be, for while we had food, clothing, and shelter, we had very little money. I wanted to leave John and again try my luck in France, but in years of scrimping I had hardly saved a small handful of silver pfennigs. To travel takes money, and to establish oneself in France takes even more.

Things finally came to a head with John one winter's night. I left our room the next morning and found that a merchant's caravan was leaving Okoitz immediately. They were going east instead of west, but it might be long before another caravan came by, and I leapt at the chance to leave, no matter what the direction. Of course, I did not tell John or anyone else that I was going.

One of the merchants mentioned that there was a new Pink Dragon Inn at Sir Conrad's new industrial town of Three Walls. I had heard long before that the waitresses at these inns could earn more money than at any other trade, no matter how sordid. They required that a woman be beautiful and a virgin, but I qualified on both those counts. They required that a waitress wear a costume that consisted of little but high-heeled shoes and a loincloth, but the barbarians of this backward land have no shame for their bodies, and indeed, the only way to bathe among them is to sit naked together in a sauna, so I was well used to exposing my body in public.

I left the caravan and spent the night in one of the barns at Sir Miesko's manor. I hid because I was well known to that good knight and did not want him to be able to tell John of my whereabouts. In the morning a small caravan left for Three Walls to deliver food, and I went with them.

The Pink Dragon Inns were all that they had promised to be, and in the first week there I made over forty pfennigs, almost as much as a belted knight with horse and armor would have been paid by a caravan. Further, my food, room, and such little clothing as I wore were provided me free, and all that I earned could be saved. All this for the light and pleasant work of serving beer and being decorative! I was wondering if I really needed to return to France at all when my "husband," John, found me.

Interlude One

I HIT the STOP button, popped the tape, and looked at it. There was nothing unusual about it. It looked completely authentic. So why had that guy acted so strangely when he'd handed it to me? He'd just walked up, put this tape in my palm, and walked silently away.

I rubbed my temples and pushed the call button for one of Tom's naked virgins. She was in before my finger was off the button, and I ordered some Blue Mountain coffee and something for a hangover. Last night's bull session had turned itself into a weapons-grade binge.

The girl was back immediately, doubtless having literally passed herself in the hallway. You do that sort of thing when you have a time machine handy. Whatever they used for Alka-Seltzer around here worked fast. I sipped my coffee and considered things.

Item: A lot of very weird things were going on. The temporal structure of all creation seemed to be shattering, even back here in 60,000 B.C. The supposition was that Conrad had something to do with it, although nobody had the slightest idea how, including Tom, and he had been one of the inventors of the time machine.

Item: Tom had agreed to meet me here this morning and

hadn't done so. That was odd. With time travel, if you didn't want to go someplace at a particular time, you could always go later and still get there on time. Tom always kept his appointments, even when he was five years late, subjectively. I'd written him a note already and put it in my letter box, and his reply hadn't popped immediately out of the other side of the box the way it was supposed to. There was nothing in those boxes but a timer and an ejection mechanism. Not much there to go wrong.

Maybe he just wanted me to watch this tape first.

I looked up at the girl who was awaiting further instructions.

"Do you have any idea what is going on?" I asked her.

"No, sir."

"Then sit down and watch this tape with me."

"Yes, sir."

I hit the START button.

Chapter Two

IT WAS a bitterly cold night, and John's hair and clothes were rimed with frost. He had lost his hat, and his eyes were red and shot through with blood. In front of everyone, he grabbed me and demanded that I return to Okoitz with him immediately. When I managed to free myself from him, he pulled out his belt knife. I was frightened and hit him on the head with a stool. I swear before God that it was never my intention to kill John, or even to seriously harm him, yet it happened.

Sir Conrad was called to the inn, since he was lord of the city. He rarely frequented his own inn and was shocked to find me there. Yet on hearing the tale, he said that I was not guilty of the murder of my husband, for it was an accident and done in self-defense, but that Count Lambert alone had the right of high justice.

On returning from Okoitz, Sir Conrad told me that Count Lambert had said that since a priest had been killed, my case came under canon law rather than civil law, and the matter would have to be taken up with the Bishop of Wroclaw.

Now, it is normally desirable for a criminal to have her trial brought before the Church. The penalties demanded by

14

the clergy are usually far less severe than those handed out
by the local lord. But in my case I felt this change of
jurisdiction was for the worse, for the Bishop of Wroclaw
did not like me, but Count Lambert certainly did. With John
dead, I knew I could easily enter the count's bed, were I
willing to share that honor with a dozen peasant girls!

Also, the Church moved very slowly on legal matters,
and many years could go by before I might be free to return
to France. I spent the uncertain months of winter working at
the inn, saving my money.

In the spring, Duke Henryk came to Three Walls to see
the wonders that Sir Conrad was building in his factories
and furnaces. The duke was a robust old man of seventy,
with an outside that was as hard as the crust of good French
bread and an inside that was just as soft. The duke made me
an offer that I couldn't refuse—more money than I was
currently making, his considerable protection from any
Church prosecution, and duties that involved only serving
the duke himself. I left Three Walls in the duke's company.

Thus I spent the next five years as the personal servant
and confidante of the most powerful man in Poland, and in
the process learned much about the politics of this new and
somewhat barbarous land. I learned who wanted what and
for what reason, who hated who for no understandable reason at all, and, sometimes quite literally, where all the
bodies were buried. As opposed to the feuding nobles of
England, Italy, or even France, Polish nobles were less
likely to go to war with one another than to resort to poison,
a trap, or a knife in the dark. Perhaps this was because the
Polish fighting man was often a member of a large, ex-
tended family and was ever ashamed to kill his own cous-
ins, who might be on the opposing side. Family loyalty
often took precedence with them over mere oaths of fealty.

My duties to the duke were not well defined. I simply did
whatever he wanted me to do. Since he wanted me to con-

tinue dressing much as I had as a waitress, my legs and breasts were rarely covered, save in the coldest weather. Indeed, it started a fad, a clothing style that many of the ladies of the court followed, at least to the extent of baring their breasts. Almost none of them adopted the short dress, feeling that naked legs were a bit much.

I always traveled with the duke and was privy to his many secrets. Indeed, an old man will always tell everything to an adoring young woman! One of the strangest things that I learned was that Sir Conrad was not a native to our own times but rather had come here somehow from the far future! Just how this was done was a mystery even to Conrad himself. All that I can think is that the future must be a grand place indeed, for if Conrad was but an ordinary man from that time, as he has so often insisted to me, what must the exceptional men be like?

I usually slept in the duke's bed, to comfort him. However, like my late "husband," the duke was incapable of actual sex, though seventy-five years on God's earth certainly gave him a fair excuse!

Eventually Duke Henryk raised me to the peerage, making me the Countess of Strzegom, with a nice manor house and a few hundred peasants. I am not ashamed of anything I did with that fine old man, and I certainly do not regret my years with him.

The duke did not die of old age, as all expected, but rather by a cowardly assassin's crossbow while he was sleeping at my side in Wawel Castle.

The duke had long and carefully trained his son to wield the sword of power, and young Duke Henryk easily stepped into his father's position. Yet the younger Henryk was not his father's puppet but did things in his own style. The very day of the assassination, all the ladies of the court were wearing dresses that covered everything but their faces and hands, knowing the new duke's displeasure with the old bare styles. Though young Henryk was absolutely honorable in all things, I knew it would not be wise for me to remain at court.

Sir Conrad—or rather I should say Baron Conrad, for Count Lambert had enlarged him—was in Cracow, and gifted the new duke with four of his marvelous horses, that they might protect him against assassins. While testing these horses, I persuaded Baron Conrad to let me go with the party, riding apillion. When we were racing through the fields, an attempt was made by three crossbowmen to kill the new duke, and Baron Conrad drew his wondrous sword and killed all the assassins while the duke's bodyguards took their lord to safety.

There was something unbelievably exciting about the chase and the fight with the assassins, bouncing behind Conrad and holding him tightly while he dealt death to the attackers. When we dismounted in a secluded wood to see if we could identify the bodies, well, to state it simply, I seduced him. I suppose I should be ashamed of myself, but in truth I was then twenty-six years old, and that is a perfectly stupid age at which to be a virgin. And how could I ever regret the wonderful pleasure that he gave me and that I had so long been denied!

Baron Conrad was then not maintaining a harem in the manner of his liege lord, Count Lambert, but was contenting himself with a single woman, a dancer from the far east who wasn't even a Christian. I had met Cilicia often, and she was a pleasant enough person, but I thought that I would have little difficulty displacing her in Baron Conrad's heart. I traveled with him to Three Walls, part of the way on his new steam-powered riverboat, an almost magical contrivance.

Yet he would not dismiss the foreign girl, but tried instead to make us join together into a single household! A foolish attempt—of course it did not work. My love, so wise in all things technical, is like a little boy when it comes to solving the far simpler problems of people. He needs my help so much and so often!

But at the time I could accomplish nothing with his other paramour, Cilicia. She seemed to think that she had prior claim on him, and indeed she was again pregnant with another of his children. After a month of trying, I left for my own estate.

Conrad contrived to visit me there at least once a month and often twice. And always I gave him a warm welcome. I wanted more, much more. I wanted a proper marriage and children by him, but I settled for what I could get.

In his own way, he was generous with me. I remember best the time when forty men and as many loaded mules came to my manor gate and announced that they were my birthday present. Since they were from Conrad, I bade them do as they would, and they fell to it with a will. One band of them put glass in every window of my manor, on frames with hinges that could open out and with screens of a coarse metal cloth that fended off insects in the summer but let the breezes through.

Another band took the roof off my highest tower and mounted there a small windmill and a huge water tank with a new well below it. Yet others dug pits and trenches in the kitchen garden and buried clay pipes and even a small stone room. My kitchens were rebuilt with a big copper stove and sinks with running water, but my favorite was the bathroom, with hot running water and a huge porcelain tub large enough for two! We used it often together, Baron Conrad and I. For years I spent much of my life waiting for his return.

Then, just prior to last Christmas, Count Lambert did a remarkably stupid thing. His wife, whom he had not seen in twelve years, died in Hungary, and his daughter, a girl of fourteen summers, came north to live with him. The count

decided that Baron Conrad would be the perfect match for
the girl and *ordered* Conrad to marry her. This at a time
when Conrad was making final preparations to defend the
land from the Mongol invaders! Conrad refused, saying that
he had never met the girl, and anyway, they didn't even
speak the same language. Count Lambert became incensed
and ordered Conrad off his lands. Conrad, disgusted, packed
his saddlebags with gold and headed west like a knight-
errant in a story, without so much as a change of underwear.

Fortunately, he stopped at my manor on his way, and I
was able to talk some sense into my poor little dumpling.
Count Lambert wanted him to marry his daughter, and to be
sure, young Duke Henryk wanted Conrad to marry *somebody* and to stop living in sin with a Mohammedan. I suggested that he marry Cilicia, knowing full well that it was
impossible. This made Conrad say that he could never become her sort of heathen and that he had been a failure at
trying to convert her to the true religion. Therefore, no
priest of either persuasion would ever marry them, nor a
Jew either, for that matter.

I then suggested that he marry me. This would satisfy the
duke, and Count Lambert would no longer force the issue if
it could not possibly bear fruit. Conrad decided that a small
wedding would be all that was needed and that things could
go on pretty much as before, with nothing changed but one
small ceremony. I, of course, knew all the players in the
game, and I knew that nothing of the kind would take place.
But a wise woman always knows when to keep her mouth
shut!

In the morning he asked me to be his wife, and I con-
sented with all my heart. His proposal was particularly welcome since I had twice missed my time and knew that I was
heavy with his child.

We rode to Cracow to talk to the duke, who, after all,
was my legal guardian, and he gave us his blessings, along

with a promise to have a serious talk with Count Lambert. Conrad was enlarged to count, since a mere baron could hardly marry a countess. We had a beautiful wedding in Wawel Cathedral, and all the nobility of Poland attended it. Indeed, there were so many that the heralds could find room in the cathedral only for barons and above, and my husband's party was almost excluded for being mere knights! He solved this problem by enlarging his entire party to baronies.

Our marriage has had no time to be blissful, for my husband has spent the months since our wedding almost exclusively in preparation for war with the invading Mongols. Conrad is facing grave political difficulties as well as military ones, yet despite the fact that I am far more adept than he at anything concerning people, he will not let me help him with politics.

The duke has invited many foreign knights to aid us against the Tartars, and he bade all the fighting men in Poland to rally to him near Legnica, where provision has been made to support so large an army. The dukes of Sandomierz and Mazovia have refused to do this, as it would involve abandoning their own lands and peoples to the Mongols and then having to reconquer them again. Further, the nobles of Little Poland were also loath to abandon their estates and start the war by retreating hundreds of miles to the west. They left Duke Henryk as a group and swore to serve under Duke Boleslaw of Mazovia, despite the fact that they had once sworn fealty to Henryk.

And Conrad, with the biggest and finest army of all, though none will credit it, felt that he could not follow Duke Henryk either, since much of his force was with the riverboats on the Vistula River, and these could hardly go west overland to Legnica. There were flying machines that flew from Eagle Nest, near Okoitz, but they could not fly from

Legnica, needing the catapult to launch them. Further, Conrad's huge land army needs the railroads that have been built for the purpose along the Vistula. They cannot fight efficiently in the west. And lastly, Conrad was loath to abandon his factories and cities to the enemy. My love therefore felt obligated to disobey Duke Henryk and rather go to the aid of young Duke Boleslaw of Mazovia, who was leading the Polish forces of the east.

But Duke Boleslaw is a boy of fourteen who has heard too many tales of knightly prowess and sees no need of saddling himself with "a lot of peasant infantry."

If ever there was a blood-soaked need for some adept political maneuvering, this is the time! Further, I seem to be the only person about with the political skills necessary to unite the military forces of this confused and barbarous land.

Yet Conrad is so naive and helpless at all things political that *he does not even realize how stupid he is*! I could not persuade him to let me smooth his path. He treats me like a pretty child who needs protection rather than as the one person who could solve at least some of his obvious problems. A few weeks ago it got so bad that he even had a guard posted at my door "for my protection," he said, but in fact to keep me from going to Duke Henryk and Duke Boleslaw and bringing them together as the old duke certainly would have done.

Three weeks ago my love marched out with the largest and finest army in Christendom to seek the Mongol foe. I stayed behind, almost as a prisoner, when I should have been aiding our efforts. Being six months pregnant didn't help, either.

And two days ago the Mongols found us! We beat off their first two attacks with our swivel guns and our grenades, and the field below is dark with their bodies. Now they are camped beyond the range of our guns, more of them than we can count with our telescopes, and they are building huge siege machines to close with us.

Conrad has not come, and we know not whether he is alive or dead. But if he be alive, he must come soon, for if he is late, it is we who will be dead, and our children with us.

Chapter Three

▽ ▽ ▽ ▽ ▽ ▽ ▽ ▽ ▽ ▽ ▽ ▽ ▽ ▽ ▽ ▽ ▽

FROM THE DIARY OF CONRAD STARGARD

Two hundred miles from my home the weather was still foul, the lightning and thunder went on without rest, and the cold drizzle had been replaced with sleet. The troops were nearing exhaustion, but three days after our battle with the Mongols, the cleanup was just about completed. By actual count, 216,692 of the enemy had been killed, and that was in our base-twelve numbers. In the base-ten numbers that I had grown up with, we had done in more than half a million of the bastards here. Their bodies had been stripped and buried twelve deep in long trenches, but their heads were set on stakes and lances in neat squares, a gross skulls to the side. There were more than two dozen of these squares stretching across the battlefield, quite a monument to Polish arms.

A ghastly sight—I'd had it done so that no one could ever doubt what we had accomplished here, so that no one could ever say that we had exaggerated.

The booty taken was equally vast. Each of the enemy had carried an *average* of five and a half pounds of gold and silver, three years worth of plunder in the Russias. There were no commercial banks available to looting Mongols, so they had to carry their spoils along with them. It was easy to see why most medieval troops were so eager to break ranks and loot. That much gold and silver was easily six years' pay. My troops, of course, were better disciplined. We would share out the loot in an equitable manner once it was taken home and counted.

Just how I was going to do that in such a manner that my entire army didn't quit and retire was a problem I hadn't solved yet. There was so much money suddenly available that it could ruin the economy with inflation, the way Spain was ruined after the conquest of the Americas. I'd have to think of something.

Since our supplies of food and ammunition were partially exhausted, each of our war carts could carry about an additional five tons, yet it took two gross of the things to haul the gold and silver alone. Another six gross carts were needed to carry the captured weapons and other gear that looked worth saving for trophies if nothing else. Each of these carts would go back toward Three Walls with a platoon of forty-three men to pull and guard it.

Most of the enemy horses had been killed in the battle and in Ilya's night raid the evening before. Baron Vladimir had felt that a half million horsehides was a prize well worth taking, and he had had the animals skinned before the carcasses were buried. Salting them down would have to wait, since we'd have to get the salt mines working again first. For now the skins were just stacked on the field, with a prayer that the cold weather would hold and they wouldn't rot. Near those stacks was a huge pile labeled "scrap iron," junk arms and armor that nobody would want to hang on a wall. The forges could always use scrap. We'd be back for it eventually.

There were perhaps sixty thousand horses still alive, mostly Mongol ponies but also some of the war-horses used by the conventional Christian knights who had been massacred on the field while we had stood by helpless. After I had discussed the matter with some of my officers, it was decided to simply let them all go free. Untrained for the job, they wouldn't have been much use as cart horses even if suitable harnesses had been available. The truth was that they would only slow us down. There was no way for us to take care of them and still get the rest of our work done. When the peasants returned, they'd find a use for the Mongol ponies. Most of the Polish war-horses were either branded or had had their ears punched with identifying marks, so they could eventually be returned to the families of their owners.

Each fallen conventional knight's arms and armor were carefully bundled along with his jewelry and personal effects, and one of his dog tags served as a label for its eventual return to his heirs. Each Christian body was properly buried with the other dog tag on a lance to mark the grave, but nothing of value was actually buried with the body. This was standard army policy, for history shows that the bejeweled dead are never allowed to rest in peace. Someday we would set up proper tombstones. Someday.

For now there was still a much bigger cleanup job to do. Far more Mongols had been killed on the eastern bank of the Vistula than had ever crossed it, perhaps as many as five or six times as many. There was probably a far greater booty to be taken, and certainly a far bigger mess to be cleaned up before the weather turned warm and rot and disease started to spread. But at least there we wouldn't have to do the sad job of burying our own people. Our casualties had all been on the riverboats, and most of them, those who hadn't gone down with their boats, had already been taken to the army city of East Gate.

I sent Baron Vladimir east to the Vistula with two-thirds of our men, there to get over to the east bank and take care of the cleanup there. That was about a hundred thousand men, eleven of our "battalions." I'd once read that God was on the side with the biggest battalions, so I'd made ours almost as large as a modern division just to be safe.

Just how Vladimir was to contact the boats to cross the river was a bit problematic, since the weather was still foul and the radios still were not working. Our spark-gap transmitters and coherer-type receivers were very sensitive to atmospheric disturbances. We'd been out of touch with the rest of the world for almost a week.

I left with the other third of our land forces, which included all our industrial workers. It was important to get our factories going again as soon as possible, since we had lost most of our riverboats and were out of some kinds of ammunition. We were taking back to Three Walls our booty, along with fifteen aircraft engines. Nine reasonably intact planes had already been sent ahead to the boys at Eagle Nest.

The pilots of our *entire air force* had deliberately crash-landed along with my former liege lord, Count Lambert, in order to take part in the final battle with the Mongols. They had taken part, all right, and had died to a man, along with most of the other valiant but undisciplined conventional knights. They had vainly spent their lives and accomplished nothing. *Idiots*, the lot of them!

One should not think badly of the dead, but *by God* I wish those planes were still flying! They could have kept our communications intact. As it was, what with the weather making our radios useless, I didn't know what was happening in the rest of the country. I had sent couriers to Cracow, Three Walls, and Legnica, but so far none of them had returned. Was Duke Henryk still waiting at Legnica for the rest of the foreign troops to arrive? Had the Hungarians been invaded at the same time we were? How bad was the destruction on the east bank of the Vistula? Was my wife, Francine, alive and well? I had no way of knowing.

Baron Vladimir pulled out at dawn, and I left with my

own troops shortly afterward, leaving two companies behind to care for our pitifully few wounded.

I was riding the new white Big Person I'd found on the battlefield. Anna, my usual mount, wasn't at all happy about this, but the new bioengineered horse understood only English, and so I was the only person in this century who could use her properly. Big People were too valuable to waste, so I lent Anna to one of the scouts who was screening our force. There were few enough Big People to do the job. I had only ten out of our total of thirty-three, and that's a thin screen for a force of over fifty thousand men, especially when there were who knows how many Mongol stragglers around. We'd spotted a few. The job couldn't be done with men on ordinary horses, since once we got on the railroad, our men could pull a war cart six dozen miles a day at a walk, far faster than any war-horse could travel.

I wished that the white mount's rider was still alive. There were a lot of questions I wanted to ask that man. In the few moments that I'd been able to talk to him, he had spoken with an *American English accent*! Further, if he was riding a bioengineered horse, he must have had something to do with whoever it was that had built the time machine that had brought me to this century. He had to be some kind of observer at the battle, or even a tourist, but he had been killed by a Mongol spear before I had had time to get some answers out of him. I'd like to know just why I was dumped into this brutal century! There can't be that many time travelers around. Would I ever get another chance to talk to one?

It took all our men to haul the carts over the half-frozen fields, but we got to the railroad track south of Sandomierz around noon, and once on it we could go much more quickly. Further, riding on iron tracks, it takes only a dozen and a half men to pull one of our big war carts, and they can pull it easily even with the rest of the men riding on or under the cart, slung on hammocks, sleeping. This let us travel day and night without stopping. The men all had full plate armor, although it was common practice to leave the helmets and leg armor in the carts while pulling.

Cookstoves were slung from the rear of each cart, with the cooks walking behind as they did their work, and dinner was being prepared when a wounded rider on one of our Big People came galloping up to me. I recognized him as being one of the couriers I had sent out, the one who had gone to Legnica. His right side and leg were drenched with blood, and he didn't waste time conveying any message to me from my liege lord, Duke Henryk.

"Lord Conrad, *Cracow is burning!*" he said before he fell unconscious from the saddle.

Chapter Four

I STOPPED the five-mile-long column that I was leading, turned to the captain of the leading company, and shouted, "Dump the booty on the ground! Dump it, I say! We have to lighten the load and go as fast as we can. Dump it and then get your men going at double time. *Cracow is burning!*"

He looked at me aghast, and it was a moment before he could comprehend what I was saying. Dump an unimaginable fortune on the ground? Victory had been turned into defeat? How was that possible? But discipline and training took over. He turned and obeyed orders. Men scurried off the carts, the big lids were taken off the six carts that the captain commanded, and thirty tons of gold and silver were dumped on both sides of the double track.

A banner had the wounded courier hauled onto a cart, and a medic bent over him. A new man was appointed scout and, with the Big Person, was added to our screen. Actually, it wasn't necessary to make a new scout. We had twice as many scouts as we had mounts for them, a fact that made sense once you realize that Big People didn't need sleep, but us Little People did. But there wasn't another scout present, so I let the man have his promotion.

As the new scout started to ride out, I called to him and had him come back. Instead of joining the screen, I had him ride back toward Sandomierz and tell Baron Vladimir about the attack on Cracow. This action turned out to be one of my major tactical errors.

"Get the pullers moving!" I shouted. "They can run while the other half of the men dump the load. Throw out everything but weapons, ammunition, and four days' food. *Double time!*"

The men on the carts behind were staring in unbelief at what the first company was doing, and I realized that this was an order that I would have to give personally to each officer. They wouldn't have believed it otherwise! I signaled DOUBLE TIME, PASS THE WORD and rode down the long line of troops and carts, shouting orders.

After a bit, one of my captains asked, "The radios, too, sir? And how about these airplane engines?"

"Hell, yes! They're not doing us any good now, are they?" There were a dozen radios with the companies farther up the line, enough in case the weather cleared.

"Just figured I should ask, sir."

I was already on my way as the expensive set went flying to smash on the siding of the railroad.

It took an hour to get the job done, and the carts were more strung out than I would have wished, but fourteen hundred *tons* of gold and silver were scattered out beside four miles of track, along with three times that weight of fancy swords, decorated armor, and other booty. Four hundred tons of surplus food were dumped as well, but we were running to Cracow.

I ordered the last company in my column to stay there and guard what we had abandoned. They didn't like it, but they did it.

Running at double time, the men pulling have to be changed every quarter hour, but the carts don't stop. Everything happens at a run, and each man is relieved when his replacement catches up with him. There were ladders on both sides of each cart to let a man climb up even when it was moving, but the warriors rarely used them. Once you knew the trick, you could step between the spokes of one of the huge wheels, let it carry you up, and then step from the top of the wheel to the top of the cart. Pity the man who trips and falls, but don't stop for him!

In practice sessions we'd been able to keep this up for an entire day and a night with fresh troops. These men were far from fresh, having started out nearly exhausted, but they did it, anyway.

We ran nonstop for the rest of the day and ate two meals literally on the run. As dusk fell, the lanterns were set out at the ends of the carts, and we pushed on into the night. I ordered a midnight breakfast since, as the Eskimos say, food replaces sleep.

I sent three of our scouts forward to find out anything that they could. I desperately wanted to go myself, but I couldn't. My place was with my troops.

The pace was deadening, mind-numbing, absolutely exhausting, but to drop back to a walk would delay our arrival in Cracow by a day. How many of our countrymen could be killed by a Mongol horde in a day? Thousands? Tens of thousands? We had to push on, no matter what the cost, for the price of anything else was more than I dared pay.

And it was costing us, how much I didn't know. Most of my men had had only four months' training, and many of them couldn't keep up the pace. Men dropped and lay where they fell, and more than once I felt my mount jump an obstacle on the path beside the track. I could only hope that we didn't trample anyone. As men began to fall and not get up, officers at the rear of the column started abandoning carts and moving the men forward to replace our losses. These abandoned carts would make Baron Vladimir's job of reaching us that much harder, but there was nothing else we could do.

The Night Fighters used a smaller war cart than did the rest of the troops, pulled by a seven-man lance rather than a forty-three-man platoon. With only four men pulling, they were having a hard time keeping up with the other, more efficient full-sized carts. Over Baron Ilya's protests, the Night Fighter Battalion was disbanded, the carts put off the road, and the men distributed to the other five battalions as replacements.

It wasn't as hard on me as it was on most of the men, since I was one of the few who were mounted. I felt guilty about it, but I didn't lend out my mount, since it was my job to be alert for any emergency. Easing the pain of one of my men could get thousands of them killed if we were ambushed and I wasn't ready to give quick orders. Yet it was still vastly tiring, and I was older than most of the men under me.

Extreme fatigue always gets me first in the eyes, and now, what with the wound I had gotten from a Mongol arrow, I had only one eye left. It felt like there was sand in it and that the sand had been there forever. At night, since there wasn't much to see, anyway, I closed my eye, held on to the saddle, and trusted to the incredible night vision of my new white mount.

We were all exhausted, the men worse than I, but I knew that once the battle was joined, we'd be awake enough. God always has a last supply of adrenaline for a man when his life is on the line.

It was gray dawn and the towers of Brzesko were on the skyline to our left when the first scout came back to report. Cracow was indeed burning, and the outer walls had fallen to the enemy. The lower city was filled with fighting, but Wawel Hill, with the castle and the cathedral, still seemed to be in friendly hands.

As a hint of the sun came over the horizon, I had the semaphores signal SAY YOUR VOWS ON THE RUN. We had all sworn to repeat our vows every morning, but I wasn't going to let anything slow us down. I could hear the troops near me gasping for breath as they chanted:

"On my honor, I will do my best to do my duty to God and to the army. I will obey the Warrior's Code, and I will keep myself physically fit, mentally awake, and morally straight."

The Warrior's Code:

"A Warrior is: Trustworthy, Loyal, and Reverent; Courteous, Kind, and Fatherly; Obedient, Cheerful, and Efficient; Brave, Clean, and Deadly."

They meant it, too.

Most of the towns and castles along the Vistula were set right on the river to make them easier to defend. Our new rail lines had to swing out and around them, to the north at Brzesko and Cracow. After the scout reported, I sent him to Brzesko to see how things stood there. He reported shortly that the castle and town were a smoking ruin, with no one there left alive. We pushed on.

I couldn't understand how all this was possible. Until the big battle near Sandomierz we had had aircraft patrolling the skies and riverboats on the Vistula. How could they have possibly missed an entire Mongol army? We had lost the planes through sheer vanity and stupidity, but what had happened to the riverboats? There had been at least nine of them left when I had parted company to join the land forces. They were equipped with lights and didn't stop for the dark. The railroad paralleled the river. Why hadn't I seen a single boat all night long?

Dear God, just what the hell was going on?

It was midmorning when we sighted Cracow, although we'd first seen the cloud of black smoke above it an hour before. The railroad was a mile north of the city walls, and the land intervening was a suburb of burned-out cottages, orchards, and smoldering barns. Not the sort of terrain where we could easily use our war carts. Furthermore, the fight was going on within the walls, in the city itself, where the narrow, twisted streets would make the carts useless. I stopped at what would be our center once we got into position. When the tail end of the line was about as far from the city as the front, I had the semaphore operators signal ALL STOP, FULL ARMOR, ABANDON CARTS ONE GUNNER EACH, and HOSTILES TO THE LEFT. That meant that we were also abandoning our swivel guns, with one gunner left behind on each cart to guard them. The guns had to be mounted on the carts to operate, but we couldn't get a significant number of carts into the city, anyway, and I didn't think the Mongols would be defending the wall against us. Not their style. I hoped.

My men were each armed with halberds or six-yard-long pikes as primary weapons and axes or swords as secondaries. All were in full plate armor, proof against Mongol arrows. Despite their fatigue, discipline was still good. In less than two minutes my entire command was lined up and ready. I signaled ADVANCE.

What with the broken terrain, I did not dare order double time. The men were tired, and we would soon have gotten scattered. Also, away from the carts we were down to bugle calls for communications, and there was no point advertising our existence. It wasn't likely, but maybe the Mongols didn't know we were here yet.

We spent two dozen quiet minutes getting to the city wall, but those minutes were not pleasant. This was the first time we had seen what the Mongols do to a civilian population. It hurts me to write about it, to even remember what I saw. Forced by necessity, I can be as hard and as brutal as the situation requires, but for the *love of God* I cannot comprehend the needless murder of helpless civilians, the

senseless torture of women and children. Why would any
rational beings do it?

The atrocity that burned most deeply into my soul was in
a small hamlet. A young woman had been stripped naked
and nailed by her feet to the lintel of the door frame of her
cottage. Around her were the mutilated bodies of what must
have been her aged parents and her four children. The
youngest of them might have been a year old, her head
bashed open on a rock. The woman's belly had been torn
open from crotch to breastbone, and dangling amid her
slashed intestines was a six-month-old fetus. She was still
alive, barely.

I dismounted and went to her. She seemed to want to say
something, and I bent close to her to hear.

"Kill me," she whispered. "Please kill me."

The laws of God and the Church make no provision for
mercy killing. To grant her wish would make me a mur-
derer, fit only for hell. Yet despite the fact that I knew that
God would damn my immortal soul for the act, there was
nothing else I could do.

"A place waits for you in heaven," I said, the tears
running down my face. I drew my sword and cleanly slit her
throat. "Though a place no longer waits there for me."

Nor was that the only atrocity that I saw on that walk to
Cracow. I do not know why an army would want their
enemies to hate them. I do not know why they would want
to turn fifty thousand tired troops into fanatics bent on their
destruction. But they did, and we were!

The city wall was an old, crumbling, useless affair only
three stories tall. The city hadn't been seriously attacked for
hundreds of years, and the city fathers had been slack in
their duties. There were enough hand-holds on the old bricks
and stone to let my warriors climb up them, especially since
wall climbing was part of the training they'd been through.
And up they went, without waiting for orders to do so. The

troops had seen the same atrocities that I had, and there was no stopping them now. Nothing would stop them until either all of the enemy were dead or every one of the warriors had died trying to kill them!

The warriors were moving, and I could see that they would be uncontrollable until the city was theirs or they died in their armor. Not that I wanted to control them. They knew what to do!

This meant that I had no further duties as their commander and was free to join in on the fun. I headed through the increasingly heavy rain for the nearest city gate, the Carpenter's Gate as memory served, since I wanted to have a Big Person under me in the battle, and while these bioengineered horses had some amazing abilities, wall climbing wasn't one of them. I hoped that this new mount was as good as Anna in a fight.

The upper city, Wawel Hill, was in the hands of the nobility, but the lower city was governed and defended by the commoners. Each city guild had its own gate, tower, or section of wall to defend, and each of these defenses had been named for a particular guild.

The wall was lightly guarded by Mongol archers, with more arriving every minute. The troops ignored them, and some had a half dozen arrows sticking in their armor as they went over the top. Pikes and halberds were tossed up to them, and they made quick work of clearing the ramparts. I saw one halberdier take the heads clean off two of the enemy with a single sideways blow and then stop and stare at what he had done, unable to believe it.

"Yes, Yashoo, I saw you do it, too!" a man beside him shouted, "now come and help us with these other ones!"

The Carpenter's Gate was ours by the time I got there, and I just rode straight through. Some of the officers had been training for battle for five years, and now they finally had a chance to put that training to use. They were in high spirits, and the mood was infectious, doubtless aided by the giddiness that is caused by the lack of sleep. Seeing the men now, no one would have believed that they had been awake for two days and had spent much of that time at a dead run. Some of our troops were laughing and a few were crying, but none of them were holding back.

Most of the Mongols were on horseback, but they soon learned not to attack our ranks. I saw three of them charge splashing through the puddles at a dozen of my warriors, or at least charge as best they could in the narrow winding streets of the lower city. Rather than cowering from the horsemen as the Mongols had obviously expected, our men fairly leapt at them. Grounded pikes skewered horses and riders! Axes and swords swung no more than once each, and all three of the enemy riders were dead before they hit the ground. None of the good guys were injured.

"Hey! That really works!" one knight shouted. "Let's go find some more of the smelly bastards and do it again!"

They left at a trot. I went over and inspected the fallen enemy soldiers. None of them had been wearing armor, though even in the rain it was obvious from the wear patterns on their clothing that they owned chain mail and had left it back in camp. My guess is that they had planned to spend the day murdering the seven thousand women and children who lived in the lower city. Encountering fifty thousand of the best-armed, best-armored, and best-trained troops in the world hadn't been part of their daily game plan!

It was soon obvious to me that if I was going to accomplish anything, I was going to have to get out ahead of the foot soldiers. That wasn't easy to do in those tangled streets. Mongols were soon abandoning their horses and taking refuge in the buildings. Seeing this, our warriors started a house-to-house search. Some were using impromptu battering rams, but a quicker technique was more often used. This was for an armored man to run at a barred door full tilt and at the last instance to flip around and smack the door flat with his back. This usually took down any ordinary doorway, and six of his friends ran through right on top of him. If it didn't work the first time, they'd try it again with two men flying backwards. There's something about good armor that gives a man the feeling of indestructibility, and he'll willingly take more actual abuse while wearing it than he would without.

I finally got ahead of most of my men and into a section of the city that was burning fiercely. The smell was enough to make me want to vomit. I might have done just that, but I thought about the results of heaving inside a closed helmet and somehow held it in. Like all the other old cities in Europe, Cracow had no sewage system. For hundreds of years people had been dumping their garbage and shit directly into the streets, and now the mess was going up in flames along with the wooden buildings around it. Actually, a good fire was what this place really needed.

Urban renewal, medieval style!

I got past the worst of the fires and into a section that was mostly burned over. One of the few buildings standing was the Franciscan church and the monastery attached to it.

There was a fight going on in front of it, a crowd of Mongols attacking a band of monks in brown cassocks. We galloped to their aid, my mount and I, and as I approached, I saw that the man leading the monks was my old friend and mentor, Bishop Ignacy.

Just as I reached the fray, a Mongol horseman swung his sword, and the good bishop went down!

Chapter Five

WE CHOPPED into the fight, my Big Person and I. I took the head off one of the Mongols and the arm off another before most of them noticed that I was there. My mount was not being a slouch, either, being every bit as good as Anna and doing at least as much damage as I was. Thunder rippled across the sky but couldn't drown the crash of sword on shield, the popping squish of a human head trampled beneath a horse's hoof.

Once the enemy noticed us, though, things got a bit hairy. I was soon surrounded and had to spend most of my effort fending off their blows rather than delivering my own. But they'd never seen a horse that could fight like mine, and she did in four of them before I could score again. Yet every time a Mongol went down, another was all too eager to take his place. I began to realize that I was growing too old for this sort of thing and that getting ahead of my own troops was maybe not such a good idea.

The cavalry came to my rescue in the form of my captain of scouts, Sir Wladyclaw, the oldest son of my good friend Sir Miesko. He was riding one of our Big People, one of Anna's progeny, and was slewing and sliving as I had done before I had become the center of the Mongols' attention. Didn't the idiots ever put out sentries?

He soon made it to my side, and while we were still surrounded, at least now I didn't have to try to watch my own back. We were soon fighting to good effect, and I think that I killed six more Mongols before things quieted down. That wasn't enough to extract full vengeance for what these bastards had done to that woman in the hamlet, but it was enough to get me a good honor guard into the hell I'd earned for putting her out of her pain.

"Well met, Captain Wladyclaw, and thank you! How did you manage to find me?"

"I didn't, my lord. This is Anna! She's been looking for you and disregarding everything I've wanted to do since we got through the city gates!"

"Well, thank you, love." I scratched Anna's ear the way she liked it. Then I saw that there was still a crowd of Mongols in front of the monks. "Whoops! There's more work to do. Let's go! *For God and Poland!*"

In the course of our fight we had drifted a gross yards from our starting point, and so we had time to get up to speed before we hit them again. Big People were larger than the usual war-horses and far more powerful than a little Mongol pony. We struck the Mongols like a pair of bowling balls, and they flew like a rack of pins. Then we were back to hacking and slashing in earnest, the blood and raindrops splashing around us.

I soon realized that the monks were not behaving like innocent victims. They were handing out as much as they took in and were tolerating an unbelievable amount of punishment in the process. They were swinging long iron maces since a man of the Church wasn't allowed to shed blood, but all the swords except mine were dulled to clubs by that point, anyway.

Then I saw Bishop Ignacy cave in the skull of the last standing Mongol and suddenly all was quiet. We dismounted, and both of the Big People started going about calmly stepping on the necks of the fallen Mongols. They always do that sort of thing, but I'd just as soon not watch.

"For this timely aid, much thanks, my son! You know, I've always wanted to say something like that," the bishop said, laughing.

"You are most welcome, your excellency. But tell me. Did I or did I not just see you go down before a Mongol sword?" I asked.

"You did, Conrad."

"Then how is it that you are standing before me? One miracle in a lifetime is enough, after all."

"There's nothing miraculous about it. I am standing now simply because I stood up again after he knocked me down! Oh, I see what you mean." He folded back the cuff of his wide sleeve to reveal a set of our regulation combat armor underneath. Looking about, I realized that all the monks were similarly attired. "The Lord said that one should turn the other cheek, my son, but he never demanded that one's cheek must be naked."

"How did you get that armor? Why are you wearing a monk's cassock instead of your bishop's robes? And why are you down here instead of up in your cathedral?" My head was buzzing.

"We got the armor by going to Three Walls and paying for it. The Church is not poor, after all. I am in the lower city because I judged that Wawel Hill would hold but that I would be needed down here. As to the cassock, well, the ladies often spend years embroidering a single one of my formal robes, and it would be rude to ruin one. Is anything else troubling you, my son?" he said patiently, standing in the rain.

"No, Father."

"Then you had best get about your business. This day's work isn't done yet. Go with God, my son!"

We mounted up and rode out.

Captain Wladyclaw and I rode through the town, taking out the enemy as we found them until we got to the Butcher's Gate by the waterfront. Quite a few enemy horsemen had apparently had their fill of fighting real warriors and were streaming out of the city.

"There's the place for us," Captain Wladyclaw shouted, pointing with his saber. "Every one of them that gets out now is one more that we'll have to catch later on!"

"Right you are! *For God and Poland!*"

We hacked our way to the gate and then turned to defend it, not against an aggressor from the outside, as is usual with city gates, but against aggressors from the inside who were trying to escape. The gate was a tunnel a dozen yards long and just wide enough to allow two men on horseback to fight while guarding it. A convenient killing ground.

The first Mongol to follow us through plunged out of the rain and into the relative darkness of the gate without realizing that we were there. Captain Wladyclaw got a lance into his horse about the time I split his greasy head open with my sword. Our eyes were accustomed to the darkness, while those of the enemy weren't. The second enemy's horse tripped over the remains of the first, but the end results were similar. The Mongols weren't expecting anyone to be trying to stop them from leaving, and in that dark tunnel a fair number went down without getting a chance to draw their swords.

A proper Christian knight would have been horrified at what we were doing, but my forces didn't believe in fighting fair. You were either out there to kill the bastards or you shouldn't be fighting in the first place. Anyway, I kept seeing in my mind that mother nailed to the door frame of her house, and I didn't feel very merciful.

Soon, however, the dead men and horses in front of us were warning enough for all but the absolutely stupid, and things started to slow down. In a few dozen minutes, my sword arm was getting sore and the dead before us were piled up saddle high. Mongols had taken to dismounting in order to climb the pile of their dead, and a Mongol on foot is dog meat to a warrior mounted on a Big Person. Nonetheless, we were being slowly pushed back out of the city gate for no other reason than that we couldn't climb the dead bodies, either. Eventually we were out in the rain again.

During a lull I said, "You know, Captain Wladyclaw, that gate is so packed that it will be hours before they can get a horse through it, and a Mongol on foot isn't much to worry about. What say we see how the other gates are doing?"

"Whatever you say, my lord. You're the commander." Anna smashed in the skull of another Mongol footman, and such had become our casualness with killing that it didn't break our conversation.

"Have you seen me command anything lately? The fight in the city is so scattered that no one could possibly keep track of it, let alone give any sensible orders. But as your brother in arms, I suggest we try the next gate east."

"Done, my lord, or brother in arms, as you would have it!" he said with a smile.

At the next gate we found two of my other scouts with exactly the same idea that we had, and with much the same results. We wished them well and continued on around the city. We found a lance of our own foot troops guarding the third gate we came to.

"Sir, our captain said we was to guard this gate, but there ain't nothing happening here. Any chance we could go back in and join in on the fighting?" the knight in charge said.

"Sorry, but you're needed right where you are. The Mongols have been trying to break out of a lot of the other gates, and we've been bottling them in. If they try it here, you'll have your hands full.''

"But there *ain't* no Mongols hereabouts, sir!''

"Your job is here. Do it!'' Captain Wladyclaw and I rode through the gate and back into the fight.

Soon we were in another free-for-all, a bloody chaos of swinging and stabbing with the city still burning around us, despite the rain.

The only water available was in a few wells, enough to provide some not particularly safe drinking water but totally insufficient for fire fighting. In the quieter areas civilians were trying to save their homes, but they didn't have much chance of success. Aside from the churches, most of the buildings in the lower city were made of wood and had roofs made of straw. What's more, they were built right next to each other with no space in between, and the upper stories overhung the narrow streets below so that the fires could easily leap the narrow gap between two city blocks. The rain helped a lot to slow things down, but the place was still a firetrap. I didn't see how anything could stop the fires but running out of fuel. That's to say, running out of city.

In one burned-out area I was pleased to note that my Pink Dragon Inn was still standing. My chief innkeeper, Tadeusz, had spent some of our fabulous profits giving the inns in the more important cities brick walls and tile roofs. I suppose he had done this more for reasons of prestige than for fireproofing, but the result was the same. Since the inn was so big that it took up an entire city block, it was isolated from the flames that had burned all around it.

I dismounted and beat on the door.

"We're closed for the duration of the battle,'' came a muffled voice from within.

"You're not closed to me! I own the place!'' I shouted back.

A peephole slid open, and then the door was unbarred. The rotund shape of Tadeusz himself filled the doorway.

"My lord Conrad! I didn't know it was you!" He was shocked by our appearance, a reasonable thing since we were both drenched with human blood.

"Very little of the blood is our own," I assured him. "Can you spare us a quick meal? We haven't eaten since daybreak."

"Of course, my lord, of course. I'll get it myself, since the waitresses and cooks have all been sent to shelter on Wawel Hill. There's none here but the bartenders and a few old guards, and they're all on the top floor with crossbows. Come in, come in, my lords, and you'd best bring your mounts in with you. They'll be wanting food and drink, too, yes, of course." He barred the door behind us.

"We're not particular about what we get so long as we get it fast," I said, leading the group into the kitchen. I put a bushel of fairly fresh bread in front of each of the Big People, and Captain Wladyclaw set out two buckets of clean water for them. We sat at the cook's worktable, which Tadeusz proceeded to cover with fifty kinds of preserved foods, most of them of the rare and expensive variety. We didn't give it the attention it deserved but just wolfed down the calories as fast as we could. We both passed up the wines that were set out for some big glasses of small beer. Fighting is thirsty work, and the job wasn't done yet.

The innkeeper was still setting out food when we got up to leave.

"You're leaving so soon, my lord?"

"There's work to do. Look, move all this stuff and as much else as you need to the front door. Thinking about it, I have fifty thousand hungry troops out there, so you'd better get some help and empty out your entire cellar. When any of my men comes by, feed them near the door. Don't let them stay in or you might have problems getting them out.

They're all so tired that they'll fall asleep if they sit down. And give them only one jack of beer each. I don't want them drunk!''

We headed back to the war.

Two blocks down we hadn't found any Mongols, but I ran into Baron Gregor, my second in command. "So how goes the battle?" I asked.

"We seem to be winning, sir, and I think that our casualties have been light. I wish I could be more definite than that, but this is the most chaotic battle I've ever heard of. I don't even know where most of our units are!"

"I don't think anybody does. I've seen a lot of Mongols escaping out the city gates. You might try and get some of our men to guard each one of them."

"I'll see to it, sir. A few men on the walls wouldn't be amiss, either. You know, this is a situation where the radios would really have come in handy."

"Yeah, if the damn things worked," I said. "You go east along the walls, and we'll go west. When the gates are all guarded, we'll meet somewhere along the wall at the other side of the city. Oh, yes. You can stop at the Pink Dragon Inn for a quick bite to eat. Pass the word on that one."

"Right, sir."

We headed back to the gate through which we had last entered. Captain Wladyclaw came with me, since he was still on Anna and she wasn't about to leave my side. Had a human acted that way, I would have busted him for insubordination, but with Anna, well, what could I do?

We got to the gate with a platoon of troops we had picked up on the way. Enemy troops were streaming into the portal, and we had to fight our way to it for the last gross yards. We got there to find the bodies of the lance of men I had met on our way in. All seven of them had died where I had left them. I should have reinforced them at the time. Another sin on my already blackened soul.

The platoon seemed to be holding pretty well, so I went on to the next gate, sending the next platoon I came across back to reinforce the first. This went on for one of our long, double-sized hours before I again met Baron Gregor. I sent him to continue his way around, inspecting and manning the walls while Captain Wladyclaw and I went outside the city to see how things were going there. It was dusk when we got to the dock area to find that one of our riverboats, the RB29 *Enterprise*, was just pulling in. I saw Baron Tadaos on the bridge.

"Baron Tadaos! What happened to your *Muddling Through*?" I shouted.

"Burned, sir!" he shouted in the darkening gloom. "Burned along with four other boats and the whole damned city of East Gate. I came here looking for help!"

Chapter Six

GOOD GOD in heaven! A *third* Mongol army?

"Tadaos! We have a third of the land forces in the city now. You collect up as many troops as you can hold and take them to East Gate. I'll follow as fast as I can with the rest!" I shouted.

"I'm low on fuel, sir!"

"Then tear down these docks if you have to, and those buildings, too, if you need more wood. But get there!"

"Yes, sir!"

The nearest city gate was the one Captain Wladyclaw and I had left stuffed with Mongol corpses, so we had to race on to the next. Damn! I should have had brains enough to mount a signalman on one of the Big People and keep him with me, but I simply hadn't thought of it. When the men were concentrated in war carts, there was always a signal-man handy in every sixth cart, so there was no point wasting a Big Person on one. Now the situation had changed, and I hadn't been bright enough to change with it. My stupidity was wasting precious time!

Once in the city, I soon found a bugler and had him sound BREAK OFF FIGHTING, MAN THE WAR CARTS, and EAST GATE IS BURNING. The first two were standard

signal tunes that most of the men knew, or at least the
officers did, and they could inform the others. The last
required the use of a special code that the signalmen had
worked out. Our bugles could play only seven notes, but if
one played two or three notes in rapid succession, there
were enough combinations to cover each letter of the alphabet as well as the numbers and punctuation marks. Messages were spelled out in a sort of code. It took a man with
perfect pitch to play and understand the code, and many of
the signalmen couldn't do it. Fortunately, the man I'd found
was one who could, and there were enough others like him
to get the message passed around.

Soon bugles all over the city were repeating my orders.
Men were scurrying to find dropped weapons — many had
abandoned their pikes as being unmanageable in the narrow, crooked city streets — and making their way to the
Carpenter's Gate. We raced across town to get to the carts
ahead of them, but it occurred to me that I'd better tell the
people still on Wawel Hill what was going on.

I went to the Inner Gate and shouted to the guards, "East
Gate is burning! The army is going to have to pull out of
here and go to their aid. I think we've killed most of the
Mongols in the city, but you people will have to do the final
mop-up yourselves. Do you hear me?"

A gray-bearded man in ancient armor stuck his head out
of a small window and looked down at me. "We hear you,
Count Conrad, but you must realize that there are few here
save women, children, and the aged. The noble knights all
went off to fight the enemy in the field! Their ladies all just
went off somewhere, I think to find a safer place to weather
the invasion. Most of the young guildsmen fell defending
the outer walls, those that did not leave months ago to join
your army. Many of those that were able to get here after
the lower city fell have died defending Wawel Hill. Women
have been manning catapults and crossbows, and children

have been bringing ammunition to them. We have nothing
left to 'mop up' with!''

"You'll just have to do the best you can," I shouted
back. "Good-bye and good luck!''

I heard him swearing at me as we left, but what else could
I do?

We went through the city, out the Carpenter's Gate, and
back to the war carts. Few of the troops had gotten there
yet, and most of the cart guards were asleep. They'd decided that one man awake out of six was sufficient, and I
really couldn't fault them. A minor attack had been beaten
off earlier in the day, but aside from that it had been quiet.
I let them sleep, since it would be good to have at least a
few men who were well rested.

More of our men were arriving all the time, though most
of them were staggering badly in the rain and gloom. Few
of them were actually wounded, but running and fighting
for two days straight is about all any normal man can take.

I waited in the rain and dark for an entire hour and then
decided that we had to go.

"But only half the men have gotten here yet, sir!'' Baron
Gregor objected. "There's only about two dozen men to a
cart, and that many could never pull nonstop to East Gate.
They wouldn't have anyone to relieve them.''

"You're right, of course. Well, move the men up to the
first carts. Get a full platoon on each cart and have them
move out at a quickstep. As more men straggle in, we'll fill
more carts and have them catch up with the rest at double
time. You'd best stay here and see that the job gets done.''

"Sir, that'll make a mess of the whole command structure! Nobody will know who's in charge.''

"Structure be damned! East Gate is burning! Just make
sure that there are six knights and a knight bannerette for
each cart, and a captain for every six of them. The field-

grade officers can sort things out among themselves as we're moving. It's not as though anybody can get lost on a railroad!''

"Yes, sir. What about the wounded?"

"Send the walking wounded back into the city to help out there. Set up a camp for those badly hurt right here."

"Yes, sir," he said, and started shouting orders. The first cart moved out in minutes, with Captain Wladyclaw acting as point man.

Even doing a quickstep was torture for the men, but we pushed on into the night. At around midnight I got word that we now had an even gross of companies in the column, and I hoped that they would be enough to handle whatever was happening at East Gate. By this point each of the men had been able to get a few hours' sleep while riding the carts, and I figured that they could take it. I gave the order to go double time.

I found myself dozing in the saddle, but fortunately a Big Person doesn't need to sleep at all. We pushed on, changing pullers every quarter hour.

I wished that there was some word from Baron Vladimir, but none had come. Had he encountered still more Mongols? Had the courier failed to make it through to him? This business of not knowing what was going on was nerveracking. I'd often heard of the "fog of war," but I never would have believed that it could take so much out of a commander.

If the Mongols had gotten to East Gate, had they gone beyond it? Were the boys at Eagle Nest under attack? The girls at Okoitz? And what about my people, my wife and children at Three Walls? Had all of southern Poland been overrun?

And what of East Gate? Was it still standing? It was our strongest fortification next to the city of Three Walls. It had six towers surrounding the castle, each nine stories tall and made of reinforced concrete, with a dozen swivel guns on top of each one . A low two-story wall connected the towers, and while that wall wasn't tall enough to stop footmen with ladders, no horse could ever get over it. Then six dozen yards inside those defenses was a concrete castle that was as strong as I knew how to make it. The walls were six stories high and protected by six more towers, each eight stories tall. The whole complex bristled with guns and had all sorts of nasty tricks to play on an attacker.

How could such a fort be taken by an enemy with only horses and arrows? How could a completely concrete structure possibly be on fire? To be sure, the fort was manned by women, but they were all properly trained and highly motivated. Much of their ammunition had had to be transferred to the riverboats during the Battle for the Vistula, but a great deal was still left to them. They were up to their armpits in refugees, but the captainette in charge should have been able to handle things. With that strong a fort, all she had to do was close the gates, and then she could laugh at the enemy. The walls were too tall to be scaled and too strong to be battered in.

Well, outside of the walls was the huge Riverboat Assembly Building, and it was made of wood.

A cold feeling went through me. Our casualties during the Battle for the Vistula were much higher than I had expected them to be. The castle had been filled to the rafters with civilian refugees, so I had the loft of the assembly building converted for use as a hospital. Those wounded men were at the mercy of the enemy, and the Mongols didn't know what mercy was!

We pushed on through the night and into the morning. The men were staggering with fatigue, and I found myself dozing off in the saddle, dreaming strange dreams and suddenly jerking back into reality, unsure of whether I had dreamed or was hallucinating or was actually trying to survive in an alien environment. I saw my pregnant wife, Francine, naked with her feet nailed to a door frame, her belly horribly slashed and her throat cut open by my own sword. I saw my children by Krystyana and Cilicia murdered on the ground, their tiny heads bashed open on the rocks. Eventually the nightmares of my dreams of torture and the nightmare of my tortured reality fused into a living horror that went on and on forever. Yet when I was sure that I could go no farther, when I knew that I must fall off my mount and sleep forever, I looked and saw the troops gasping, running, staggering, splashing on the muddy boards beside me. If they could go on, then so could I. I drew strength from their dedication and pushed onward.

It was well past noon when we got to East Gate. The Riverboat Assembly Building was gone, reduced to a few blackened stumps sticking up from rain-soaked foundations. The *Enterprise* was at the docks, next to four hulks burned to the waterline, and the city was guarded by my own troops.

A sentry waved us through, but I stopped to talk to him. "What's going on here, warrior?" I asked.

"We got here at dawn by riverboat, sir. Everybody was dead."

"Dead? How many Mongols were involved? Which way did they go?"

"I don't much know anything else, sir. I've been standing guard ever since we got here, and nobody's told me nothing. Maybe you'd best talk to Baron Tadaos. He's back on the boat, I think."

I told the men in my relief column to pull into the railroad yard and rest, and once there most of the men pulling just lay down in the cold spring rain and fell asleep. Those on the carts were already sleeping.

Captain Wladyclaw was near at hand. I told him to get

fresh scouts out on Big People and to find out what he could.

Baron Tadaos was in his cabin, debriefing a young corpsman who was crying and shaking in his chair. The man's clothes were badly burned, his hair was mostly gone, and there were blisters on his hands and face.

"Come in, sir, and sit down. There's some terrible things happened here," Tadaos said.

I sat, grateful to sit on something that wasn't a saddle. "Maybe you'd best tell me the story from the beginning, Baron."

"Yes, sir. I got here yesterday around noon and saw the boat house was burning. I'd put off my company of troops with you almost a week before, so I was down to the boat crew and the signal group under Baron Piotr. Mongols was all over the place, but we docked between two of the other boats that was here. See, half my boats was in port for lack of repairs, fuel, and ammunition. We only had a dozen rounds for each of the guns, but I figured that we'd see what help we could be, anyway."

He was interrupted as an armored boatman came in with a big tray heavily laden with food and drink. "We found a storeroom in the castle that hadn't been broken into, sir. You haven't eaten since yesterday, and I promised your wives that I'd take care of you, sir."

He set the tray on the desk and left without another word.

"I can only pray that the girls are still alive somewheres. I guess we all need to eat. Dig in, gentlemen," Tadaos said.

"But like I was saying," he said with food in his mouth, "we left three gunners on the bow to do what they could, and the rest us went out with swords and pikes. I was even out of arrows, so I left my bow behind. Never did see it again.

"We joined up with what was left of the boat repairmen,

the crews of the other boats, and the medics that was taking care of the wounded in the hospital here. A lot of the walking wounded was with us, too, but we was still way outnumbered. Them Mongols being on horseback didn't help none, neither. We lost us a lot of men, and they pushed us back to the boats.

"Only by then most of the boats was on fire, except for this one on the end, the *Enterprise*. The engineman on the boat had brains enough to have a head of steam up, and we had no choice but to push off and look for help.

"I didn't like doing that, since all five of my wives was in the castle, or so I thought, and it felt like I was murdering them and the kids, too. But it was run for help or die right there for no good reason, so we ran.

"Those damn radios of yours haven't worked for a week, but when we got to Cracow, we saw that it was burning, too. That's when I ran into you. Doing what you said, we collected up four companies of troops, all of which I could get aboard, seeing as how they didn't have no war carts, and we ripped down the docks and a dozen sheds nearby to fuel our trip back here. It damn nearly wasn't enough. I'd already given the order to start tearing down the boat when the lookout spotted East Gate, and we made it on our head of steam with the boat still intact. Just as well, since this just might be the last boat we got left!

"The place was empty when we got here first thing in the morning. Empty of living people, anyhow. You could see where there'd been a fight in front of the boat house, and our boys sold their lives pretty damn dearly, let me tell you. But there wasn't no fight around the castle. There was just a massacre, I think the worst massacre the world has ever seen! I just come back from there, and what I saw would make the worst sinner in the Christian world fall down and cry!

"There must be twenty or thirty thousand people dead in there, sir, and every one of them women or children or a few old gaffers. Ain't a one of them could have done the Mongols a bit of harm, but the filthy bastards murdered them all, anyway. Shit, sir, I ain't got words bad enough for them . . . them . . . whatevers."

Chapter Seven

THE BARON was crying, and I let him have a few moments to get a hold of himself. After a while he continued.

"Sir, I didn't find any of my people, but there was so many dead in there that I knew we'd be weeks sorting them all out. I figured my family was done for, but then some of the troops found this young feller, and what he says is that it wasn't our people who was murdered in there. I mean that they wasn't army families. He says that all them women and kids was the families of nobility from Cracow, Sandomierz, and points in between! But maybe you better hear about it straight from him."

"Maybe I'd better, Tadaos. How about it, son? Are you up to repeating your story for me?"

"Yes, sir. I think so, sir. I was a corpsman working in the hospital that was set up in the loft of the boat house, I mean the Riverboat Assembly Building."

"Relax, son," I said. "You're among friends here. Just tell us the story the way it happened. And tell me, how old are you?" It was maddening to take all this time listening, but unless I knew what had happened, I wouldn't know what to do next.

"Yes, sir. I just turned fifteen. Anyway, I heard my

captain telling one of the banners that he had just come back
from the fort and that they couldn't give us any help. He
said that the women's army contingent there was pulling out
with all the commoner refugees in the whole fort. He was
pretty mad about it, but he said that there was nothing he
could do to change things. He didn't command the stupid
cunt in charge of the fort. Excuse me, sir, but that's what he
called her.''

"Yes, yes. But *why* was she abandoning her post?" I
said. A captainette was the woman left in charge of an
installation when the men went off to war. It was an unusual
position in that it was temporary in nature. For example,
Captainette Lubinska, who had been in charge of East Gate,
was ordinarily in charge of the accounting section there, and
during normal times she had no authority at all outside of
accounting. But once the men went off to fight the enemy in
the field, she was in absolute charge, subject only to a
clearly defined chain of command that ended with me. She
even outranked the six baronesses that ordinarily lived at
East Gate, for example, and they were expected to obey her
orders.

The reason for all this was that men rarely chose their
wives for their ability as battle commanders, and it was
important to have the most competent woman in charge, no
matter who she had married.

But nobody except me and Baroness Krystyana could
have legally ordered Captainette Lubinska from her post.

"Sir, I was just overhearing somebody else's conversation, and my captain's at that, even though he was pretty
loud about it. He said that Count Herman's wife came up
with a few dozen bodyguards and a large group of other
noblewomen, and the captainette wouldn't let them in. She
said that fort was full and that these new refugees would
have to continue on down to Hell, I mean the Warrior's

School, thirty miles away, for shelter. But the countess
talked the captainette into coming down and talking to her,
and then the countess said that the fort wasn't your property, sir, so it wasn't army property. The fort really belonged to Count Lambert, her brother-in-law, and Count
Lambert wanted her to take it over and shelter there, since
it was the strongest fort in Poland, and everybody knew it."

"That wasn't true," I said. "Count Lambert paid for the
fort, but I was to see to the manning of it. He wouldn't have
changed that without talking to me about it. I can't believe
that he would ever have given anything to the countess. He
hated her! Not that we'll ever know for sure. Count Lambert
died days ago on the battlefield west of Sandomierz."

"Yes, sir, but she got the captainette to believing her,
anyway. They went into the fort. Then an awful lot more
nobility kept coming, and the countess turned every commoner out the fort to make room for them. Some of them
went on to Hell, or the Warrior's School, I mean, and some
went up to the hills to take their chances up there."

"And this happened three days ago?" I asked, trying not
to vent my anger at the captainette. It was really all my fault
for appointing that woman to so important a post in the first
place. I'd had a bad feeling about her, but I'd done nothing
about replacing her.

"I think four, sir. Then about noon yesterday, I was
outside taking a breather, and I saw about a hundred old-
style knights ride up in chain mail and all. I thought it was
kind of funny because they were all riding little horses, but
their leader spoke real good Polish to the sentry, and their
shields were all painted with Polish arms. Anyway, the
leader said that they had word from Cracow, and I heard the
countess yell that they should be admitted. I saw the gates
go up and the drawbridge go down, but then my break was
over and I had to get back to tending the wounded. I didn't

think much of it at the time, but I guess I should have. That must have been how the Mongols tricked their way into the fort.

"Then, about a half hour later, one of our men came up shouting that the place was crawling with Mongols, that they were streaming in on us from the south. We all armed ourselves, but my captain said I was to take care of the wounded, since some of those men were badly hurt. I was the only corpsman left behind. I didn't like it, but orders were orders. I could hear screams from the castle and shouts from the fighting down below. All the wounded who could move had gone down to join the fight, even some guys with only one arm, but there were still more than two dozen of them up there that were helpless.

"A while after that, one of my patients started shouting that the building was on fire, that we all had to get out somehow. From the smoke and the smell, I could see he was right, but there were so many of them and only one of me! I picked up one of the men who was near the stairway and carried him down to the ground floor and outside, but the fighting was so bad out there that he was killed by a Mongol arrow before I got out the door.

"I went back up, and the fire had gotten real bad. Men were crying to me, begging me to not let them die by burning to death. One man, a captain with his legs both messed up, he grabbed me by the arm. 'You know what you've got to do!' he says, and I said that I didn't. He says, 'You can't let all these men die by fire! That's the worst possible way to go. It's so painful that any man doing it would die with a curse on his lips, and then what happens to his soul? You've got that axe, boy. Use it! And use it on me first!'

"Then he starts singing 'Te Deum,' sir, real loud, and the rest of the men starts singing with him, those who were conscious. I'd armed myself when everybody else had, and my axe was sharp and new in its sheath. I'd never used it, not till then, anyway.

"Sir, I chopped that captain straight across the neck, and it took his head almost off. Then I went down the line of wounded men and did the same to almost every one of them. They kept on singing until I was done. Some of those men I killed were already unconscious. Some of the others gritted their teeth as I came up to them, and a few nodded to me that it was okay, what I was doing, but only one of them said I shouldn't do it. He was Robby Prajinski, and I knew him because he was from my own village. He screamed and begged me not to hurt him, so I didn't. I just went to the next man. I guess the fire was real bad, because I couldn't see so good. Maybe it was the smoke, or maybe I was just crying, but I hit every one of those poor men square, sir, even the last one where the floor burned out under us. He was singing until I hit him. I guess that's where I got these burns.

"I lost my axe in the fall, and I could hear Robby screaming somewhere, but I couldn't find him in the fire. I got outside somehow, and all of our men out there were dead. I was thinking I should go back in to try to find Robby, but my clothes outside my armor were burning. It was like the Mongols didn't see me somehow, because I made it into the river, and that put the fire out. I drifted downstream for a while, and I was kind of surprised that I floated in my armor. Maybe it's the goose-down in the gambesons. Anyway, I crawled out, and I guess I mostly slept until the sentries found me."

I buried my face in my hands, unsure whether I was crying as much as the young corpsman was.

"You did what you had to do, son. Fate put a horrible job in front of you, but you did your duty, and you did it well. May God bless and forgive you," I said. After a bit I added, "You did right, son, but maybe you'd better go to confession. There are a number of chaplains around here somewhere."

"Yes, sir." The boy got up to leave, and Tadaos put some more food in his blistered hands before showing him out.

"Take care of him, won't you," I said to Tadaos.

"Will do, sir. Now, before you leave, do you have any spare ammunition? We'd stripped most of the ammo from the fort for the fight on the river, and it seems like the Mongols burned all the rest of it they could find."

"We can give you a few dozen cases. You're going to see what you can do about patrolling the river?"

"There's nothing much else I *can* do, sir. That, and there are still three of my boats unaccounted for, and I mean to find them. Baron Piotr's getting downright antsy about it."

"Piotr still lives, then?"

"Yeah, he was one of the lucky ones."

"I'm glad. Well, good hunting." I stood to leave.

"You too, sir."

It was now late in the afternoon, and if we left within the hour, well, there were a dozen targets for the Mongols within two dozen miles of here. We'd probably get wherever we were going before dawn. I ordered that all of our Night Fighter companies be re-formed and put in the front of the column, that all of the relatively fresh men who had come in by riverboat be put on the line behind them, and had the two companies in the worst shape left behind to man this installation and start cleaning it up. While I had been talking to Tadaos, eight more companies had come up from Cracow. The city was now secure, even if most of the wooden buildings in the lower city were totally burned down. At least there were no Mongols about, or rather, no live ones.

But there was no word from Baron Vladimir. Two-thirds

of our army might as well have vanished from the earth for all I knew.

Baron Gregor just about had things reorganized when Captain Wladyclaw galloped up.

"It's definite," he said. "The entire Mongol force somehow regathered into a single body, and then it went east. There was some fighting at Sir Miesko's manor, but it did not fall to the enemy, or at least it hadn't when one of my scouts saw it through a telescope an hour ago. He said that a bunch of crazy old ladies were up in the towers there with swivel guns and a few gross Mongols were lying dead around them, while the other living enemy troops were keeping at a respectable distance. But he said that the bulk of the Tartars had turned south and are heading for Three Walls, sir."

Three Walls! My wife, my children, and most of my ex-mistresses were at Three Walls. My first impulse was to take my entire force there at a double time, but Baron Gregor talked me out of it. Or rather, he shouted me out of it.

"Sir, these troops are simply not physically capable of running all night long three nights in a row! Nobody could possibly do that. Furthermore, at a quick march, where the men can get at least some sleep, our forces can get to Three Walls by dawn. Getting there sooner won't accomplish anything except telling the enemy that he is about to be attacked! It makes sense to send Baron Ilya ahead with his Night Fighters to see what they can accomplish, but the rest of our men are best off being fresh to fight at dawn.

"Three Walls is even stronger than East Gate here was, and Baroness Krystyana's in charge there. You know that girl even better than I do, and you know she wouldn't fall for a Mongol ruse the way that silly twit of a countess did here!"

"Yeah, I guess you're right, Gregor." I swung into the saddle.

"And another thing, *sir*! Every man here has gotten at least some sleep in the last four days except you. Have you gone crazy? Do you think you can direct a battle with half your brain not working? Do you think we'd trust our lives to someone who was about ready to keel over? Now, you get off that goddamn superhorse and stretch out on one of the war carts! Go to sleep! We'll get you to the war on time, never you fear."

"But . . ."

"But nothing! Shut up and soldier!"

"Yes, sir," I said.

Chapter Eight

MY SECOND in command was shaking me awake. "It'll be dawn in half an hour, sir."

Sleeping in well-fitted plate mail is fairly comfortable, sort of like relaxing in a good contour chair. I threw off my old wolfskin cloak and shook my head to clear it. "What's been happening, Baron Gregor?"

I sat up on the moving cart, and Gregor, riding beside me on the white Big Person, put a bowl of soup in one of my hands and a mug of beer in the other. Not quite what I needed. *God*, but I wished that something was available with caffeine in it.

"We're about three miles from the hedge at Three Walls, sir. The rain stopped just after you started snoring, and a while later the radios started working after a fashion. Duke Henryk *still* has not pulled out of Legnica. Baron Vladimir has arrived at Cracow and is advancing on us. The transmission was pretty poor, and that's all we have been able to find out about him."

"The duke's conventional knights wouldn't be of much use to us, anyway. Look at the fiasco they caused at Sandomierz. I can't see waiting for Baron Vladimir. He'll be days getting here. What about the rest of our installations?"

"Okoitz, Coaltown, Eagle Nest, and Copper City are all safe and sound. They haven't been bothered. The boys at Eagle Nest say that they have one aircraft rebuilt and ready to fly. A second should be ready later this morning, sir."

"Good. Tell them that I want that plane flying over Three Walls as soon as possible. We need all the surveillance we can get."

"Yes, sir. The granary in the Bledowska desert was taken by the Mongols—we only had a platoon guarding it, and it was never meant to be seriously defended—but the Mongols left it intact. They probably considered it useful booty, to be used later. Sir Miesko's manor was hit, but the attack was squashed by a hundred lady schoolteachers under Lady Richeza. Our ladies at Three Walls have beaten off two serious attacks, and the Mongols have laid siege to the place. Your wife tells me that a siege tower and some wheeled catapults are being built just out of swivel gun range."

"Francine is well, then?" I finished the beer and started in on the soup. It had a lot of meat in it, but very little grain and no vegetables. It was Lent, but the men fighting to defend their country had been given dispensation to eat meat by the Bishop of Wroclaw. When we had thrown out some of our supplies to lighten the load, the troops had kept the foods they craved the most, and two weeks on a high-protein diet had not made up for the lack of meat in the weeks before that.

"She said she was, and she sends you her love. I sent her yours, of course, but I didn't see any sense in waking you. So far, casualties at Three Walls have been almost nil. An arrow hasn't much force left by the time it gets to the top of a seven-story wall. The catapults are something else, however."

"Yeah. Especially if they're like the ones they used on us in the riverboats. We'd better hurry."

"We'll get there at a walk in time for an attack at gray dawn. There's no point in getting there sooner than that," Gregor said.

"Oh, I suppose you're right. Do the Mongols know we're coming?"

"Possibly not. Baron Ilya's Night Fighters did a pretty fair cleanup job while you slept. The Mongols seem to have a real general in charge. At least they left plenty of sentries and scouts out. 'Course, they still haven't learned not to do sentry duty sitting around a campfire, but the thought was there. The last bunch Ilya taught that lesson to weren't in any shape to pass on the education they got! He had the horses slaughtered as well as the men so that none of them would find their way back to the enemy camp and tip our hand. I think our scouts took out all of theirs. When a Big Person starts to sniffing on the trail of a Mongol, you just know there's going to be bloodshed, and those girls can really fight in the dark!"

"So Captain Wladyclaw gets another feather in his cap, and Ilya'll be harder to control than ever," I said. "What do you know about the enemy positions?"

"Best as we can tell, they're all camped on the killing ground, this side of the kitchen gardens, on the place we used to use for a parade ground. There's some wells down there, and they probably figure that the big hedge of Krystyana's roses offers them some protection."

"Nice. Better wake all the men and get some food in them."

"The cooks have been at it for an hour, sir. During the night I had all the cart wheels greased so they're real quiet."

"Good. Make sure that the men stay that way, too. Semaphores and hand signals only from now on."

"Right, sir."

"And give me my mount back!"

It was still dark as we approached the city. I was in front

of our silent column to make sure that things were the way I thought they were. The double-tracked railroad went through a simple gate before it entered the killing ground.

This gate was never intended as a military defense; its main job was simply to keep animals in. Nonetheless, I was surprised to see that it was manned by our own Night Fighters. Baron Ilya was there waiting for me.

"I got maybe a company of my men just inside the gate in Mongol outfits, sir, so's they wouldn't know we was here. I just wanted you to know so's you wouldn't shoot them down."

"Okay. I'll signal you just before we start the attack, and you pull those men behind our lines in a hurry. Once things warm up, the gunners won't be too choosy."

"Right, sir."

Baron Gregor had a man using hand signals to split off our troops, sending a column of war carts in each direction on our side of the rose hedge. Save for the snap of branches as the big carts were pulled through them, the columns were silent as snakes. We could hear the Mongols a dozen yards away from us on the other side of the hedge, but we didn't hear them give any alarm.

As each cart reached its assigned position, the men quietly took the big armored lid off the vehicle. This was slung on spare pikestaffs six yards to the side of the cart to act as a shield for the men pulling it. At the same time, the pins were pulled from the casters of the big wheels, the wheels were turned at right angles away from the line of march, and the wheels on the armored side were locked in that position. The carts were pulled sideways into battle.

Harnesses were attached to the armored side of the cart, and the pikemen tied them to the ring on their backplates with a slipknot. Gunners quietly mounted the pinions of their guns into the "oarlocks" built into the sides of the carts. They lit the ignition lamps in the base of each gun, loaded them, and set out their spare ammunition. Cookstoves and other nonessentials were set on the ground. Pikes and halberds were handed out, and men checked each other's arms and armor.

Having been practiced hundreds of times, the conversion from transport vehicle to war machine took only minutes, even in silence and nearly total darkness. Some of the halberdiers had to be reminded to get in front of their shields, since this wasn't their usual position, but Baron Gregor had briefed the captains on our plan of attack.

Six hundred carts take a long time to move two miles quietly in the dark and over unprepared terrain, even when everything is well coordinated. At any moment the Mongols could find us sneaking up on them, and a well-planned surprise attack could be turned into a bloody chaos. But despite my sins, God was still on our side.

At the first hint of dawn I saw my troops lined up and ready, stretching a mile on each side of me. I called to Ilya in a stage whisper, and a few hundred ersatz Mongols poured quickly through our line, heading back to where they had stowed their armor.

Still using hand signals, I gestured ADVANCE, and every captain passed it on.

The hedge was five yards high and thickly tangled with long, sharp thorns. The seed package had claimed that a hedge of these Japanese roses was proof against man and beast, and for once the seed company hadn't lied. I think it gave the Mongols a false sense of security. No man or animal smaller than an elephant and bigger than a mouse could possibly go through it, but good steel could!

Thirty-six hundred halberdiers started making toothpicks out of two miles of Krystyana's roses. The hedge had been only two yards thick when we'd planted it seven years earlier, but it had somehow spread to a dozen yards and more in some places. This surprised me, and perhaps it gave the enemy more time to get ready for us, but I think they wasted a fair amount of time trying to figure out what the strange noise was, so it all balanced out. We finally broke into the clear, and the gunners opened fire.

We went across the Mongol camp and trampled it flat in the process. It was huge. Judging from the size of the enemy camp near Sandomierz and the known number of men that had been in it, there must have been two hundred thousand Mongols here, yet at first the resistance was surprisingly light. No more than five thousand men came against us, and many of them were obviously wounded. They went down quickly, and I signaled CEASE FIRE.

A panicky thought shook me. Had the bulk of them somehow escaped our trap? All my forces were facing Three Walls. Were the Mongols behind us, waiting to hit our unprotected rear?

Anna came up to my side, carrying the protesting Captain Wladyclaw with her.

"Captain Wladyclaw! I'm glad you're here. Look, we aren't finding enough Mongols in front of us! If they're to our rear, we're in big trouble. Get your scouts way behind us and get word back in a hurry if we're walking into their trap instead of springing our own. Here," I said, dismounting. "Take the white person with you as well and put another man on her. I'll ride in on the carts."

"Yes, sir, but Anna has stopped obeying me again."

"Anna, if you love me, go with Wladyclaw and help protect my back." She hesitated a minute and then galloped back through our lines.

Chapter Nine

A WHILE later we topped a rise, and I saw where the missing Mongols had gone. They were pulling a dawn attack of their own. Lovely! If they were getting set to attack, their minds would be off defense. The war carts went ahead at a quick-step. We were still two miles from the main wall as the sun came up. We recited our morning oaths as we advanced.

Except for one week of the year when we thinned our stock of wild animals, the lower portion of the killing field did duty as our parade ground and as pasture for our dairy herd. The evidence was that the Mongols had slaughtered our cows, but they'd soon pay for them in full. Fortunately, this was not our prize herd, or they would have made me *mad*!

We were advancing over the very ground that many of my officers had practiced on for five years. We knew every hill and rock on it. What's more, there is a certain psychological advantage to fighting on your own home turf.

Three Walls was built where I had found a number of minerals in a boxed canyon. I'd given it its name because God had already built three of the city walls for us, and we only had to build the fourth. Since that time we had added a second wall made out of bricks that doubled as a housing unit outside the first wooden one. Eventually a third wall, concrete this time, was built outside the second, and now most people thought it was named for the three combination wall and apartment buildings we'd built there.

We topped another rise, and I could see a commotion ripple through the Mongol ranks. They knew we were here, and they knew that they were caught between the proverbial rock and the hard place, with the walls of the city to their south, impenetrable hedges to their east and west, and seven ranks of armored men coming shoulder to shoulder at them from the north! Further, there were 3,600 guns pointing in their direction, and if they didn't know what that meant, they were about to learn.

The Mongols had built four huge catapults mounted on wheels, along with a wheeled siege tower that looked to be eight stories tall. The catapults were built fairly close to the ground, and were pulled along by men with ropes as well as pushed forward by men leaning into long poles, without needing much in the way of direction by the Mongol officers. The officers were there anyway, though, keeping all four catapults in a neat, straight line, a dozen yards behind the siege tower.

The siege tower was being moved in much the same way, except that many long ropes were attached to the top of it as well. Directed by a wildly gesticulating officer at the top of the tower, men were pulling on these ropes to keep the ungainly structure from toppling over. The great wooden machines moved slowly toward the city wall as we advanced on the enemy.

Our ladies manning the swivel guns on top of the wall were firing constantly at the enemy troops who were laboring to get the machines into position, and were killing them in droves—but as soon as a man fell, he was replaced by one of the seemingly inexhaustible Mongol reserves.

Suddenly, the siege tower started to tilt forward, toward the wall. The men on the ropes behind the tower strained to keep it upright, while the officer at the top directed those pushing and pulling it forward to continue at their task. The effort was well coordinated, and the front two wheels were actually lifted slightly into the air, with all of the weight of the siege tower on the rear two wheels, as it continued inexorably forward.

I could see what the officer in charge was trying to do. Some castles have big clay jars buried around the walls that will be crushed when any great weight rolls over them and will stop or tip over a siege engine. If the officer could get his machine past the hidden jars that had just been crushed by the front wheels, it would be in position to attack our walls. The only problem with his plan was that we didn't have any such jars planted.

I'd never really studied a modern sewage treatment plant back when I had the chance, but I had once helped to install a single-family septic system. Needing to do something with the sewage generated by the four thousand families living in my city, I had simply scaled up that single-family system by a factor of four thousand. Three Walls had a tile field that covered almost a square mile, which made the kitchen garden above it one of the most fertile in the world. There was also a bodacious septic tank that was as long as our outer wall. It went from hedge to hedge, and was thirty yards wide and ten deep. And the roof of the tank wasn't any stronger than it had to be.

Watching them through my binoculars, I could see that the Mongols were racing hundreds of men into the moving tower, all of them eager to be among the first to attack the women on our city wall. The Mongol officer looked supremely self-confident until the rear wheels of his siege tower encountered the holes that had been punched into the roof of the septic tank by the front wheels.

With a certain calm deliberation, the huge siege tower dropped three stories into the dark grey muck below. Many of the men pulling from the front were dragged down with it, and those at the back, pushing on the long poles, were suddenly catapulted into the back of the tower, to slide helplessly down into the slime with the others. Then the tower started to tip sideways, and fell with apparent slowness onto the tightly packed horsemen who were escorting it forward. I saw the face of the officer in charge, looking vastly annoyed as he and they and it went through the roof and sank out of sight.

Smelly grey muck splashed over the catapults and those propelling them forward, but with a stoic lack of imagination, they all continued their advance, thinking perhaps that it can't happen here.

It could. Simultaneously, with military precision, all four catapults broke through the roof of the septic tank and sank out of sight, along with most of the men propelling them.

A cheer went up from our ranks, and from our ladies guarding the city wall.

"A rough way to die." One of the pikers laughed. "Drowning in sewage!"

"Laugh all you want to," another said. "Odds are we're the ones that are going to have to fish out and bury them smelly farts."

"Would you do it for five pounds of gold and silver? That's what every one of them bastards carry! I tell you I would!" a third trooper shouted .

"I believe you! 'Course, in your case, nobody could smell the difference!" a fourth yelled.

My men were outnumbered at least eight to one, and they were on foot while their enemies were mostly mounted. Yet not a man of them seemed to have even considered the obvious possibility that they might lose! Considering their spirit, I thought that it was an unlikely possibility, too!

An airplane came and circled overhead. He didn't drop any messages, so everything must have looked okay to the pilot.

A few squadrons of Mongol horse archers rode past our line and let fly at us. I ignored them. Best we save our ammunition until we were firing at point-blank range into crowds of them. Their arrows couldn't do us much damage anyway.

Through my binoculars I could see the occasional puff of smoke from the swivel guns atop the wall, but I could also see that Krystyana hadn't fired her wall guns yet. Smart girl! She was saving her best for the last.

The wall guns were cast into the two yards of reinforced concrete that made up the first story of the wall. Imagine a shotgun with a bore you could stick your leg into or a primitive sort of breech-loading claymore mine. The muzzles were still covered over with their thin coating of plaster, a surprise that was yet to be presented at the party.

The field narrowed as we marched south, and the carts on the ends had to drop out and follow behind. This caused no confusion because we'd practiced on this very field so many times before.

A half mile from the wall the Mongol general must have decided that a breakout was in order, for at least half their horsemen formed up and charged our line. It was time. I ordered FIRE AT WILL, and the bugles played it along our whole line.

Our swivel guns let loose, and noise and smoke covered the field. Through patches of clarity, you could see where single bullets had plowed rows through the Mongol ranks, killing three or four of them at a time. Very few of that first wave got through to hit the pikers and axemen, and I don't think any horseman who got into our pikes lived to try it again.

This was exactly the sort of fight I had envisioned from

the beginning, the sort we had armed and trained for. And it was working beautifully. The men were elated! After the huge losses we had suffered on the riverboats, after the helplessness the troops had felt watching the conventional knights being slaughtered west of Sandomierz, after the confusion of the battle at Cracow, after seeing the senseless slaughter at East Gate, and after all the mind-numbing running and pulling in between, finally, at last, something was working perfectly!

Naturally, somebody started to sing, and the troops along the entire line picked up the tune.

Poland is not yet dead!

Not while we yet live!

I could see that up on the wall, despite the fact that they were both pregnant, Cilicia and Francine were manning swivel guns right next to each other, firing down at the enemy. And I saw that two of Krystyana's sons — my own children! — were running ammunition to them. I waved, and they all waved back.

But you don't kill a quarter of a million men in a minute, and we kept advancing as best we could, but no longer at a full quickstep. Going over the fallen enemy and making sure they were really dead slowed us down. Our center was soon bowed back as the edges advanced more quickly, and we had them surrounded. I had to order the wings to slow down so we wouldn't be shooting through the enemy troops and back into our own.

About then Krystyana decided that it was time for the wall guns, and all nine dozen of them let loose at once. The effect astounded even me, and I'd designed the bloody things. Suddenly, everything within two gross yards of the wall was either very dead or trying very hard to get that way! Bits of shrapnel and dead Mongol were blown as far as our own troops. The enemy still standing were stunned and made easy marks for the swivel guns.

Then one knot of horsemen turned as their leader pointed directly at me. Suddenly, some three hundred men and horses wheeled and charged straight for my cart! Everything had been so beautiful, but suddenly things didn't look too good.

The gunners tore into them, and many riders went down. The Mongols knew that they were all dead men, but they wanted vengeance for their own deaths, vengeance in the form of *my* life! They kept coming, and as their ranks thinned, I saw in the center of them two faces I recognized. One was that of the Mongol ambassador, and the other was General Subotai Bahadur himself.

Standing in the center war cart, I drew my sword and waited. There was nothing else I could do.

"Thank you, our Lord, for these thy gifts, which we are about to receive, from thy bounty, through Christ, our Lord, amen," one of the gunners on my cart said. I didn't know if he was being sacrilegious or just thanking God for the targets, so I kept my mouth shut. It was pretty dry just then, anyway.

The two older Mongols seemed to be leading charmed lives, or perhaps the gunners were reluctant to shoot a man with white hair and wrinkles when there were so many younger targets available, but in the end they were the last two left alive. Together, their horses jumped my cart's big shield and came down directly on top of the pikemen. As they leapt from their dying horses toward the cart, a wounded piker caught Subotai in the gut with a grounded pike. I don't know which of the three us was most surprised, but the old general was suddenly airborne. He actually pole-vaulted right over my head!

The ambassador landed in the cart between two startled gunners and swung his sword at me. I parried it and gave him a slash to the forearm. His hand and sword went flying.

He pulled a dagger with his left hand, and I took that one off as well.

He said, "Damn you, Conrad!" and slumped to the bottom of the cart.

I looked at him and decided that we could use a Polish-speaking prisoner. I put tourniquets on his stumps.

The roar of gunfire slowed to a rattle and then to occasional pops. Slowly, it stopped completely. Troops looked wide-eyed over the smoke and the smell of the carnage, not quite ready to believe that it was finally over. Slowly, the truth dawned.

Victory! The tops of the walls and towers were covered with our women and children, cheering for us and for themselves. Baron Gregor had the men unleash themselves from the carts, and they walked to the wall, axes and pikes in hand so that they could chop up the fallen enemy and make sure that dead Mongols stayed that way. A brutal business, but a necessary one. There was no exchange of prisoners with the Mongols, and any who escaped would have to rob and murder their way home just to stay alive. Best to kill them clean here and now.

The prisoner I had taken was another matter. I had one of our medics sew up his stumps and left orders for him to be guarded.

Actually, our medics outnumbered our wounded, and we had less than a hundred killed. A remarkably one-sided victory.

I climbed down from my war cart and joined the others streaming toward the now open city gate. As I passed our wrecked septic tank, I saw a number of warriors around it, pikes in hand. Quite a few Mongol troops were floundering around in the wretched stench below us.

"Do you think they'll want some prisoners?" one of the warriors asked a friend.

"They didn't say nothing about wanting none," his friend answered. "Anyways, it 'ud be easier to catch them some fresh ones than it would be to clean these bastards off." And with that, he reversed his pike and used it to hold one of the dog paddling Mongols under the stinking grey mud.

"I guess you're right," said the first, reversing his pike.

I just shook my head and walked on until I ran into my second in command.

"Give the men leave to enjoy themselves until tomorrow morning," I told Baron Gregor, "except for two companies that you don't like. Somebody had better stay on guard. We'll be needing some radio operators as well."

"Right, sir."

"Try to get through to Baron Vladimir and tell him the news. Have him send half his men back to where we dumped all that booty and bring it here. The rest of his men should stop at East Gate and clean the place up. Send a scout to him if the radios aren't working. And I want the planes to fly over all of the country that they can and make sure that there isn't yet another Mongol army out there."

"Right, sir."

"Can you think of anything else we have to do?"

"Not offhand, sir, aside from spreading the word about this victory."

"Then after you get those messages out, go see your wives. I'm going to mine right now!"

I went back to my old apartment in the first wall through the cheering crowds of soldiers and their dependents. I smiled and waved back, trying to be the good politician, but my heart wasn't really in it. I had been going on my own adrenaline for weeks, and now at last it was leaching out of me. I felt incredibly tired, drained, and weak. I was sick of war and blood and dirt and saw nothing glorious about wallowing in them. What I really wanted to do was get out of this filthy, stinking, blood-soaked armor, take a long, hot bath, have a stiff drink, and kiss my wife, and not necessarily in that order.

I went up to my rooms and found both Francine and Cilicia waiting for me. Inwardly I groaned. The last thing I wanted now was more confrontation, and the Chinese symbol for an argument is two women under one roof.

They both smiled at me.

"We have decided," Francine said. "When we were shooting at the Mongols, we decided that we should share you. We both love you, and you love both of us, so we can make it work."

This statement surprised me as much as a new Mongol army. I sat down to take it all in. The horse really had learned how to sing!

The war was over, and now we'd have to get busy and build the peace.

Chapter Ten

FROM THE JOURNAL OF COUNTESS FRANCINE

Once I heard that our men were coming, I was no longer afraid. I knew that Conrad would never let us be harmed. Captainette Krystyana allowed me to operate one of the swivel guns, even though there were other women who were better at it than I. She said that seeing me in battle would encourage Count Conrad. I suppose that it was for the same reason that she put Lady Cilicia at the gun next to mine.

There is something about fighting in the company of others that gives one a strong sense of camaraderie, and I wonder if this isn't the reason why men like to do it so much. Certainly I could no longer hate Cilicia when she was shooting at the same murderers that I was.

"He loves both of us," she said to me during a lull in the fighting. "And we both love him."

"What you say is true. We can't help ourselves. Truly good men are hard to find," I said.

"Many of the women here share a man. Couldn't we do the same?" she said.

And so it was that after Conrad had rescued us from the Mongol horde, we both gave him a warm welcome. Knowing him well, we had a warm tub of water waiting for him, and together we stripped off his filthy, blood-drenched armor and clothes.

He had not had the chance to change his clothing for two weeks, and his outer clothes were spattered with so much blood and gore that they were stiff and hard even after we removed the metal from them. We didn't even consider having them laundered, but sent them out to be burned!

With one of us at each side of the tub, we washed him down like a little baby, and he loved it. We scrubbed him and rubbed him and even made little baby noises at him. We had to change the water twice before we got him really clean, and he drank an entire pitcher of cold beer while we did it.

Our love had been through a half-dozen fierce battles and had only one small injury. He didn't tell us then that this wound had cost him the sight in his right eye.

We hesitated in giving him a really proper hero's welcome, for we were both in our sixth month and feared to harm our children. Before he got there, we had debated what to do and had finally called in one of the maids to attend to his needs. The poor girl was disappointed, though, for once we got him out of the tub and dried, he went into his chamber and fell sound asleep on top of the covers. He didn't wake until noon the next day, and by then I was gone.

Leaving the maid to attend to Conrad in the unlikely event that he awoke, Cilicia and I dressed in our best and went down to join the army in its celebration. It was important that we make an appearance among the warriors. We first went and sang a mass at the church, as many of the men were doing, though Cilicia sat quietly through it, not being a Christian.

Then we went to join the party. The ladies had brewed vast quantities of strong beer for the occasion, and it was being consumed with gusto. We were both dying to find out all that happened, and Baron Gregor was most helpful. Baron Ilya was even more so, for I think that he is the only one of my husband's barons that does not have even one wife, so we had him to ourselves. As he talked on about the fighting on the riverboats, the battle near Sandomierz, the burning of Cracow, and the murder of the people at East Gate, the full horror and magnitude of the slaughter came to me.

And also the priceless opportunity that all this represented!

Think! Almost the entire nobility of the duchies of Little Poland, Sandomierz, and Mazovia had been killed. And not only the fighting men but most of their wives, children, and grandparents had died as well. In all of eastern Poland, there was no one left with the strength to defend the land except my husband, Conrad!

And there was no one left alive to inherit it all!

By himself, Conrad had defeated the biggest invasion Christendom had ever suffered, and he had done it almost without losses, except for his riverboats and aircraft. His huge land army was completely intact.

Those three duchies needed Conrad's protection, and I intended to see to it that they got it in the traditional manner! The few surviving nobles and freemen of eastern Poland were going to make Conrad their duke. Dukes! With the right persuasion, they'd make him the duke of all three duchies!

To do that, I was going to have to speak to all of them, and I'd have to do it before Duke Henryk got off his slovenly rump in Legnica! He hadn't fought for eastern Poland, and I was not about to let him reap the prize of victory.

First I went to Baron Gregor and told him of my plan. He was very enthusiastic about it and agreed to stop sending messages to Duke Henryk. He felt that it could be disastrous to tell the duke actual lies, but he thought it might be possible to convince his grace to stay in Legnica for another week by slight misdirection. I left that to the good baron and got myself ready to go to Cracow.

You see, the only way to talk to every one of the scattered people of eastern Poland was to use Conrad's magazine. For years everyone had relied on it for the news, and it had a perfect reputation for always telling the truth. Yet it hadn't occurred to anyone to use it to persuade.

The magazine was printed in the Franciscan monastery in Cracow, and Baron Gregor said that the monastery still stood, even though the buildings around it were in ruins. I intended to be there by dawn.

My condition was such that I could not safely mount a horse, but Conrad had had a number of railroad carriages built. One of the smallest was light and fast, though it carried only five people. I had two of my maids pack for themselves and me and went to the stables. Luck was still with me, for I found Anna there.

She was in surprisingly low spirits, and I had to take her to her ''spelling board'' to find out what the matter was. It took an hour to get the whole story out of her, but it was time well spent.

Conrad had found another mount like her, but white in color, and this person could not understand Polish as Anna and all her children could. She could only understand the English of the future that my husband came from. Conrad, acting with stupid male practicality, had kept the new mount to himself and had been ignoring Anna just when she felt he needed her most.

I had long admired Anna, and now she really needed a friend.

''Oh, you poor baby,'' I said to her. ''So Conrad went running off to battle, first on a riverboat without you and then on this new white hussy. Shame on him! To do such a thing to his oldest and best friend. As soon as we get back,

I'm going to scold him for what he has done to you. But right now there's something that we must do that is very important for him. I mean, he's been a bad boy, but we are still his ladies and we must take care of him, yes?''

She nodded yes.

"We have to go to Cracow and get the monks there to print a special issue of the magazine. This will tell everybody that Conrad should be the new boss. Can you get us there by morning if you push that new little railroad cart?''

She nodded yes.

It took some struggling to get the cart out of the building, for there were no attendants about. Everyone seemed to be at the victory party.

"My lady, you shouldn't be doing such heavy work!''

"Oh!'' I was startled and looked to see a young officer standing in the limelight. "You're Sir Miesko's son, aren't you?''

"I have that honor. Captain Wladyclaw of the scouts, at your service, my countess,'' he said, bowing deeply.

"I'm so glad you're here, Sir Wladyclaw. Can you get this carriage on the track?''

"But of course, my lady. Yet what do you want with it?''

There was nothing to do but take him into my confidence and explain the whole thing to him.

"Well, if Baron Gregor approves the plan, then so do I,'' he said. "Lord Conrad *should* be a duke, or better yet a king! But I think that he would not approve of his wife going all the way to Cracow unescorted, especially as there could be a Mongol or two still hiding out there. However, my men and I are free at the moment and would be honored to do the task.''

"But Sir Wladyclaw, that would make you miss the victory celebration.''

"It matters little, my lady, since my own men have their wives at the Warrior's School and not here. I myself am yet a bachelor, and there are six hundred platoons of young men in earnest competition for the regretfully few single ladies at Three Walls. Also, if we do not go to Cracow in your service, we will likely have to spend tomorrow burying dead Mongols, a task worth avoiding if it can be done with honor. So you see that it is you that do us the favor, Countess. I shall have a lance or two of scouts here before your servants arrive with your luggage."

The captain was always true to his word, and we were on the road in minutes, the captain with ten scouts, all riding Anna's children, and in Anna's carriage two of my maids and myself.

Conrad must have designed the carriage with Anna or one of her identical children in mind. Its wheels were placed under springs, with some sort of oil-filled pot that Conrad called a "shock absorber." Suffice to say that it ran with remarkable smoothness.

Conrad called this sort of carriage a "convertible," since the railroad wheels had very thick flanges that permitted it to be driven on ordinary roads as well as on railroad tracks.

At the back, there was a sort of lower half of a horse collar that perfectly fitted Anna's neck and shoulders. This let her push the cart without being encumbered with a harness, and the cart was so low to the ground that she could easily look over it. Pushing this collar to the left or right permitted her to steer the cart when it was off the railroad. Also, this arrangement permitted the passengers to talk to the person pushing it, and Anna and I still had a lot to talk over, one girl to another.

Later in the evening, when conversation was starting to ebb, Sir Wladyclaw rode to the side of the carriage and begged leave to introduce his men to me. I was of course delighted to meet them, for besides its being good politics, I enjoy meeting with young people, and these were all very young men.

It was rather like holding court, save that we were all moving down the railroad at a pace that no ordinary horse could keep up for long. They couldn't all line up at once, since some must needs ride "point" and others "flank." I resolved to have Conrad explain these strange terms to me, but just then I did not want to expose my ignorance to Sir Wladyclaw.

Somehow it was necessary to shift men to and from various positions before each could meet me, but this had the advantage of letting me speak at length with each of them. Or rather I should say shout, for our speed was such that the wind was strong.

It also allowed my maids to size them up at length and to speak of them in a most immodest manner when we were between visitors. It has always been my custom to let my servants speak as they will when we are alone, for one learns much from one's subordinates. The girls were quite pleased with Sir Wladyclaw's men, and for good reason. Not only was each a fine specimen of young manhood, but each was also from a very good family. I found that while I did not know any of them personally, I knew friends and relatives of every one of them. We spent some pleasant hours discussing mutual friends. When the lengthy introductions were at last over and Sir Wladyclaw was again at my side, I spoke to him of this.

"But of course, my lady. A scout must be a well-traveled man or he will get lost trying to find the enemy or even his own army. The work is vigorous, so he cannot be too old. He must be a born horseman who can spend days in the saddle without tiring. That was necessary enough in the days of ordinary horses, but in these modern times, why, a Big Person can run for days without stopping. Who else but a nobleman could have this experience? Oh, think not that I'm being snobbish! Both of my own parents were born commoners, for my father was knighted on the battlefield for valor, not because his father was noble. But the fact remains that I got my first horse when I was four years old, and I made my first visit to Cracow when I was six! A commoner simply doesn't get the benefit of the sort of up-bringing that I got. And some of my men were better off than I, since their fathers, grandfathers, and uncles were all widely traveled horsemen. What I am trying to say is that when we formed up the scouts, we knew that we would have very few Big People for the first few years. We had to get the absolute most we could get out of them. That meant that we needed the best horsemen we could possibly find, and I think we did a very good job.''

"You did indeed, Sir Wladyclaw," I said. "But you said that there would be very few Big People *for the first few years*. There are less than three dozen of them at present. Surely they can never be numerous!''

"Though it pains me to disagree with so gracious a lady, I fear I must do so. There are but two dozen and ten adult Big People now, counting the new white one that Lord Conrad found, but there are also two gross, six dozen, and four young ones growing up right now. Further, in the next month or two, nine dozen and eight fillies will be born, assuming that we haven't lost any Big People in the war. A few are missing, you know. In two years' time we shall be able to equip an entire company with Big People, and in twenty years they could well outnumber all the Little People in the rest of the army!''

"Then you can expect considerable promotion as your little command expands," I said.

"That is my hope, my lady. Indeed, I voluntarily took two demotions in grade in order to get this post, and I don't think I'll regret that choice in the long run. Also, it means that the men under me will be promoted as well, and I have chosen them for command ability as well as for horseman-ship.''

"But you haven't explained why they're all so handsome!" one of my maids said.

"But they're not," Sir Wladyclaw said. "You only think that they are because of your essential lechery, my young lady, and I love you for it!"

"Well, you haven't done that yet!"

"Patience, my love. There was a slight matter of an army to train and a Mongol horde to vanquish first. But now that these trivial chores seem to be accomplished, I shall devote myself to honoring my noble mother's dearest hope, the getting for her of some grandchildren. It is my earnest intent to spend as much of my time as my lords permit in the next few years in the granting of my dear mother's wishes. The assistance of healthy young ladies is earnestly sought!"

"I don't know if you're serious or not," she said.

"Alas, it is a thing known to but a few. But we shall study the matter with deliberation as soon as my lords and your lady permit."

And with that, our gallant Sir Wladyclaw rode out to inspect his men. The girls were both giggling at the exchange, and in truth I was smiling about it, too, me, a pregnant woman of thirty.

To be sure, much of what he had said was surely nonsense, but he had said it with a smile on his lips and a twinkle in his eye. More importantly, he was fit and lean and strong. He was clean and polished and remarkably sexy. He had a good mind, a decent education, and a proper attitude on things. Indeed, he was a young man who would go far in this world.

Chapter Eleven

AT FIRST light we went through the bloodstained gates of Cracow, which Conrad and Sir Wladyclaw had completely stuffed with dead Mongols, if the tale could be believed. We could have found rooms at Wawel Castle, but it was not convenient to the Franciscan monastery, and I was beginning to find walking difficult. Also, there is a great deal of time-consuming ceremony at the castle, and I did not want to waste a moment on anything but the task at hand. Thus, we proceeded directly to the Pink Dragon Inn and obtained lodging there. Oh, the innkeeper said that the place was completely filled with people whose houses had been burned, but on realizing who I was, he quickly agreed to clear the rooms necessary for my party.

We ate a remarkably spare meal, even for Lent. There was only oatmeal porridge and new beer, for the inn's huge cellars had been completely cleared to provide a quick lunch for a twelfth of my husband's army. Even rare wines that had been aging in the bottle for *three entire years* had been given away, for Count Conrad had said ''Empty out your entire cellar,'' and the innkeeper had taken him exactly at his word. A sad loss.

We then went to the monastery, arriving as the monks

were chanting Prime. Soon the new abbot was with me, for the old one had died in the fighting. This new man, Father Stanislaw, had been in charge of the print shop, and he, too, fell completely in with my plan. There was much anger in Cracow at Duke Henryk, for that nobleman had once sworn to defend the city but now had failed to do so, or even to come when the city was under siege.

To be fair to Henryk, the nobles of Cracow had so disagreed with his battle plan that they had left him as a group and gone to fight the Mongols under the leadership of Duke Boleslaw of Mazovia. But the nobles who had done so were now almost all dead, and the commoners have a short memory about such things. The abbot said that to a man, the people of Cracow wanted Conrad for their duke.

The abbot had supplies on hand for a "print run" of twelve thousand copies and set aside all other work to get it done.

Together we talked of an entire issue that treated nothing but the recent war with the Mongols, as opposed to the usual format, where there were a dozen short articles on everything from current events to cooking recipes. We would have a dozen or so witnesses of the various battles each tell their story, stressing how it was that Count Conrad had saved all of Christendom. Near the end there would be an article stressing the danger that eastern Poland was in without a properly confirmed duke to defend it. Then there would be an appeal, hopefully by Bishop Ignacy, for all the freemen and nobles of the duchies of Little Poland, Sandomierz, and Mazovia to meet and elect Conrad duke. Or maybe even king.

The story of the battles had yet to be written, and several monks were put with Sir Wladyclaw and his men to get some of it down on paper. I left to secure Bishop Ignacy to our cause, but as I boarded my carriage, word came that a riverboat had come to port. I had Anna take me there immediately for fear that the boat might leave before I had a chance to talk to the captain. The magazine would have to be delivered, after all.

The boat proved to be the *Enterprise*, with Baron Tadaos himself commanding. This was a stroke of luck, for he commanded all the boats on the river and knew more of the river battle than did any other man.

The baron gave me a warm greeting, and he, too, liked my plan of making Conrad Duke of eastern Poland. He promised all assistance in delivering the news but would not take the time to write the story of the river battle. His duty, he said, was to patrol the rivers and search for his several missing boats. However, he lent me Baron Piotr for the task of writing the history of the Battle for the Vistula, as he called it, and I had to agree that this intelligent young man was certainly up to the task.

As I drove Baron Piotr to the monastery, I said, "You realize that it is important that as much credit as possible must go to Count Conrad himself. You know that if Conrad himself were writing the tale, he would praise everyone but himself, but we must see to it that the truth is told."

"My lady, the only way that Conrad could have done more than he did would have been for him to have killed every single Mongol with his own sword! I shall praise him to the stars, not because you have asked but because he deserves it," the baron said.

Leaving Piotr in the care of the monks, I went to Wawel Cathedral in search of Bishop Ignacy. He was important to my plan because he was so well known and loved. He wrote a sermon every month for the magazine and thus had great influence in the country, indeed in the world, for many copies of the magazine found their way to all the countries of Europe! He was very patriotic and had long worked for the unity of Poland.

Thus, I was very taken aback when, having explained my

plan, I found that the bishop was less than totally enthused by it.

"My lady, I have my doubts as to the wisdom of all of this."

"But your excellency! Eastern Poland lies defenseless! Only Conrad has the power capable of defending it."

"I quite agree with you, my daughter, but Conrad would defend it in any event, whether he were duke or commoner."

"But the people want him for their duke!"

"I don't doubt it. Furthermore, they're right. He'd make a fine duke!"

"Then, your excellency, why do you oppose this plan?"

"I am not opposing it. I simply have grave doubts. You seem to forget that I am Conrad's confessor. I know the man very well, perhaps even better than you do. I have no doubt that he would be very good for the country. Indeed, since Duke Henryk controls most of western Poland, were Conrad to control the east, Poland would once again be a united country, could they but agree. And I think that they would. I tell you that Conrad could be made the first King of Poland for a hundred years!"

"Then why do you doubt him?"

"I don't doubt him! Conrad would make a great king, but would being the king make a great Conrad? Do you think that he would be happy with such a position? I don't! Do you know, when once I suggested the throne to him, he said that it looked very stiff and uncomfortable and that he had a fine, soft leather chair in his office that tilted back and suited him. When I suggested the crown, he said that a crown was nothing but a hat that let the rain in. You may want Conrad's enlargement, and the people of Poland may want it, too. But does Conrad want it? I doubt it! He wants to be free to work on his technical devices, and he considers them to be far more important than the fleeting glories of temporal power."

"Your excellency, I cannot believe that any man in his secret heart would turn down absolute power."

"Conrad has very little of this 'secret heart,' as you call it. Indeed, he truly wears his heart on his sleeve, most of the time, to his considerable pain. True, he likes power, but power to him is a very different thing than it is to you. The power he glories in is the power of a white-hot spray of liquid steel pouring from one of his furnaces or the thundering power of one of his huge engines turning at great speed. He cares nothing for the brutal power that permits a king to put some offender to death. He doesn't dream of crowds chanting his name. He avoids crowds as much as he can! He does not want the honor of sitting at the high table of a banquet. He makes excuses and tells lies to avoid banquets altogether! He has dreams, yes, but his dreams are of great cities gleaming white in the sunshine with not a bit of trash in them, of steel tracks that crisscross all of Europe, connecting every hamlet, of mighty ships traveling swiftly to far lands with neither sails nor oars. That's what *power* means to your man! Not sitting on a gilded chair wearing a golden hat."

I was much taken aback by all the bishop had said, for there was more than a grain of truth in it. Yet I was not about to let half a country slip through my fingers.

"You speak the truth, Father. I realize now that when the seym, the local parliaments, meet and they choose Conrad as duke, he will refuse them. After all, they can't *force* him to become a duke. But think of what this will mean, your excellency! Without Conrad, they must then choose someone else. If they are all met together and have already decided to choose a single man, Poland is united! The eastern half, anyway, or all of it if they then choose Duke Henryk, who is Conrad's only real competition. Father, you have changed my reasons for what I'm doing, but you have not changed my intention to do it! Doesn't

Poland need to be united? Won't you help me with this plan?''

"Hmm. On that basis, where we would only be using Count Conrad's current popularity as a device to get the people together, yes. To that I would lend my support.''

"We need more than your support, your excellency. We need your active help and leadership! With so many of the noblemen dead, I think that you alone would have the prestige to call together all the seym here to Cracow and have them come. Or do you think that Sandomierz would be more centrally located?''

"Sandomierz is not only more central, my daughter, it is also intact! Surely you have noticed that lower Cracow is a smoldering ruin. No, I'm afraid that we must definitely choose Sandomierz.''

I left the good bishop working on his proclamation and his sermon and had Anna drive me back to the inn. And then I went to sleep.

Chapter Twelve

FROM THE DIARY OF CONRAD STARGARD

I woke to see that it was broad daylight outside. The second thing I noticed was that I had an attractive young lady in my arms and that she wasn't one of my wives. I thought about it a bit and decided that they had probably provided me with this substitute since they were both in advanced pregnancy, and that it would not be gallant to look a gift lady in the mouth. Of course, if she were not here with my wives' permission, there could be fireworks, but what the hell. I had been two weeks and more without, and that's an absurd amount of time!

So I found out that her name was Mary and that she was one of Cilicia's new maids. I had never known Cilicia to have a maid before. She was picking up Francine's bad habits already. I told Mary that all this was wonderful and topped her for the better part of an hour. About fifteen years old, she was an enthusiastic and healthy girl, if not particularly skillful. At least she wasn't a virgin.

Then I began wondering what the army was doing.

Promising the girl that I'd see her later, I threw a cloak over my bare shoulders and walked over the catwalk to the second wall. The few people I met gave me a smile and a nod, but left me to my mood. The three walls, which doubled as apartment buildings, were connected with narrow, lightweight wooden bridges at each floor that let you go from one apartment building to another without having to go all the way down and then up again. They were built such that if the first wall was taken by an enemy, the catwalks could be easily knocked down and the fight could be continued from the second or even the first wall. Fortunately, this had not proved necessary against the Mongols, but every little bit of safety helps.

I got to the fighting top of the outer wall and saw that the cleanup job was well under way. A start was being made at repairing the septic tank. Dead Mongols were being stripped and decapitated, with the bodies being hauled away for burial somewhere out of sight. In the distance, heads were being stuck on poles lined up on both sides of the railroad tracks. Different from what we had done before but just as effective. Maybe even more so, to someone traveling down the track. I wondered if anyone had calculated just how long a double line of a quarter of a million heads was. I did the arithmetic in my head and came up with six dozen miles! Perhaps Baron Gregor was in for a surprise.

The dead Mongol horses were being skinned, and a fair number of the young and healthy ones were being butchered. Many of them were being salted down. Krystyana always was a tightfisted little manager.

Things were being done, they didn't need my help, and I found this to be good. I went down to the showers, which were empty at this hour, and then to the dining room. I was surprised to find that lunch was already over, but I wanted a breakfast, anyway. I hadn't had an egg in two weeks, and I not only ordered six of them, over easy, I had the cook go out to the chicken coop herself and get some that were absolutely fresh. I had them make me some fresh biscuits, too. Rank hath its privileges, and for a day or two I intended to wallow in them!

Yet still I missed a cup of coffee, and no amount of wealth or power could get me one. Most modern Poles prefer tea, but I had developed a taste for good coffee during my college days in Massachusetts and had kept with it after going home. An expensive habit, but worth it.

After eating, I went to the church, feeling guilty for not having gone there yesterday as soon as we had won the battle. Even with most of the people working on the cleanup, there was still quite a crowd in the church, most of them silently praying, giving thanks. There was a long line of people waiting for a chance at the confessionals, one of the things I had introduced to this century. They were standard in my own time, and the priests here had accepted them almost without question as a convenience. My own soul was blackened almost beyond redemption, and I knew that soon I would have to go to Cracow to see my own confessor, Bishop Ignacy. I prayed for an hour and it helped.

My next stop was to the Big People's barn. All of them were gone except for the new white one. Out on patrol, I supposed. I needed to talk to the white person, anyway. I took her over to the big letter board so she could spell out words and answer my questions. The Polish alphabet isn't quite the same as the one used in English, but they are similar enough to get by. Like Anna, she knew that she was a bioengineered product of a civilization in the distant past. Like Anna, she hadn't the slightest idea how a time machine worked. She knew her former rider only as Tom. If he had a last name, she hadn't heard it. In fact, she had absolutely no new information for me at all, except for her name. It was Silver. I should have guessed.

I told her that she was on the payroll now and that she was welcome to swear allegiance to me. She didn't know what that was, so I put it off until later. Somewhat disappointed, I went back to my apartment.

I never developed as close a relationship with Silver as I had with Anna. She didn't like to come up to the apartment and listen in to the conversations, since she couldn't understand them. She couldn't develop friendships with the local children the way Anna did, for the same reason. And I was now a far busier man than I had been ten years earlier. I just didn't have as much time to spend with her as she deserved. I hired two young boys to stay with her and try to teach her Polish, but she proved absolutely incapable of learning the language. A bad situation, but I didn't know what to do about it.

Back in my apartment, I passed Cilicia in a hallway. She smiled and gave me a quick kiss, but she knew enough about my moods to know that I needed to be alone.

I went to my office and told Natalia, my secretary and Baron Gregor's first wife, that I didn't want to be disturbed by anything less than Duke Henryk or a new Mongol army. I closed the door, and if I had had a telephone I would have unplugged it from the wall. I had some thinking to do.

For the last nine and a half years I had been busy building the seeds of an industrial revolution and building an army to defend Poland from the Mongols. The second objective was now accomplished, for we had given the greasy bastards the soundest beating that they had ever gotten. They'd be a generation sucking their wounds before they dared try us again. By that time, we'd be invincible. We'd likely be attacking them!

As for the first objective, well, there were a lot of improvements still to be made in our technology. Indeed, many had been made in the last few years and had been shelved because we were so involved in war production that we didn't have time to mess with them. The idea that war encourages technology is a myth. War encourages war production and very little else.

The alchemists had come up with an improvement on our

method of making sodium bicarbonate, an important chemical in the production of glass, medicines, and the biscuits I had just eaten. The old method mixed salt water (sodium chloride) with carbon dioxide from heated limestone (calcium carbonate), and ammonia from our coke ovens. This yielded sodium bicarbonate and ammonium chloride. The problem was that we couldn't find much of a use for the ammonium chloride and didn't get all that much ammonia from the coke ovens. This greatly limited the amount of the stuff we could produce.

Zoltan's improvement was a way to take quicklime, calcium oxide, and combine it with the ammonium chloride to get all the ammonia back, which we could then recycle. We were still throwing away the calcium chloride. Well, it melted snow, and eventually we came up with the idea of using it as a dehumidifier as part of an air-conditioning system. But mainly, now there was no limit to the amount of glass we could make! Within a year, glass would be cheap enough to use for making canning jars.

Some experimental work had been done on electricity, too. We now had a varnish that was a fair insulator, provided that the voltage was low and you didn't expect much flexing. We had plenty of copper, and all the new towns I had built were very compact, so they could be easily defended. If we put a generator within each city, we wouldn't have to send the electricity very far, so using a low voltage made sense. It eliminated the need for ugly power towers that couldn't be defended, and for half the year we could use the waste heat from the generators to heat our buildings. The usual modern method of doing things wastes about two-thirds of the energy in the fuel in generation and transmission losses. With my system, much of this waste was eliminated, at the price of having a power station next door.

Electric lights would be nice, and although I didn't know where we could get tungsten for the filaments, Tom Edison made a decent light bulb using a carbon filament, simply a baked thread. It's easier to make a low-voltage light bulb than a high-voltage one, since the filament gets shorter and thicker. And once you have a light bulb, you have solved most of the problems in making an electronic tube.

Well, we'd have to work on it.

Nonetheless, the big job ahead of us was simply to do more of what we had been doing.

The simple fact is that mass production is necessary to produce goods and services in sufficient quantity to maintain a decent standard of living. Mass production cannot exist without mass distribution. The larger the market you are serving, the more specialized and efficient you can make your productive machines and processes.

It was critically important that we build more railroad tracks so that industrial and agricultural products could get from place to place more easily.

The failure to emphasize the importance of transportation is one of the Russians' greatest failings. Karl Marx, in his nineteenth-century evaluation of the world economy, lived much of the time in a British industrial area. He not only was never a railroad man or a seaman, he seemed to think that these things were unimportant. All his thoughts were on the making and consuming of things. As a result, orthodox communistic thinking stresses production and treats transportation as a necessary evil.

This philosophical bias has resulted in an inadequate transportation network in Russia, and this in turn is one of the causes of that country's incredible inefficiency.

The railroads were a top priority, but the more I got to thinking about it, the less important a railroad engine seemed to be. Pulling carts with mules, as we were doing now for civilian transport, was a hundred times more efficient than using pack mules in caravans, which was the only competition. It takes almost as much manpower to tend one of our primitive steam engines as it takes to tend a string of mules. More important, in twenty years we'd have so many Big People that we could use them to pull the carts. Then we wouldn't have to expend any manpower at all! The motive power would also be the driver. A Big Person can pull a ten-ton cart six hundred miles in a day. That ought to be fast enough for anybody. Pulling one cart at a time, we wouldn't have to bother with railroad hump yards and all that sort of time-consuming nonsense. And Big People don't consume nonrenewable resources or pollute the environment the way mechanized transport does. Best to leave mechanically powered transportation to the rivers and oceans.

Then there was the problem that in the last half year we had multiplied the size of the army by a factor of six, to 150,000 men. This was accomplished by giving them an abbreviated course at the Warrior's School. They had learned to handle weapons and take orders, but they hadn't been taught to read, write, or do arithmetic.

This necessary expansion was a tremendously big bite for us to take, and I rather wished that it was possible for us to chew it up. At present, though, we had housing and permanent jobs for only about twenty-five thousand families. More housing and more factories and more farms were obviously needed. But the only thing I could see to do for now was to at least temporarily discharge everybody below the rank of knight who hadn't worked for us before. Then, in time, those who wanted to come back in could finish up the Warrior's School course, and if they passed, they could come back into the army.

No! Stop! Dumb idea. We might need those men again at any time, especially if I had judged the Mongols wrong. Rather than discharging them, I had to form them into active reserves. That would mean regular pay, regular practice sessions, a reserve command structure, and a dozen other headaches. And doing all this while they were scattered all over the country! I'd have to delegate the authority on this one, since I certainly didn't want to bother leading it myself. I wondered if Baron Vladimir would want the job.

The reserve force would have to be a temporary thing, designed to phase itself out as the men came on as full-time workers or retired after ten years or so.

Construction was going to be the big game on campus for quite a while. I had long dreamed of building a line of company-size forts along the Vistula and the Bug as a defense against Mongols, and a similar line along the Odra and the Nysa against the Germans. Oh, except for the German Teutonic Order, the Germans hadn't given us much trouble lately, since they were mostly involved in conflicts in Italy and with the Pope, but from a historical standpoint they repeatedly invaded us, and it was just smart to be ready for it.

We had already built a good working model of a stand-alone fort, the one at East Gate. It had been taken by a combination of trickery and stupidity, but there had been nothing wrong with the design that I could see. It was easily defensible and looked like a castle, but actually it was mostly an apartment building for two gross families. It was really a small town, with factories, a school, a library, a store, an inn, and everything that such a community needs. Two gross families is about the right size for a town, too. At that size, you have enough neighbors to have somebody interesting to talk to and there are enough of you to support a full set of community services, but you are not so big that people get lost in the crowd. Three Walls, for example, was already too big. Despite the fact that everybody was well taken care of, we were getting a crime problem. I don't mean relatives getting into fistfights, either. That sort of thing will always be with us. No, I mean real organized crime, like that fair-sized theft ring we broke up a year ago.

In a town of under three hundred households, things like that aren't likely to happen. Everybody knows what's going on!

Each fort would be situated on twenty or thirty square miles of land, and that land would be farmed by the troops. In the off-seasons there would be light industrial work available to keep them busy. They would spend one day a week in military exercises, but mostly they would be a working community.

I had long been toying with the idea of a factory that would build large precast concrete sections that could be shipped by railroad or boat and assembled on site into a fort. They'd have to go up fast, since I wanted to get the army back up to its present size in a hurry. To house an additional hundred thousand men and their families in four years, I'd have to throw forts up at the rate of two a week!

And there wasn't only the concrete to think of. There was plumbing, wiring, power plants, heating systems, weapons, school-books, and beer steins. I got to sketching out what was required, and it was very dark before I quit.

We were going to have to build a factory that built factories that made the components of the forts, which were themselves partly factories! I wrote a note to Natalia to have all drafting and engineering personnel relieved of all military duties and back at their desks immediately. I needed help!

I woke up in the sunshine again, with the same girl in bed with me. I had missed the sunrise service two days in a row! There was some cheering going on outside, and I went to the balcony to see what it was all about. The women and children from East Gate were back! Not the nobles who were murdered there by the Mongols, but our own people who had left the fort two or three days before that. The women and children had wandered around in the hills for a week before they had found their way back here.

I got some proper clothes on in a hurry and went down to the mob scene below. Understandably, the men whose families had been missing were delighted to find that they were safe and sound. They were hugging and kissing and laughing and crying, sometimes the same person doing all four at the same time. What annoyed me was the fact that the captainette who had brought the dependents in was being carried around on some of the men's shoulders as though she were a hero.

I got over to them and wrenched her down. "You stupid bitch!" I shouted. "You're under arrest!"

"But what for, sir?" one of the men asked.

"What for? For dereliction of duty, for abandoning her post, for treason, and for contributing to the murder of twenty thousand women and children!" I shouted.

Then suddenly everybody was quiet.

Chapter Thirteen

THREE WALLS still didn't have a jail, so I had a blacksmith put leg shackles on her and followed the two knights who took our prisoner to the storeroom we used as a lockup when necessary. The room was already in use for the hand-less Mongol ex-ambassador, but I had her thrown in with him. He stank the way all Mongols do, but I didn't owe her any favors. I was on my way back up when I realized that I was going to have to judge the case.

You see, "count" is a judicial title, like "judge" or "justice." A man holding it had the right of high justice within his realms. That is to say, he could hold a trial for a major crime and punish the offender as he saw fit. His word could have a man hanged. I had held the title of count since the Christmas before, but that meant that I was count of Francine's tiny county of Strzegom, where there never was much crime. Here, at Three Walls, I had remained Count Lambert's baron despite my right to use the title of count. Up until a week ago, that is. When Count Lambert had been killed by a Mongol spear and I had inherited his lands in Poland, I had also inherited his responsibilities. I couldn't fob off my serious criminals on him anymore. I was it!

I went back up to my office to ponder this latest problem.

For years I had been ducking my legal duties by having somebody else do them. On Sir Miesko's recommendation, I'd appointed Baron Pulaski to be my judge. The baron had four subordinates, a court recorder, a bailiff, and two prosecutor-defenders. These last two took turns. They went around my extensive and scattered estates, hearing cases and writing up their recommendations to me. I almost invariably went along with them or, in the case of serious offenses, handed their recommendations up to my liege lord, Count Lambert. In time he got to following their recommendations as well.

But they really didn't have any official sanction for their existence. Since they normally tried trivial matters and only conducted hearings on serious ones, nobody had seriously complained about it. But Captainette Lubinska's crimes were hardly trivial. Whether I tried her or had Baron Pulaski do it, I would be setting a precedent.

After some hours of agonizing over it, I decided that the baron was more competent a judge than I was, and he was certainly more unbiased. Furthermore, I didn't want to spend the rest of my life being a trial judge. I had better things to do than sit on a gilded chair deciding if some poor bastard deserved to die. If my liege lord, Duke Henryk didn't like it, he could start by telling me so.

If, indeed, he still was my liege lord! The last I'd heard from him, he was damning me for failing to go to Legnica and join his forces there. For all I knew, he considered me to be an independent duke now.

The simple truth was that the military forces that obeyed me were vastly superior to his, and I controlled quite a bit more money than he did, although as a good socialist, I had difficulty thinking of all this vast wealth as being my own. Actually, I could probably declare my own independence and make it stick!

Not that I'd want to.

I could see no advantage to independence and quite a few disadvantages. Being part of a greater whole, I could expand my industrial and agricultural revolutions as fast as necessary simply by doing it and paying a fee or buying land if it was required of me. A little persuasion was all that was usually needed. As an independent king, or whatever, I'd have to fight a war every time I tried to open up a new market. Insanity!

I sent a runner to find Baron Pulaski and ask him to come have a talk with me.

My designers and draftspeople had all shown up at dawn and had spent the morning getting their work area cleaned up and ready to go. It had been more than a year since we'd used it, what with the war and all. Most of them were back in civilian clothes and feeling a little unusual about it.

"I'm not going to enforce any dress codes around here," I told them, "but if you have to go out to the field or even to the shops, I'll expect you to be in uniform. You're still in the army, after all. Now then, we have some factories to design, and we'll need at least the foundation drawings finalized in two weeks so the troops can start on them as soon as they finish cleaning up the mess we made on the Vistula. Now here's what we need . . ."

Once I got them going, I went back to my "manager" office, called for my secretary, and asked if there were any messages. She brought in a stack as thick as my arm, sorted as to what they wanted. An efficient lady.

Baron Gregor wanted to release all his men who had been workers at Three Walls to get the factories going again. He was particularly worried about the ammunition situation. I wrote "granted," with a note that all men who had served in the Construction Corps should be sent under Baron Yashoo to East Gate to rebuild the Riverboat Assembly Building. Since almost all these workers had at least a half-dozen new subordinates who had gone through only four months of training, these subordinates would be assigned to other knights at no more than a dozen new men each.

There were six dozen letters of congratulations and then a request from a priest that in the future all Mongols should be baptized before they were beheaded. Denied. The bastards didn't deserve to go to heaven.

There were a lot of requests for discharge, mostly so the men could search for their families. Denied, put your request through channels. There wasn't much to worry about, since most army personnel had their dependents at army installations that had not been attacked, and nobody had gotten killed at any of them.

I made an exception in the case of Captain Targ, whose family was far to the east, near what would be Zakopane. I owed him a serious favor, since he had saved my life, and I thought this was a good way to pay it. I sent orders to his baron that he and his brother should be given indefinite leave and lent horses if they wanted them. I really meant to do him a favor, but I guess it didn't turn out that way. The two brothers headed east, crossed the Vistula, and were never heard from again. Their family was also among the missing.

Lady Natalia came in after a while and asked me if I wanted my dinner brought up, but I decided that the men should see that I was still alive, and we went down to the cafeteria, not that there was any "café" to justify the name.

The chow lines there were absurdly long, worse than what happens when the communists try to sell six refrigerators in Warsaw. I told Natalia that she should put out the word that the cafeterias would have to be restricted to dependents, officers of the grade of captain and higher, and men who had originally worked at Three Walls. All others would have to eat at their war carts, though the cooks could draw on the stores here. Natalia and I, of course, took cuts in front of the line. RHIP.

The next week was spent in meetings and similar boring but important trivia. The aircraft had found no trace of other Mongols, even though we all knew that there had to be a lot of stragglers hiding out there somewhere. Francine was in Cracow playing hostess to some political nonsense, but she seemed to be having fun and staying out of trouble. I supposed that she needed to get away from it all for a while after the tensions of the war, and I let her have her own way. The cleanup at Three Walls had been completed, and the original workers from each of my other installations were sent home to get things productive again. Getting things back to normal seemed to take as much work as getting us on a war footing had.

Then Baron Vladimir arrived.

I gave him a hug when he got to my office. "God, Vladimir, it's wonderful to see you! What took you so long?"

"What took me so long, my lord? I think that the problem started when I was entirely too efficient in getting across the Vistula. You recall that as we left the battlefield west of Sandomierz, you were to return the booty here to Three Walls, and I was to take the larger group of our men to cross the Vistula and clean and loot the killing fields there. We found no riverboats running, but we found two of those river ferries of the sort you invented so many years ago, during that delightful journey we made with our ladies to the River Dunajec. You know, the sort that uses a long rope to force the river itself to carry one back and forth. Three dozen big river barges were available at Sandomierz, as was a good supply of rope, so we quickly built three dozen more of the things. By dint of efficient organization and hard work, I was able to get my entire command across by midnight.

"Now I have a question for you, my lord. What ever possessed you to entrust so important a message as the fact that Cracow was burning to an absolutely untrained peasant? The silly fool had never before in his life been more than six miles from the village in which he had been born! He had never been on a Big Person before. He had never even seen one! Is it any wonder that he never thought of telling her who they were trying to find? He had not the slightest concept of geography, and he couldn't have read a map even if he'd had one! He couldn't read, period! Is it any wonder that he missed us in the dark and rode all the way to the Crossman city of Turon? He was two days finding us! Why did you do this thing to me? Two-thirds of your men missed out on half of the war!''

All I could do was to bury my face in my hands and say, *''Mea culpa, mea culpa, mea maxima culpa.''* Through my fault, through my fault, through my most grievous fault.

''Baron Vladimir, I'm sorry. At the time he was simply a man on a Big Person, and I didn't even think about what I was doing. A courier had come in badly wounded with the news about Cracow. One of the officers assigned a man to ride the Big Person and help out our flankers. Then I realized that you must be told as soon as possible, and so I changed the man's orders. I never stopped to think about how limited, how restricted the average peasant is. I'm sorry.''

''And I accept your apology, my lord. You made a mistake, but as it turned out, no great harm was done. You had sufficient forces with you to handle the problems that happened to come up. My men could have given you more power, but they could not have given you more speed. Yet it could have turned out otherwise! The Mongols might have caught you strung out on the road with your men half-armed and armored, with your pikes stored for transit, and your guns unmounted. They could have met you with locally superior forces and wiped you and all of your men out! You were lucky. But while I was waiting to see you—''

"They made *you* wait?"

"The Baroness Natalia is sometimes overly protective, my lord. But while I was waiting, I heard the tale about Captainette Lubinska. She made a mistake as bad or even worse than yours, and she didn't have your luck! Now you plan to have her hanged for it. Do you realize that she was born a peasant girl on a farm just outside of Cieszyn, where Count Herman's wife held sway for so many years? For all of Lubinska's life, the countess was an authority figure whose word was not to be questioned. Then, one day, the countess lied to her, usurped her authority, and ordered her away from her post. Is it any wonder that she obeyed the countess's orders even if they weren't exactly legal? What did the captainette know about the law? She was only a peasant, for God's sake!"

"Again you shame me, Vladimir. Look, I've turned the matter over to Baron Pulaski. Why don't you speak to him, and also speak at her trial?"

"All right, my lord, if you wish it. But remember, the right of high justice is yours now. You may delegate the duties, but not the responsibility!"

"You are entirely too right. For now, though, what happened once you got the word about Cracow?"

"Well, once I got the message out of the peasant—he hadn't slept in days and was babbling—we had to drop everything and recross the Vistula. The railroad tracks are on the west bank only. I sent troops south in battalions at a walk until the rest could catch up. After that we went to double time. When we got to the company you left behind to guard the booty, we absorbed them in our van, since they were fresh by then, and eventually left our hindmost company on guard. At Cracow I left a battalion to secure the city and relieve the wounded you left behind there. We had just arrived at East Gate when we got the word about your victory here. As per your orders, we cleaned up East Gate and sent men back to the dumped booty to pick it up. Half of my men are now on the way back to clean up the killing grounds on the east bank of the Vistula. Also, I sent a battalion west to the salt mines to dig and bring back all the salt they could. We'll need it if we're to save the horsehides we've taken. The rest of them are here now with your booty and what we collected at East Gate.''

''What booty at East Gate? We lost there!''

''Many of those women and children had jewels and money secreted about their persons, my lord. Perhaps the Mongols were in too much of a hurry to search them all properly. But for whatever reason, there was quite a lot of it, and policy is that the dead should never be buried with anything of value, not if you want them to rest undisturbed.''

''You're right, of course. Is there any chance of returning the money and jewels to their next of kin?''

''No, my lord. Only a few of them could be identified. We never thought to issue dog tags to noncombatants.''

''Well, we can hardly keep it for ourselves. Looting Mongols is one thing. Robbing the Christian dead is quite another. Perhaps we should donate it to the Church.''

''That was to be my suggestion, my lord.''

''Well, get some rest and see your family. There's a meeting at one tomorrow that you should attend, and then I guess you'll be going back to the Vistula.''

''I can delegate the cleanup, my lord. I have a trial to attend first.''

Interlude Two

▽▽▽▽▽▽▽▽▽▽▽▽▽▽▽▽▽

I HIT the STOP button, leaned back, and stretched. Tom still hadn't gotten here. I was almost to the point of worrying about him, but not quite.

"It's getting to be lunchtime, don't you think?" I said to the nude girl snuggled next to me.

"Yes, sir."

"Well, why don't you get me a couple of salami sandwiches, a side of onion rings, and a cold Budweiser. And get anything you want for yourself."

"Yes, sir."

An untalkative girl, but she was pretty and obedient, and I guess you can't have everything. Nice outfit, too. She was back almost immediately. She spread my lunch out on the control desk and stood waiting.

"Aren't you hungry? Why don't you eat?" I said.

"Yes, sir." She brought in a bowl of something that looked like custard and spooned it quickly down.

"Is that all you're eating?"

"Yes, sir."

"Don't you want anything else?"

"No, sir."

I shrugged. Well, she was pretty young, and kids that age can survive on nearly anything. I put it down to some sort of fad diet.

I sat back, put my arm around her, and hit the START button.

Chapter Fourteen

CAPTAINETTE LUBINSKA'S trial went on for five days. I managed to scrupulously avoid it, except when I was called in to testify as to exactly what orders she had been given. Baron Vladimir spoke at length in her behalf, but when the sorry affair was over, a jury of her peers, twelve captains and captainettes, found her guilty. According to the code of military justice that I myself had written, the punishment was death by hanging, and that's exactly what Baron Pulaski sentenced her to, to be carried out first thing in the morning.

My own rules required a speedy sentence, provided that the case could be reviewed in time, since to keep a condemned prisoner waiting for months or years, as is often the modern practice, seemed to be unnecessarily cruel to the criminal. Enough time for the condemned to say a good confession, go to mass, and spend a night in prayer was all that could be morally justified. Also, much of the reason for punishing someone is as an example to others, and if the thing drags out for years, people forget what the crime was all about. The hanging, when it finally happens, becomes a simple, needless murder by the state.

Baron Vladimir came to see me that evening. He repeated

all the arguments he had made before, and also said that much of the fault for the incident was mine, for I had put a weak and stupid peasant woman into a position that was too far above her.

"My lord, if you loaded ten tons of iron onto the back of a mule and it collapsed, would you blame the animal? Would you kill it for having failed in its duty?"

"We're not talking about a dumb animal here, Vladimir. We're talking about a human being!"

"True, my lord, and I would not be arguing so strongly if it were only a dumb animal you were abusing, though I would still call your failings to your attention. You are my liege lord, and I am obligated to give you my best counsel, even and *especially when you don't like it*! Furthermore, the difference between a dumb animal and a dumb peasant is less than you may think. We are knights, you and I. Our function is to protect the peasants, not to hang them for *being* peasants!"

So that was the crux of the problem. Baron Vladimir was a traditional member of the old nobility, while I was a man born in the twentieth century. Vladimir was a good friend and a valuable subordinate, but his world outlook was very different from mine. And he hadn't stopped explaining things to me yet.

"We were put here by God to protect women, my lord, not to kill them for having feminine weaknesses! I say again that the fault is yours for putting her in the position that you did, for elevating her far above her station, and for trusting a woman to do a man's job. You had men who were sound of mind but could not join us in the field. Baron Novacek, for one. He may not have hands, but he could have commanded East Gate and done a good job at it. Why you insisted on having all your women's companies led by women is beyond me."

Why indeed? It had seemed good for morale, and it ensured that a man wouldn't take advantage of a female sub-ordinate, but the main reason was my twentieth-century belief in equality. If women were doing the defending, they should lead the defense as well. Now it seemed that I was equalizing the captainette right out of her life.

I let Vladimir continue until he started repeating himself, then I said, "Baron, I don't know what I'll do about this mess yet, but whatever I do, it won't be done lightly. Tell me, that courier who missed you in the dark near Sandom-ierz. What did you do to him?"

"Him, my lord? Well, he was incompetent as a scout or messenger, so I could hardly leave him with a Big Person, but he had done his best within his limitations. I let him sleep while we recrossed the Vistula and then put him back down in the ranks as a pikeman. It doesn't take much brains to do that job, simply courage, strength, and obedience, things that a peasant is often good at."

"But you didn't punish him?"

"Would I punish a fish because it couldn't fly? *Peasants are stupid!* You can't expect one to do a nobleman's job."

"I see. To change the subject, what about you, Baron Vladimir? You've done a wonderful job these last six years with the army. Have you done any thinking about what your reward should be? About what you want to do now?"

"Hmmm. I've had some thoughts, my lord, or perhaps I should call them dreams. I have saved much of my salary over the years, and I'll get my share of the booty. I wonder, well, there is the castle you got from Count Lambert, the one Baron Stefan used to hold. You've never used it for much of anything. Would you consider selling it to me?"

"No, but I'd give it to you if you wanted it. You've certainly earned it, and as you say, it's just going to waste. Or better still, how about the new castle I built for Count Lambert at Okoitz? It's a dozen times larger and comes

stocked with a renewable supply of attractive young ladies.''

"A portion of me is tempted by Okoitz, my lord, but my
better parts say that I'd be happier with my wife and family
without the count's fabulous harem. You see, what I want
is to live in the old traditional way, with the wife and
children that I haven't seen enough of these past years. My
oldest boy is eight years old now, and he has seen very little
of his own father. I don't want to live as Count Lambert did,
and I certainly don't want to live like you! Further, I think
that there are a lot of the peasants on the lands that you've
gotten that prefer the old ways as well. With your permission, I would gather together those peasants that would
swear to me and take them from these mines and factories
of yours.''

"Permission granted, old friend. From my standpoint,
you'll be relieving me of some of my malcontents. The
castle is yours, along with as much land as you can find men
to farm it.''

"And a bit more, some forest for a hunting preserve, my
lord?''

"Fine, so long as you don't go and reintroduce wild
boars and wolves on it. And the people you talk into joining
you, well, don't get *too* traditional on me. I'm going to
insist that they have schools, stores, and modern farming
methods.''

"Of course, my lord. I never intended to throw out any
of your *improvements*! It's this business of changing jobs all
the time, and promotions, and not knowing the grandsons of
your grandfather's friends that troubles me. I don't know
quite how to put it, but it's as if things have gotten like a
river that is running too wide and too shallow! I want to go
along in a deep, old channel, where the human things go on
as they always have and always will. Glass in the windows

and flush toilets and good steel plows are fine things, and a man would be a fool to not use them, but it's the human factors that I worry most about.''

One of the failings of the communists was that they had a vision of the future that they thought was good, and they tried to make everybody conform to their ideas of goodness. To my own mind, well, it's a big world and it takes all kinds of people to fill it. If some peasants prefer a life-style that I would find oppressive, well, as long as nobody is forcing anyone, I say let them do as they wish. I don't need *everybody* on my bandwagon.

"Then you shall have it as you want it, Baron. Just remember the ancient right of departure. Some of the children of the men who swear to you may not feel the same way as their fathers. But I'm not minded to lose your good services entirely. If you wish to live in a feudal manner, then you must do feudal duty to me. What I want you to do is to command the active reserve forces of our army. You see, this time we had warning about when the enemy would attack, but next time we might not be so lucky! Now, my plan is . . .''

We talked for hours about what the reserves should be, and when we parted, we were in agreement.

At least about the army.

As he left, Vladimir said, "Do you know yet what you are going to do about the captainette?''

"No.''

I left word that I must be up before dawn and sent notes to both Baron Pulaski and Baron Gregor that the execution must not take place without me. God forbid I should cause a woman's death because I overslept.

Then I tried to sort out the problem of Captainette Lubinska. I sent away the servant girl I found in my bed, and I tossed and turned for half the night. On the one hand, Lubinska was legally guilty of abandoning her post during time of war, and that had started a chain of events that had ended in a terrible massacre.

On the other hand, Vladimir was right. She had been put in a situation where she was in way over her head. But then, every person in the army had been thrown into deep water, including Vladimir and myself. A lot of people had died because they were too weak or too stupid to perform the task before them. A lot of people had died because they had a problem that nobody, no matter how strong or brilliant, could possibly have solved. I saw one boatman get squashed flat when a two-ton rock came down on him, and where was justice then? Nowhere, that's where. But had he lived, he wouldn't have had to stand trial for not stopping that rock.

So why do we try anybody?

It has often been argued that a person is the result of his heredity and his environment, that we are what we were made to be and therefore are not responsible for our failings.

Well, if human beings are just things that were made, then it doesn't matter if they are punished or not. It only matters whether they act as desired. If a pot was made badly, throw it out! It's not the pot's fault, but that doesn't matter. The whole idea of guilt doesn't come into it at all. Once you think about it, you have to conclude that *people don't matter at all* unless you grant them a moral sense, unless you grant them a soul. Maybe that was the root cause of many of Stalin's atrocities.

I gave up trying to sleep. I put on some clothes and walked to the church. I sat down in a pew, but soon I was on my knees.

Well, then. You can say that God made people and everything else. It's all His problem! Let Him solve it! Why should we poor fallible mortals ever judge anybody? What right do we have to judge His work?

Except that we all know that if nobody was ever punished

for doing anything, crime would soon be so rampant that nobody would be safe. Many people would live by stealing, and people would be murdered every time somebody got angry. Life would hardly be worth living in such an environment. Like it or not, we sad, confused, and fumbling mortals have to do something about criminals. We have to do it for simple, practical reasons. We can't blame it on God, and we can't let Him do the punishing, since He waits until the sinner is dead before doing the job of judging him, and that's a little late by human standards if we want to have a safe society.

Good. This was getting me closer to the mark. Forget about the moral reasons for punishment. They rest on sandy ground. We have to punish wrongdoers in order to (A) stop them from hurting the rest of us again, that is to say, in group self-defense, and (B) as an educational mechanism to convince others that they should not imitate the wrong-doer.

So. Were we going to hang Lubinska because she was likely to abandon her post again and get another 21,000 women and children killed? Of course not! Well, obviously, she should never be trusted with an important post again, but we wouldn't have to kill her to accomplish that. Discharging her or busting her down to the lowest rank would be sufficient. Certainly she presented no further danger to society.

So we must be killing her as a teaching aid. Well, would it be an effective teaching aid? By this time everybody knew how and why she had screwed up. Everyone realized now that to abandon a post can cause a great tragedy. Would one more death added to 21,000 make any difference? No. It would be insignificant.

Then what were we gaining by hanging her? Were we providing ourselves with a sacrificial lamb to cleanse the guilt from our hands? A scapegoat? I never could go along with that strange bit of theology.

Actually, you couldn't blame the captainette for the deaths of all those people, not directly. The Mongols had killed them, and we had killed the Mongols. Case closed.

The Mongols had been let in by Count Herman's wife, and they had killed her for it. Again, case closed.

The captainette had believed the wrong person as to who should be in charge at East Gate. She had believed her traditional boss instead of me. She had been given her command by me, and I had done it because Baroness Krystyana had recommended her.

Night was fading into gray dawn when I finally knew what I had to do. Somehow I was immensely comforted by the certainty of it.

There was quite a crowd in front of the outer wall when I got out there. The sun was about to peek over the horizon, a gallows had been built, and a lot of people were standing around it, including all of my barons who were at Three Walls. The Lubinska woman was near the scaffold, attended by a priest and two guards. I went to her and said quietly, "You're not going to die this morning." Stunned and unbelieving, she looked at me and said nothing.

Baron Vladimir led us in our morning services, and a priest, not the one attending the captainette, said a very quick mass without a sermon. The people were expecting Captainette Lubinska to climb the scaffold, but she didn't.

I did.

Chapter Fifteen

FROM THE JOURNAL OF COUNTESS FRANCINE

The job of writing the articles for the magazine was done in but two days, and work had already begun on the casting of the drums of type to print it. But then the time seemed to drag, for there was much work to be done in the casting of type and the printing of the half gross of pages that the magazine would contain, and none of it could be done by me.

It would be a plain magazine, for there was no time to carve the woodcuts that usually adorned its pages, except for a few old commercial messages that were used to fill otherwise blank space. Since there was no time to contact the merchants and obtain payment from them, you may be assured that all the "ads" that we used were from my husband's factories.

Indeed, it seemed for a time that the cover, too, would be blank, until a friar named Roman came down from the cathedral and painted three lithographic blocks for the purpose. He was a merry man, grown pudgy and red-nosed from drinking too much wine, but he was a fine artist for all of that. The cover he made had on the front a fine portrait of Count Conrad in his armor and with our battle flags flying behind him, and on the back a lively scene of our gunners shooting at the Mongol enemies over the heads of our footmen. Further, all this was done in inks of three colors, the first cover that had been done so. I think that some may have purchased the magazine only to have the fine artwork!

I persuaded the abbot to give his men dispensation from the saying of their prayers eight times a day so that they might spend the time in work, and I made arrangements with the inn that they should be fed as they worked at the machines that Conrad had built for them. The monks were at first much taken aback by this, for the waitresses of the inn did their work, as always, nearly naked. Yet there were soon far more smiles on the monks than scowls, and I bade the waitresses to continue as they had. I was something of a heroine to these young ladies, for I had once been of their number and now was of the high nobility. I suppose that my success fed their dreams. Yet when they asked that I dress in their fashion and help serve, I must needs turn them down. My waist had grown too large with pregnancy, and anyway, Conrad would certainly not have approved! Still, I was tempted.

The monks worked from before dawn straight through to the dark of night, but still, the job would be a week in the doing, and always I feared that Duke Henryk would arrive and take the whole thing into hand himself.

I took myself to Wawel Castle and spent the day there talking to any that I could meet about the seym that was soon to be held in Sandomierz. All that I met, the old and the infirm, were enthusiastic for Conrad's enlargement, yet there were very few of the nobility there. All too many were gone or dead.

The city council *came to me* with the plea that Count Conrad should be their duke and protector, and we talked long as to how this could be accomplished. They then sent representatives to every incorporated city in eastern Poland to plead for our cause, and they did this at their own expense, as well! Not that I was in lack of funds, but when those tightfisted burghers had their *own* money involved, you can be sure that they would give it their best effort!

While I was thus employed, Sir Wladyclaw was also busy. The weather was now fair and the radios were at last working properly, so his men were no longer needed as messengers. Keeping only one at his side, he sent the others about the countryside in search for Mongols and, when time permitted, to tell the gentry of the victory won by Count Conrad and of the seym to be held at Sandomierz. They found no large groups of the enemy, and we were growing daily more certain that victory was truly ours, but more than once scouts brought back heads barbered in the strange Mongol fashion as proof of their prowess!

I sent occasional messages to my husband, telling him that I was well and that I was helping to organize a meeting of the seyms of eastern Poland, since because of my association with the old duke, I knew so many of the people in this area. I never exactly told him that the feeling here was that *he* should be duke of all three duchies, for fear that he would decline the offer before it was even made to him. Bishop Ignacy was entirely too accurate in his estimation of my husband! When the time came, I wanted him to think that the nomination was entirely spontaneous and that it was his duty to accept it.

Until the time was right, I wanted him to stay in Three Walls, doing his little engineering things!

He *should* come to Sandomierz, I told him in the messages I sent, for he did have lands that he had purchased along the Vistula, and thus he was obligated to come, but to be there a little late would cause no harm, I said. My intent was that when he got there, the matter would be already settled. Once he was duke, he would find reasons of his own for remaining duke. I knew it as I knew him.

When the print run was almost done, a scout brought

back from the army camp west of Sandomierz a list of the Polish nobility that had survived the battle there. To publish a list of those who had died would have taken a book three times longer than our entire magazine, though we promised that such a magazine would be published in the future. For now, all that we could do was add eight pages with the names of the living. *So few!*

At last the printing was done, and all the monks fell to the task of combining the pages and binding them together. I was able to get many of the town's folk to help with this task, and as soon as a stack of finished magazines was ready, one of Sir Wladyclaw's scouts was there to take them to all the towns and hamlets of eastern Poland. Of course, we were careful that none were sent to the west for fear that Duke Henryk would hear of it.

The riverboats helped distribute the magazines as well, for Baron Tadaos now had three at his command. Two of them had been found up a small creek, intact but devoid of their crews. There was evidence of a fight, but what exactly had happened there was something that we would probably never know. The baron had found men to operate them and ammunition for their guns, but what he was happiest about had nothing to do with men or arms. His many wives and their children had been found, and all were alive! Indeed, they were helping him operate his boat.

Sir Gregor sent me a message that said that our radio operators at the duke's camp at Legnica told of sickness there and that the duke was taken ill with it. He was not likely to die, yet he would not be fit to travel for at least a week. The message ended with a request that we should pray for the duke's recovery, and indeed I did pray for his health, but that it be returned to him later. *Much later!*

Once, in our long fireside conversations at my manor before we were married, Conrad had told me of a land in which once he had lived where all the leaders were chosen every few years by all the people. He talked of candidates for office shamelessly putting up great pictures of themselves and hanging many posters with slogans on them as though they were so many cattle to be sold at auction! At the time I laughed at the thought of the old duke thus pandering himself, but as I later thought on it, I could see the necessity of it all.

It took far less time to print the covers, which were done on a separate machine, than to print all the pages of the magazine. Since the facilities and supplies were available, I persuaded Friar Roman to make some posters as Conrad had once described. Some were just the front cover of the magazine, with my love's portrait. Others boldly said, ''I want Conrad for my duke!'' Many thousands of these were made, though at a price for the friar's services. I promised that after I had my child, I would pose for him in any manner that he wished while he painted me. Well, perhaps it would be fun.

I wanted to get to Sandomierz well ahead of the crowd, to set the stage, as it were. Soon we were on the road again, my maids crowded out of the carriage by stacks of posters and magazines and riding apillion with two of Sir Wladyclaw's Scouts. None of those involved seemed to mind the arrangement in the least.

The captain felt that an escort of five would be safe enough, but I persuaded him to bring all his men to make a better appearance as we rode into Sandomierz.

The city of Sandomierz had been under siege, but it had not been taken. The city council had long looked to the strength of its walls, which were well built and defended. These people were among the few burghers that had purchased sufficient guns and armor from Conrad's factories. Further, they had heeded his thoughts and the suggestions that he often wrote in the magazine and had been ready when the Mongol hordes had come against them. Thus, while the suburbs had been devastated, all that was within their walls was safe. Also, those who had been on the walls had been treated with a view of the major battle of the war, at least in terms of the number of enemy killed. It was here that the riverboats had made their greatest slaughter, and dead Mongols had been heaped up on the bank opposite until they were twenty bodies deep! Even as we arrived, battalions of my husband's men were still stripping and burying the dead, for Conrad was afraid of the pestilence and disease that follow battle. The heads were all up on pikes, a huge monument to Polish arms. Also, the Mongols had looted widely in the Russias, and he wished to see this wealth back in Christian hands.

On arriving, I went directly to the inn. It had been doing very good business, but for months the innkeeper had not been able to deliver its profits to Conrad. I drew on these funds at need, in part to rent most of the rooms at the inn itself. Thus, when an important person could not find lodging in the town, I could offer it to him as a favor from Conrad. And surely no decent man could speak publicly against his host!

We spent much of the next week talking to all who would listen, which was practically everyone, about the upcoming seym and about Count Conrad. It was easy to persuade the town's people to adorn their storefronts and homes with our posters, for it seemed to them that to do otherwise would be to slur the man who had saved their city! They all knew that had Conrad not killed the Mongols west of the city, they and all they had would be gone. And once a burgher had Conrad's name and face on his home, he could hardly say anything but that he favored him! Thus, as the first notables came to attend the seym, it must have seemed to them that the matter was already settled. Not many men will go against their neighbors once the matter has been decided!

Further, I hired men who could read well in public to

stand in the squares and read the magazine to any who would listen. Thus, we told our story to everyone, including the majority, those who could not read at all.

The good Friar Roman had also written some poems in Conrad's honor, and we were able to find minstrels who put those poems to music. Soon they became all the rage, and other minstrels began to write songs of their own in his honor just to compete!

All things were going beautifully, and I was having a wonderful time.

Chapter Sixteen

FROM THE DIARY OF CONRAD STARGARD

"There will be no hanging this morning," I said to the crowd from the vantage point of the scaffold. "The right of high justice is vested in me and me alone. Baron Pulaski, you and your jurors did your jobs properly. By the letter of the law, Captainette Lubinska is guilty of abandoning her post in time of war, and the punishment for that is, and ought to be, death by hanging. But the ultimate responsibility is mine, and I choose not to permit the sentence to be carried out, despite her guilt. Perhaps this guilt is mitigated by the fact that she was lied to by a woman who once was her liege lord's wife. Perhaps it is softened by the way she got her charges safely back here to Three Walls.

"But the real reason why I will not hang her is because her death would accomplish nothing. She is not guilty of causing the death of those twelve thousand, five gross, ten dozen, and five women, children, and old men who were murdered at East Gate. The Mongols killed them, and our army killed the Mongols. All but one, the one in fact who tricked Count Herman's wife into letting the enemy into the fort! That man is now my prisoner, kept alive because we might one day need a messenger who can speak both Polish and the Mongol tongue. He'd probably prefer death to imprisonment, since both of his hands were cut off in the fighting.

"If any of our fellow Poles is guilty of the tragedy at East Gate, it must be Count Herman's wife. She was the one who improperly took charge of the fort and then allowed the Mongols in. Well, the Mongols killed her for the favor, and she's in God's hands now.

"Captainette Lubinska's crime was therefore one of bad judgment, and if her judgment was bad, she never should have been given such an important post in the first place. I should have relieved her when I saw that she was acting erratically. I gave her the position because she was recommended to me by Baroness Krystyana. So.

"For exercising very poor judgment while in command of a major post, Captainette Lubinska is busted to the lowest grade and is to be given only the most menial of duties for the next five years. After that time she may never again be promoted beyond the third level.

"For recommending a person of poor judgment to an important post, Baroness Krystyana will be demoted to the lowest level for a period of one month during which time she shall be given the most menial of tasks. After that month, she shall be returned to her present position and pay grade.

"For believing Baroness Krystyana and for failing to replace Captainette Lubinska at a later date, Count Conrad Stargard will be demoted to the lowest level for a period of one week, during which time he shall be given the most menial of tasks, and after which he shall be returned to his present position and pay grade.

"I have spoken. It is done."

My proclamation was met with stunned silence. Well, if punishment is supposed to be an educational procedure, I think that these people were being properly educated. At least I was making them think!

For the next week I worked in the kitchen, washing dishes, while designing a dishwashing machine in my head. The job involved using a whole new set of muscles, and I came home every night just a bit stiff. And you know? It felt good!

Krystyana was less gratified working the tub beside me, but then, she always was feisty!

Soon people started coming down to the kitchens so that I could solve their problems. I referred them all to Baron Gregor, since Baron Vladimir had left for the Vistula. I was a lowly worker, and it wasn't fair to expect much from a warrior basic. Soon I had to post my secretary to fend off these people so that I could attend to my proper duties, the washing of dishes from dawn to dusk, with a timed lunch break.

On my last day of playing bubble dancer, when Krystyana was out feeding the chickens, Natalia let one visitor through to me. It was Warrior Lubinska.

"You shouldn't be doing this, sir. You humiliate yourself."

"There's nothing humiliating about honest work. Actually, I'm rather enjoying it. It's good therapy. Anyway, you shouldn't call me sir. My army rank is now the same as yours. How about 'my lord,' since it would take the duke to change my civil rank."

"You should have hanged me."

"Nonsense! If you had deserved hanging, I would have done it. You got what you had coming, nothing more and nothing less."

"No, that's not true at all."

"Well, what *is* true is that you were ordered to do menial labor, and you're not doing it. Take off your jacket and roll up your sleeves. You can help me with these dishes."

I did my clumsy best at talking her out of her depression, but after a few hours of working next to her I could see that

I hadn't helped much. I think that much of her problem was what I'd heard called "survivor's guilt," the strange, irrational guilt that a survivor feels after almost everyone has died but her. Lubinska wasn't the only one feeling it. There were reports from the field hospital we'd set up near the battlefield west of Sandomierz that a number of the surviving knights had committed suicide. But what could I do? I just didn't know.

When our work shift was over, I told her to buck up, that things would get better. The words were phony, but what else could I say?

The next morning I was told that during the night Lubinska had tied one end of a rope around one of the merlons on the outer wall. She'd tied the other end around her neck and jumped.

Since she was a suicide, there was no mass said for Warrior Lubinska, and she didn't receive extreme unction. They couldn't bury her in hallowed ground, so they buried her alone, a bit away from the Mongols.

It was bad being a battle commander, but being judge was far worse! I was never trained for this kind of thing. I had no aptitude for it. I just couldn't take it! I had no business being a count.

As soon as Duke Henryk was well, I intended to ask him to make me a baron again and take back the right of high justice. That is, if he'd still talk to me. He hadn't answered my last dozen letters and radio messages, but I guess he was still pretty sick.

The next day I was informed by Francine that it was time for me to show up at the seym in Sandomierz. It seemed like a tedious thing to do, but good citizenship requires that you vote whenever you have the chance, and I supposed that I should set a good example. Anyway, it would do me good. I needed to get away from things for a while.

When I asked her, Cilicia wasn't interested in going. She had always been a quiet and stay-at-home type when she was pregnant. I was getting ready to set out alone at dawn when Captain Wladyclaw showed up with a dozen of his men to give me an escort, an honor guard, he called it. I thought it a silly waste of manpower and told him so. But they were already at Three Walls, and their proper post was in the east, looking for Mongol stragglers, so they might as well go back east in my company. The captain also said that my wife had insisted that I wear my fancy gold-plated parade armor, which my smiths had once made for me as a Christmas present. I'd worn it at my wedding, but I hadn't touched it since. The captain was fairly adamant about it until I relented and changed out of my practical combat armor. But if I hadn't, Francine would have acted hurt, and that can get hard to take.

"Your wolfskin cloak sets well against that gold armor, my lord," the captain said.

"More importantly, it's warm. We've wasted enough time already. Let's ride," I said.

Big People can run as fast as a modern thoroughbred racehorse, the difference being that they can do it with big armored men on their backs instead of little jockeys, and they can keep it up all day long instead of for a single mile.

We went nonstop until we got to East Gate. Baron Yashoo had the new Riverboat Assembly Building more than half up. In the past seven years we'd cleared more land than we'd used lumber, and what with the new sawmills, it had made sense to saw and stack the wood for proper seasoning. Baron Yashoo was drawing on our lumberyards. I complimented him on his progress, and we were on our way again in minutes.

I wanted to make a stop at Cracow to see Bishop Ignacy and go to confession, but Captain Wladyclaw said that he

thought that the bishop was at Sandomierz attending the
seym, and anyway, Lady Francine was waiting for us. I saw
no point in arguing with him, and we rode on.

Running along the side of the railroad track, or on it
sometimes, we made good time, arriving just after noon.
Our railroad tracks were far straighter than the twisting
trails that passed for the roads that covered most of Poland.
The girls could really stretch out and move! After a few
weeks of being in a city, it felt good to have a fine mount
like Silver between my legs. I was smiling as we went
through the city gates, and the crowd there was lively.

I supposed that it was natural for people to cheer for a
visiting general, a patriotic sort of thing for them to do. It
was a few moments before I realized that they were shouting "Duke Conrad!" at me, and a few more before I saw
my name and pictures of my face plastered over everything
in sight.

All I could think of was that as duke I'd have a hundred
times as many court cases to worry about. I'd have to go
through the agony of the Captainette Lubinska affair six
times every week from now until forever! No way did I like
or want that sort of life-and-death responsibility.

No!! Not me! No way, gang!

The crowd was soon so packed that we couldn't move
except in the direction in which we were heading, and instead of going to the inn, as I had expected, we were forced
toward the main square of the city.

"Captain Wladyclaw, just what the hell is going on
here?" I shouted at him.

"They seem to be taking us to church, sir," he said,
pointing to the great Church of St. James across the square.

"That's not what I mean, and you know it! What's with
all these posters and pictures and people calling me duke?"

"Well, they need a new duke, and there's nobody else
left! I'm afraid that you're stuck with the job, sir."

"No! No, I won't do it!" We were being slowly moved toward the church, the crowd acting like some fantastic undertow pulling me to my doom.

"Sir, I believe you've already been elected."

"The hell I am! They can't elect me without my permission."

"I'm not sure of all the legalities, sir, but by tradition, the seym doesn't need anybody's permission to meet and hold an election. Certainly not yours."

"That's not what I mean, and you know it! They can't make me! They'll have to find someone else!" I swear that everybody was smiling and cheering except me. Dammit! Wasn't it enough that I had helped wipe out the Mongol invasion? Did they have to saddle me with a job I didn't want just because I'd helped them?

"Who, sir? I tell you that all of the normal candidates were killed by the Mongols!"

"Duke Henryk! He'd be great for the job." Not only did everybody want to cheer for me, they insisted on touching me, patting my mount, and pawing the legs of my armor. I was getting a sort of claustrophobic feeling.

"They'd never have him, sir. Don't forget that he abandoned eastern Poland to the Mongols and hasn't gotten off his rump in Legnica since."

"He's been sick! Anyway, his conventional knights couldn't have accomplished anything important except getting themselves killed. Legnica is a good place for him. And them!"

"He *says* he's been sick, sir, but none of these people have seen it. He's a villain in their eyes, whereas you have saved all of their lives. If your forces are far superior to his, all the more reason to want you!"

"Nonetheless—"

"Nonetheless, we're at the church, sir. You'd best dismount and greet your wife."

"I'm not through with you, Captain, but this mess is more her fault than yours!" I swung out of the saddle into the crowd and pushed my way up the church steps.

The captain came up behind me and removed my helmet. I turned and stared at him, wondering why he had done this strange thing.

"But sir! You can't wear a hat in church!" he said.

I just shook my head and went on.

Francine was standing in front of the Romanesque portal.

"Welcome, my hero, my love!" she said.

"Like hell it's a welcome! It's an abomination! I know that this is all your fault, and I won't do it! Get somebody else to be the damn duke. Not me!"

She turned me toward the altar and began walking slowly toward it. "But you must, Conrad, if only for a little while." She spoke in a low voice, and I had to bend my head to hear her.

"What do you mean for a little while? Being a duke is a lifetime job with no retirement benefits!" I followed after her. It was that or lose her in the crowd.

"It is until you abdicate, my only love," she said softly.

"Abdicate? Then why do it in the first place?"

"Because Poland needs to be united, that's why. For the last hundred years, Poland has not had a king. It has been nothing but a collection of independent duchies where the people happen to speak the same language. Right now, for the first time in a century, the people of Mazovia, Sandomierz, and Little Poland are willing to unite under one man. Only one man. You! They would never do that under Duke Henryk, even though the western half of Poland swears fealty to him, for they think that he has betrayed them. They would never pick some distant relative of one of the dead dukes, since that would give a huge political advantage to the new duke's home duchy, and the other two duchies would lose out. It has to be you! But only for a little while, my love. Then, when things settle down, you can work out an arrangement with Duke Henryk, and Poland can be united under a single man. The land will again have a king!''

"Yes, but surely, if I talk to the seym, I can sell them on some other guy—''

"But nothing! Do you know anyone else who could be trusted with such a temptation? Is there anyone else but you who would willingly give up power when the time comes? Go ahead! Name me one man!''

I pondered for a minute, and the slow procession to the altar stopped. "Bishop Ignacy! He could be trusted."

Francine tugged me by the sleeve and got me moving again. "Nonsense! The bishop is a good man, but if he held the eastern duchies, he would put them under the control of the Church. Admit it! The eastern duchies are still exposed to the Mongols. Consider that you have defeated an enemy army, but you have not yet defeated their nation! Poland needs a war leader, not a churchman, in power.''

"Yeah, I suppose so. What about Baron Vladimir?''

"I tell you that no man but you could be trusted. This much power would tempt any other man.''

"Then why trust me?''

"Because you don't want to be duke in the first place! Your very arguments defeat themselves. Darling, this is your duty to your country. You must not fail Poland!''

I'm a ponderer by nature. I can usually come up with the right answer, but it takes me a while. I never was one of those glib, fast-talking sorts who can sell farm machinery to Mongols. I'm not really quick thinking on my feet in a confusing situation. As I was trying to sort this one out, Francine knelt down at the communion rail, and so I just naturally knelt down beside her, out of habit, I suppose. As I did so, the Bishop of Plock put the ducal crown of Mazovia on my head! The crown of Sandomierz was quickly put right on top of that, and the crown of Little Poland was promptly placed on top. I was stood up, wondering how the Church that I had trusted could do this thing to me. I was turned around, and everyone in the big, crowded church started cheering. I tell you, it was annoying!

Chapter Seventeen

I STARED at the shouting crowd, and it was all that I could do to not scream right back at them. I took the crowns from my head and looked at them. Someone had modified them so that they all interlocked into the silliest-looking thing imaginable. I handed the contraption to Francine.

"Here! You wanted it! You take it!" I said. She was so shocked that for once she didn't have anything to say.

"But you *must* keep it!" the bishop said, horrified.

"The only thing I *must* do is die, and I have *some* say-so as to when that's going to happen! And as for you, your *excellency*, there are fourteen tons of gold and jewels that I was going to donate to the Church. You're not going to get them now! I trusted the Church, and you went and pulled this shit on me!" I turned from him and looked to the back of the church. *"Silver! Come here to me!"* I called out in English.

Somehow she heard me above the crowd and came straight in. Silver didn't have Anna's religious side, and the church was just one more building to her. The people had been taken aback by my taking off the crowns, and even more so by my speaking in a strange, harsh foreign language, but they got out of her way as Silver came straight up the church aisle.

I mounted up and rode out.

At the church door Captain Wladyclaw was still standing there, dumbfounded. I took back my helmet from him and said, "As for you, Wladyclaw, you have been telling me lies all day long. If your father wasn't one of my oldest friends, I'd have you court-martialed! As it is, well, you'd better stay far out of my way."

The inn was almost empty when we got there. Everybody except the innkeeper seemed to be out in the streets, cheering. The door of the place was big enough to ride through, and that's just what we did.

"My lord!" The innkeeper looked up at me, shocked and afraid.

"Right! I want your best room. Send up a meal for me and my mount. And bring up a pitcher of beer, a pitcher of wine, and pitchers of anything else you have around!"

He knew better than to argue and led the way to a room marked DUCAL SUITE. I ripped down the sign, dismounted, and told Silver that no one but the innkeeper was allowed in.

She nodded YES.

Someone else's things were in the room, but the innkeeper just picked them up and went out with them. To hell with him, whoever the last tenant was!

The innkeeper returned quickly with four nearly naked waitresses carrying food, six pitchers of potables, and fresh sheets. I had to tell Silver that the waitresses were okay before she'd let them in.

"What's this stuff?" I asked, pointing at one of the pitchers.

"You said to bring some of everything that I had, my lord. That is from a barrel that was sent to me years ago from your inn at Cieszyn. It's called 'white lightning,' but no one liked it. Still, you said . . ."

I poured some into a glass. It had been clear white when

I'd made it nine years ago, but it was a golden amber now. I tasted it and smiled for the first time in a while. Nine years of storage in an oak barrel had done amazingly good things to it.

"Good. Now go out and find me a block of ice! This stuff is just what I need!"

The innkeeper made the sign of the cross and left. The waitresses scurried about, changing sheets and towels. This suite had its own bathroom, a rarity. Finished, they hurried off after their boss, frightened.

I started in on a monumental drunk.

I was too upset to sit down, and so I paced the room with a glass in my hand. A waitress came in with some ice, cut from the river during the winter and stored in one of my icehouses. I put some in my drink and told the girl to sit in the corner and be quiet, since I might want something else later.

After a while I was over being absolutely angry and could think again.

Now, what was I going to do about *this* mess? Unifying the country was certainly important, but dammit, I'm an engineer, not a politician, and certainly not a hanging judge! All I wanted was to be left alone to do my job, the truly important job of getting this country and this century industrialized. I had neither the talent nor the ability nor the inclination to wander about the countryside playing God in a gold hat!

There was some commotion out in the hall, but I ignored it. Everybody I knew was smart enough not to argue with a Big Person who had her orders, especially one who didn't understand Polish!

I'd played at being a battle commander, but only because it was absolutely necessary. Without my army, my training, and my weapons, we'd all have been killed! But I hadn't been very good at it. In fact, I'd screwed up a lot of times and had come through on sheer luck. Well, that and the fact that the enemy was even dumber than I was. Some recommendation!

What to do about the election? Well, I could take the job of duke and then delegate away all the power. Set up men in each duchy as my deputies and let them do things their way.

Right. And in ten years' time the men I had delegated would effectively be dukes, and all their cronies would be counts and barons. Eastern Poland would stay feudal and backward. Peasants would stay peasants, and the infant mortality rate would stay such that half the kids born wouldn't make it to their fifth birthday, and it would be all my fault.

It got louder outside the door. I sent the waitress out with the message that if they didn't quiet down, I'd have the entire inn cleared. It quieted down.

Damn them all! Or I could take the job and do to these duchies what I'd done to Baron Stefan's barony: put in schools where there weren't any, subsidize the new farming methods, and bring the people into the industrial sector as fast as possible.

Except that eastern Poland doesn't have the natural resources that Upper Silesia has. This area never would be heavily industrialized. Damn.

Since most of the nobility was dead, probably most of the land would escheat back to me if I were duke. I could just parcel the land out to anyone who wanted to farm it and make the area a land of yeoman farmers. That might be the best bet. But to do it, I would be involved with lawsuits with every fifth cousin of the previous owners. Thousands of lawsuits! It would be a full-time job for the next twenty years, and I'd never get the chance to work on electric lights.

Well, if I did take the job, the first thing I'd have to do

was to take a survey of just what lands and properties were
mine. Probably a good job for Baron Piotr, with Sir Miesko's help. The school system under Father Thomas Aquinas
probably had information as to which major family had
what. We'd pulled all the schoolteachers west in February,
so they were all still alive.

No, that would have to be the second thing I'd have to
do. Everything east of the Vistula was probably destroyed,
and there was a lot of work in disaster relief to be done. At
least there was plenty of money to work with, but that was
yet another problem to solve. How to divide up the booty
we'd taken without inflating the economy to destruction?

There was a writing desk in the suite, with paper, ink,
and some of our new steel pens. I started taking notes but
was hampered by my armor, which I was still wearing.
Army-issue combat armor can be gotten into or out of in a
hurry, but this gold stuff I was wearing had dozens of straps
and buckles. I had the waitress help me out of it, and the
gambeson as well, since I was hot. The inns were always
overheated because of the waitresses' costumes, or rather,
their near lack of them. Taking off the gambeson had me
down to my long johns, but what the heck. I was still
wearing a lot more than the girl was.

Actually, she was a pretty little thing, if still a bit frightened. She was about fourteen, fair and bare, with long,
straight blond hair, a nice body, and nipples so small and
pink that you could barely see them. And she was a virgin,
the inn's rules being what they were. I told her to relax and
have some wine. I wasn't going to hurt her.

I went back to my notes, and started making up a PERT
diagram of all the things that had to be done assuming that
I actually accepted the job of duke. After a while I noticed
that the whiskey pitcher was empty and sent the girl out for
some more. She took an empty mead pitcher with her as
well.

Eventually the job started to look possible. I'd have to swear fealty to Duke Henryk as soon as possible, with the price tag of a nationwide system of courts in the modern fashion. He'd be in charge of it, and I would never get involved. Would the military courts be under him? I wasn't sure if that would be good, since I'd be keeping command of the army, of course. I put a star next to it, as I had on all the other problems I didn't know how to answer.

The three Banki brothers would each be put in temporary charge of a duchy, say, for two years, until things settled down. They'd each have to have a list of instructions limiting their power. We really didn't need any more conventional counts or barons, for example.

Halfway through the second pitcher of whiskey, I started to feel very tired. I went over to the bed, crawled under the covers, and fell asleep.

I awoke to find the waitress in bed with me, and, yes, she had taken off the shoes, stockings, bunny hat, and loincloth that were her uniform. At least I think she had done it. I didn't remember being responsible. She was snuggled up under my arm and seemed contented enough.

I had only a slight headache, and heavy drinking always makes me horny. I woke the girl up, and she smiled.

Somehow, during the night I had decided that I had to become a duke, and as such I could do anything I wanted, at least until I swore fealty to Henryk. I didn't know if I had taken the girl the night before, but I rolled over onto her and did so now. She seemed to be waiting for me to do it, and eager.

As it turned out, she'd been a virgin when I'd started, but not for long thereafter. Good, though. Some fine natural talent there.

"Thank you, your grace," she said when we were done. "I always hoped my first one would be a hero."

"Well. You're welcome, uh, what was your name?"

It was Sonya, and after a bit of talking I gave her a job in my household as a maid, since I'd just deprived her of her job as a waitress. She no longer qualified.

I got up and stretched. I would have to tell the world that I'd take them up on their job offer, but I was in no great hurry to do so. First a bath and breakfast. I sent Sonya down to get some food and checked on Silver. She was still doing guard duty, and the innkeeper had seen to it that she had been unsaddled, fed, and rubbed down. Her saddle and bags were there beside her in the hallway. I took my saddlebags into the room and drew an oversized tub of hot water.

Sonya came back and joined me in the tub without asking. Soon she was scrubbing me down, and I found myself enjoying the pampering. She washed my hair, cleaned my fingernails and toenails, and even shaved me, saying that she had always shaved her father. A very well-trained young lady! Up until now I'd always resisted the notion, but maybe having a personal servant wasn't such a bad idea, after all. Efficiency isn't everything!

After being toweled off, I was sitting nude and letting myself get completely dry when two other waitresses came in with our breakfast. The food and service were good, and I found myself wondering if I didn't want three or four servants instead of only one. Later, perhaps.

The sun was coming through a window, and I said my Warrior's Oath, which impressed the girls no end. Then they helped me into one of my best embroidered outfits, buckled on my sword, and kissed me good-bye. All three of them. I went out feeling fit to face demons, dragons, and even a politician or two. Someone had saddled Silver, but I didn't ride out as I had ridden in. I was no longer mad at the world.

Chapter Eighteeen

VVVVVVVVVVVVVVVVVVVVVVVVVV

My wife and a few dozen dignitaries were waiting for me in the common room of the inn. They all looked at me apprehensively, more than a little frightened.

I turned to Francine. "I take it that these gentlemen are what is left of the authorities of the eastern duchies?"

"There are many others, my love, but these men are the most powerful."

"Well, then," I said, "if you still want me to be your duke, I'm minded to take the job."

That got them all cheering. I really must have had them worried.

"I hadn't planned to be your leader, and you really should have asked me about it first. Be that as it may, I'll do it because the job needs doing. You understand that if I'm going to do this, I'm going to do it in my own way. I am not going to maintain three courts full of unproductive people as my predecessors did. I'm not even going to have one of the silly things. The proper function of government is to provide law, order, and security. It is not constituted to provide amusements for idle people. Agreed?"

The bishop who had crowned me stood up and looked about to see if anyone objected to his speaking first. No one did. "Your grace, we shall be content to follow you in whatever manner you choose to lead. We all know by your past actions that what you will do will be good."

"Where I come from, they call that a blank check. Thank you." I got out the notes I'd made the previous night and found that I could read most of them, except for the last page or so, where the scrawl became drunkenly illegible. I read them to the group to let them know what I had in mind, leaving out the part about my swearing to Duke Henryk.

"There are still a lot of points that have to be worked out, but in general, that's the program I have in mind. Do I hear any objections? No? Then I'd best get on with it."

Francine stood. "Then if you are to be my duke as well as my love, would you please take these back?" She handed me the three crowns, and I took them. That got another round of applause.

All my inns had a radio transceiver and a post office, although the posts had been shut down during the war and were not yet working again. I sent messages to many of my key people, asking them to come to Sandomierz. Then I sent to the granary in the Bledowska desert, ordering all carts available to be filled with the new grains and shipped north and east. Spring planting was almost upon us, and I doubted if there was any seed to be found east of the Vistula. The millions of Mongols who had been through surely would have eaten everything they could find.

Next I rode to the ducal palace to take possession of the place. I could have done everything from the inn, but that would have lacked class. Also, it would have cost me money in lost revenues, since while the rooms of the inn could be rented out, those of the palace couldn't. At least not now. In the future, once some more efficient government buildings were up, all the old palaces and castles around might make very charming hotels. An interesting thought, anyway.

The palatine of the ducal palace was a venerable gentleman who had been working there all his life. He showed me around, and it wasn't bad at all. I'd visited the place a few years before, but as a mere baron from a distant duchy, I hadn't gotten the grand tour. It was a smaller version of the castle on Wawel Hill, which I also owned now, thinking about it. It was built of red glazed brick, and a fine collection of old weapons, furs, and tapestries gave it a certain barbaric splendor. There was indoor plumbing, though, and glass in the windows. Except for adding some radios, there wouldn't have to be much in the way of needed changes.

I made some, anyway. I had lunch and fired the cook. I think that if the last duke could stand the cooking at his palace, he must have gotten his taste buds chopped out in a tournament. I figured that anybody who could ruin roast mutton couldn't possibly be retrainable. He was replaced by the cook at the inn. In the same message to the innkeeper, I explained about Sonya and had her sent over along with my clothes and armor, and the barrel of nine-years-in-wood whiskey, which was declared to be my own private stock. All other innkeepers were to inventory their supply of the stuff and reserve it for my own exclusive use. RHIP. While I was thinking about it, I sent a message to Cieszyn, ordering the cook who had helped me make that first batch to run off another six thousand gallons of it and store it in oak casks. I promised to call for it in nine years.

Baron Wojciech was the first of the Banki brothers to arrive, since he had been in charge of the cleanup on the battlefield directly across the Vistula from Sandomierz.

He came into my chambers at the palace with a cloth-wrapped package under his arm and looked admiringly at the tapestries, the furs, and the brightly painted wood carvings.

"You know," he said, "saving the country must pay pretty good. Someday I'm going to have to try that myself, sir! Or I guess I should call you your grace now."

"Sit down and have some mead," I said, pouring. "Woj-ciech, you can call me anything but an atheist, and you did your share in saving the country!"

"Thank you, your grace. I have a present for you, or at least a present I can give back to you." He unwrapped the package to display my pistol, the one I had lost during my fight at a pontoon bridge on the other side of the Vistula. It had been polished and cleaned and was only slightly rust-pitted. It had my name engraved on it, since the smiths always seemed to do that sort of thing whenever they made anything for me, along with a note as to who had made it. Advertising, I suppose.

"Thank you. I see that you provided a new belt and holster."

"I didn't know if you'd thrown the old ones away, your grace."

"Just as well. I left them on the *Muddling Through*, so I suppose they were burned when she was. I take it that you like this palace?"

"Of course! It's beautiful, your grace!"

"Good, because you have a present coming, too. This palace is going to be yours for the next two years. I want you to run the Sandomierz duchy for me as my deputy."

"Thank you, your grace! I'm honored. Yawalda is going to be thrilled! I know she will fall in love with this place."

"Well, don't get too attached to it. Remember, it's only temporary."

"Yes, your grace. I'll be able to choose my own subor-dinates?"

"Within reason, yes. You'll have a battalion of regular army troops under you, but it's going to take some sorting out, since most of the warriors have farms or businesses to get back to. I want to keep three battalions of full-time fighting men together, though, in case we're attacked again. That's one here, one at Cracow, and one at Plock. Your brothers will have the other two. Baron Vladimir will command in time of war, and he'll have about a dozen battalions of part-time active reserve forces to back you up.

"Still, I don't think we'll be bothered for a while, and your main job will be to get every farmer who wants it seed, tools, and all the land he can farm. We can give them credit on supplies, and there should be more than enough land, what with all our losses to the Mongols."

"There were more losses than you know about, your grace. The Mongols took the city of Sieciechow, on the east bank of the Vistula, and I don't think that they left a single man, woman, child, or domestic animal alive. They just murdered everybody, even the cripples and the priests. We even found somebody's pet dog nailed to a church door. And the young women . . . You don't want to hear about what they did to the young women. And there were worse things. You know those big Mongol catapults? Well, it looks like all the people that were pulling the ropes on them were Polish peasants! Many thousands of them were killed by our own guns, it looks like."

I put my face in my hands. "Oh, my God! I was there! We killed them ourselves! We thought that they were Mongols. Those catapults were destroying our riverboats! What else could we do?" I was crying. At the time, we'd been laughing at the way they died so easily, the way single bullets would take out whole rows of them. Would there be no end to my sins?

"You didn't know, your grace. You couldn't know. And even if you did, like you said, what else could you do?"

"Nothing, Wojciech! There wasn't a damn thing we could do. But I'll tell you this! Once we get things squared away around here, in a few years, we are going to go out east and get those filthy bastards. We are going to hunt them down and kill every Mongol in the world!"

"Good, your grace! I'll help you do it! I've seen the

figures on the number of Big People that will be available in ten years, and with them we can chase the Mongols right off the edge of the world.''

''That we will! Or right into the sea of Japan, anyway!''

''Just don't forget me when the time comes. Don't forget that I was the one who had to bury those poor peasants.''

''I won't. Tell me, what are things like in the east?''

''Empty, your grace. I think that there were three million Mongols who invaded us, and what they didn't eat, they fed to their horses, and what their horses didn't eat, they burned. You know, I think that's why they had to cross the Vistula so badly during the war. They had eaten everything on the east bank, and it was either cross over or starve! There are a few of the scouts who claim to have even found the remains of half-eaten humans, but you couldn't prove that by me. Just the same, folks are scarce over there. In the weeks that I've been on the east bank, I don't think I've seen over a thousand of our own people, except for the army. We put them all to work, you know, digging graves, mostly. We pay them, of course, and feed them, which is more important. But there are so few of them left!''

''A lot of people believed us when we told them to run to the west. Most of them will be returning. It's important that we repopulate that area. If we leave it empty, somebody else will move in. Maybe some of the warriors we'll be discharging will want land there. Write up an order for me to all commands, telling them that there is land east of the Vistula free for the farming. We can give them credit on tools, seed, and so on.''

''Yes, your grace, but our people won't need credit. The booty hasn't been counted yet, but I can tell you we're all rich! I think there was more gold left on the banks of the Vistula than ever crossed it.''

''Indeed? I would have thought that the Mongols would have looted their own dead.''

"They did, your grace, but I think only on the sly, you know? I mean, there wasn't much to be found on the bodies on the tops of those piles, but there were dead men two dozen deep in some places! They never got to the ones at the bottom."

"Wow. It looked like they were piled that deep when we were shooting them, but I'd convinced myself since then that it couldn't possibly be true. Well, get yourself settled in and send for your wife and family. I'll be leaving here in perhaps a week, and you can take this chamber for your own then."

The next few days were spent getting organized. Word came that two Big People had been killed in the war, both while carrying couriers from the battlefield near Sandomierz. Judging from the mess we found around their bodies, they and their riders had spent their lives very dearly, but they had spent them nonetheless. Jenny and Lucy were gone, and they would be missed.

Of their remaining sisters, ten Big People were assigned to the postal service, and the mails started to move again. Six other Big People were assigned to the Detective Corps, since crime was on the rise in the wake of the social disruption of the war. The rest of them were assigned to the scouts, since I was still worried about our borders, and the few planes we had up couldn't be everywhere.

Captain Wladyclaw was sent to patrol the eastern marches, a good place for him. I got the feeling that he was more attached to my wife than to the army, and nonsense like that belongs in *The Three Musketeers*, not in Poland. He was promised the twenty Big People that would be coming of age in the fall, but for now he was just going to have to make do with what he had. I kept Silver, of course, and Anna seemed to have attached herself to Francine, so I let them stay together. And there were still four Big People with Duke Henryk.

I'd never thought to stockpile farm machinery, war production being what it was, and major orders for plows, cultivators, and harvesters were placed with the factories.

The last of the booty was finally sent to Three Walls, and Baron Piotr was put in charge of counting it. Working with the Moslem jeweler we'd picked up years ago, he simply had it all melted down, refined it into bricks of pure gold and silver, and then weighed it, except for some pieces that were judged to have sufficient artistic merit to be worth saving. Silver City, the zinc smelting and casting works in the Malapolska Hills, was put into full production making coins. We'd decided that the men should be paid in standard army currency rather than in actual silver and gold. One currency around was enough.

Jewels were sorted as to size and type, and some wooden warehouses were thrown up to store the war trophies. Just how those fancy swords and armor were to be divided was still unclear. Was it worth sending the entire army back to Three Walls just so each man could take his pick?

After much discussion, we decided that each warrior should be paid his back pay and one thousand pence as an advance on his share of the booty. Knights would be paid two thousand, and so on up the line. Not that they *had* to draw that much immediately, but they could.

A major headache was determining which men wished to stay with the army and which wanted to return to the semi-civilian life of the reserves. And after that there was a major reshuffling of personnel to make up the three battalions of troops that we were keeping on a full-time basis.

None of this concerned the people who worked at my factories, of course. They were aboard forever!

There were crowds of refugees that needed to be fed on their way home and thousands of lost or orphaned children that needed taking care of.

The details kept us up night after night.

Francine was being very quiet and subdued, realizing that she had overstepped her bounds by far in conning me into taking the dukedoms. I finally got it through to her that had she let me in on the plan from the beginning, there wouldn't have been any problem. But you shouldn't surprise a guy that way!

Anyway, she didn't say a word about Sonya. Whether this was because she thought it normal for a nobleman to have a servant or because she was just afraid of another row, I don't know.

Sonya had shown up at the palace in a waitress outfit, and my only comment was to tell her to get rid of the rabbit ears. She worked that day topless, not having her other clothes with her, and the next day all the rest of the women working at the palace were doing the same, even Francine's maids. Old Duke Henryk, the father of the current duke of that name, had in his last years ordered that all of his palace serving wenches should bounce around bare-breasted, and I guess the local girls figured that old Duke Henryk's styles were back. While I never told anyone that she should work with her top off, I knew better than try and stop women when they pick up on a new fad. I just passed the word that the style should be restricted to unmarried girls over twelve or so, and then only in warm weather, saying that there was nothing pretty about a girl who was freezing to death. A bit of sanity returned.

In a week the worst of the trivia seemed to be beaten down, and it was time to go to Plock. I invited Francine along, since I knew that some politicking might be needed there. Plock hadn't been hit by the Mongols, and the German Crossmen had their main base of Turon not far away. If I was going to have any resistance, I'd be getting it there. Then I changed my mind. Plock might be the most politic place to go, but I was way overdue for confession. We went instead to Cracow and Bishop Ignacy.

Chapter Nineteen

FROM THE JOURNAL OF DUCHESS FRANCINE

In the early morning we were set to visit Plock, the capitol of Mazovia, when Conrad abruptly changed our destination. Baron Gregor was removed from my carriage to take the horse ridden by his brother, Baron Wiktor Banki. This worthy knight was put into my carriage to join me, my maids, and that annoying little trollop Conrad had picked up for a servant. The others were told to follow us along the track, but Conrad insisted that we should run to Cracow immediately. The other four carts of our party, being pulled by ordinary horses, might be able to get there by sundown if they could find a change of horses, but the Big People could run us up to Wawel Castle an hour before dinner. Conrad laughed off the idea that we wouldn't be safe without a bigger escort, saying that his sword was better than most, and anyway, the Mongols were all dead or gone. Of course, he was wrong.

Conrad had made such a horrible scene at his coronation that I refuse to write about it! It was all I could do to convince the leaders of the three duchies that he was still suffering from the war and get them to wait on him the next morning. Fortunately, by then Conrad had gotten his wits about him and had done the sensible thing. After accepting the crowns, he went about taking control of Sandomierz with a wise program of ignoring the existing power brokers who had elected him, since he no longer needed them, and putting the whole place under the control of his own trusted men, his army. Those men would follow him into hell—or go there alone if he commanded it! I was so proud of him that I didn't complain about his new blond-haired chippy.

Sometimes he is absolutely brilliant, and at other times such a total fool! Or could it be that the whole scene in the Church of St. James was just an act to get them to accept his new program absolutely and without question? Could he actually be that astute? So many times he has done such seemingly dumb things, yet always he ends up on top. No! It was impossible! He was just lucky! I think.

He wasn't so lucky when we were attacked on the road. Conrad was a few gross yards ahead of us when two Mongol warriors rode out of the bushes a gross yards from the road and attacked him in the early morning. Baron Wiktor had his sword out as soon as he saw them, and vaulted to the top of our carriage to defend it. But from there he could accomplish nothing, for Anna had already gone alone to Conrad's aid, and the Mongols were putting all their efforts to the killing of my beloved husband!

Anna screamed a warning, but Conrad was far ahead of us when the fight started. She raced to his aid, but before she got there, it was all over. The first Mongol threw one of those deadly spears at Conrad, the sort that all the warriors I had met complained of. At close range, those spears could puncture even our best armor.

Conrad turned in the saddle and slashed the spear in half as it flew at him! His second blow came downward at the spearman's neck, and head and arm came off the rest of the body in a single piece. He then wheeled his mount and charged at the second Mongol, who was shooting arrows at him. Two of the missiles struck my love in the chest and stuck there, but he paid them no attention. He simply charged straight in and knocked them over, man and horse! As the enemy started to get up, dazed, a last blow of that amazing sword chopped through both helmet and skull, and suddenly all was quiet.

"Well done, your grace!" Sir Wiktor shouted as our carriage coasted to a stop. "I have heard of your prowess often enough, but that's the first time I've ever had the chance to see it."

It was the second time I'd seen my love in battle, and it affected me this time just as it had before. I wanted nothing more than to take him into the bushes and love him on the spot, the child in my womb notwithstanding! A glance at the maids told me that the effect was universal, and the new blonde was chanting, "Yes. Yes. Yes," with a silly grin on her face.

Duke Conrad dismounted and called to Baron Wiktor, "Come help me round up their horses! The people behind us were worried about spare mounts. Now we can leave them some. Francine, get out your writing kit and write them a note that we can leave behind."

There wasn't much time lost in getting the enemy horses, since Anna and Silver cooperated nicely in rounding them up. Soon Conrad came to the carriage with two large purses filled mainly with gold. He looked at the arrows stuck in his golden breastplate as if he had noticed them for the first time, and pulled them out.

"Well, there's a mess for the jeweler to worry about. And here's some booty that we won't have to share with the whole army! What do you say to an eight-way split, for Anna and Silver deserve a share as well."

And that's just what he did. The maids were ecstatic! They each got four years' pay.

The horses were tied to the track along with my letter to Baron Gregor, the dead Mongols were left for the others to dispose of, and we were back on our way to Cracow in minutes. And still I wasn't sure. Was he that lucky or simply that good?

Finally I asked him about it as he rode along by my side. He said with an almost perfectly straight face, "My strength is as the strength of ten, for my heart is pure."

So I still didn't know! He wouldn't tell me pure *what*!

At Cracow the carriage was taken from the track at the station, and Anna pushed it slowly through the burned-out cottages of the suburbs. It was a sorry sight, yet the first greenery of spring was on the land, promising the healing of old wounds. At the city gate, Conrad left us to go to the bishop's palace on Wawel Hill, and we followed slowly afterward, for to push the carriage over a plain road without iron rails made Anna's task more difficult.

The guard at the inner gate at Wawel Hill gave us a joyful greeting, saying that Conrad had gone before and that Duke Henryk was here as well. Baron Wiktor and I were more than a little apprehensive as we went to Wawel Castle, for confronting the duke was a thing that neither of us looked forward to. Yet it had to be done, and it was better that we should do it before Conrad was through with Bishop Ignacy. There was no telling what my love would do if the situation was left to him alone.

As we entered the ducal chamber, Duke Henryk ˙was sitting behind the desk that he had used so many times before, that he himself had once ordered made in imitation of the one Conrad had given to the bishop. But it was a chamber that had been promised to Baron Wiktor by my husband, in a castle that no longer belonged to Henryk!

"Welcome to Wawel Castle, your grace," Baron Wiktor said.

"You bid *me* welcome, Wiktor? To my own castle?"

"Yours no longer, your grace. The seyms have elected

Conrad duke of Little Poland, and of Sandomierz and Mazovia as well.''

"The nobles of Cracow all swore fealty to *me*," Henryk said. I could see that this would go as badly as I had feared.

"True, your grace," Baron Wiktor said, "but since that time, you abandoned the city to the Mongols, and the men who swore to you have been killed almost to a man. The nobles and burghers who are left would never obey one whom they think has betrayed them, and Conrad is now duke.''

"So I have been told by the churlish louts, may their souls be damned! I never abandoned Poland!''

"Yet you were not here when the city was attacked, your grace. Duke Conrad was.''

"He was here in disobedience of my orders! I told him to come to me in Legnica!''

"He could not obey you, your grace. Your battle plan was foolish, and he had to obey a higher power.''

"What higher power? *I* was his liege lord!''

"Your grace, can you possibly have forgotten the night five years ago when you and he and I, along with three dozen others, stood vigil in the mountains? Can you have forgotten that morning when God Himself put a holy halo about each of our heads and blessed the work that we were going to do? Can you have forgotten that you yourself knelt before Conrad and were knighted by him into our Holy Order of the Radiant Warriors?''

Duke Henryk was cringing before the baron's onslaught. I was surprised to see Baron Wiktor standing up to the duke so forcefully, so masterfully. There was more to the man than I had suspected, and he wasn't through with the duke yet!

"You must have forgotten, for when the time came for us to do the work that God had ordained, you went and came up with a silly battle plan without even consulting with the man who headed your own order. You had a fine time writing and consulting with every king and duke in Christendom, but you had never a word for the man with the finest army in the world! The man whom *God chose* to do the job! So you sat and hid in Legnica while Conrad fought the war without you, and now you have the gall to sit in his castle as if the spoils of that war were yours to take!''

"There was sickness in our camp. The foreign troops were slow in arriving. We could not advance," the duke said weakly.

"The sickness could have been avoided had you heeded Conrad's book on camp sanitation. *We* had no sickness! And to hell with the foreign troops! *We* didn't need them!"

"Well, the foreign knights have now been sent to Hungary to aid our allies in accordance with my agreement with King Bela. More than half of my own men went with them as well."

"Good, your grace. We no longer need them. What remains to be seen is whether or not we need *you* any longer, either!"

"You threaten me, Baron Wiktor?"

"No, your grace. I merely suggest that when you meet with my liege lord, Duke Conrad, you assume a properly grateful attitude. He, not you, saved the country, and he, not you, commands here. Remember that he now controls half of Poland, and he could take the other half by force at any time if he was minded to!"

"I . . . I will bear your words in mind, Baron Wiktor. If you'll excuse me, Duchess." And with that, Duke Henryk left the chamber, his back bent.

"Baron, you were magnificent," I said as soon as the door closed. I couldn't resist throwing my arms around him!

"I merely spoke the truth," Wiktor said as he disengaged himself and sat behind the desk. "Duke Conrad has made me his deputy here, and I would have failed him if I had let someone else usurp that power. Please be seated, my duchess. Our lord can't be too much longer with his confessor."

Chapter Twenty

FROM THE DIARY OF CONRAD STARGARD

My session with Bishop Ignacy was one of the longest that we ever spent together, and the vespers bell rang long before we were done. We had supper sent up to us, and my confession continued well into the night. With most priests, confession is a fairly short, perfunctory affair, but it is never so with Bishop Ignacy. I was deeply troubled, and he took all the time that was necessary to dig into all the bloody, crowded doings of the last month.

In the end he gave me his usual scolding about my sexual affairs, but absolved me completely for all that had happened in the course of fighting the Mongols, and for the Lubinska business as well. I felt clean for the first time since we had headed out for war. Clean, but still I bore scars within that would always be with me.

When we were through, I said, ''By the way, what did you think of those inquisitors that I had sent to you, Father?''

''What inquisitors? I have met no one from the Holy Inquisition.''

''Well, the day before we marched out to war against the Mongols, two members of the inquisition came to speak to me.''

''And what did they have to say?''

"I'm not at all sure, Father. You see, neither of them could speak Polish, and I can speak neither Italian nor Latin. Furthermore, they had apparently been forbidden to speak of the matter with anyone else but me, so they could not explain the thing to our translator. Also, you have forbidden me to talk about my transportation to this century with anyone but you, Father. Therefore, I made sure that they had a good map to Cracow and directions on how to get here and told them that they should talk to you. Now you say that they never got here."

"Well, that's reasonable enough, seeing as how you probably gave them one of your 'army maps' with south at the top and everything else topsy-turvy. No wonder they got lost! Everybody knows that *east* belongs at the top of a map! After all, the Garden of Eden was in the east, and we are all descended from Adam and Eve, who lived there. Since we are descended from the east, it must be above us, and therefore it belongs at the top of the map. It's perfectly logical!"

"Yes, Father. So you haven't seen them?"

"No, and by this time I think it unlikely that they will arrive. They have either been killed by the Tartars or they are going back to Rome in disgust! Now I will have to write a formal letter of inquiry, explaining what little I know of this matter and asking what happened to the inquisitors."

"Yes, Father. Could you please ask them to send someone who speaks the language next time?"

"Good night, Conrad."

A sleepy castle page showed me the way up to the suite that had been reserved for me, the duke's apartment. I found that Francine was already asleep, but Sonya was waiting up for me, good little servant that she was.

In the morning, bathed and shaved, I was having breakfast, when Francine joined me.

"Good morning, Francine. You slept well?"

"Yes, my love, though perforce alone." Sonya brought

us some more sausages and hotcakes, and I could tell that
Francine was trying to ignore her. She had accepted Cilicia
and had offered me her own maids on occasion, yet she
didn't seem to like me having one of my own, somehow.
Oh, well. Women are strange. It was best to ignore the
situation and wait for the horse to sing.

"Well, you were sleeping when I got back. I didn't see
any point in waking you."

"You took so long in confession?"

"I had a lot to confess. Millions of people are dead
because of me," I said.

"And many millions more yet live because of your dil-
igence and prowess. Have I ever told you how much the
whole of Christendom owes you?"

"Hmph. I'm just a man who's trying to do his job."

"Then there is more work yet for you to do, my love.
Duke Henryk is in the castle."

"And we're in his old room. I guess I'll have to have it
out with him today, though I can't say that I'm looking
forward to it."

"Much of the way has been cleared for you, my love.
Baron Wiktor and I talked long with him yesterday. There
is much to the baron that I had not seen before."

"He's a good man, though his brother Gregor is the truly
wise one of that bunch. That's why I'm giving Gregor command of Mazovia. Sonya, would you please go to Duke
Henryk and ask him when it would be convenient for him to
talk with me today? And, uh, put a dress on first. Henryk
has this problem with feminine skin."

"Wait!" Francine said as Sonya was about to leave. "Is
that wise, my love? *You* command here, and you should tell
him when it would please *you* to meet. And if it pleases you
to have your wenches nearly naked, you should not change
your custom to suit a visitor."

I shook my head and said, "Okay. We'll compromise.

Sonya, ask the duke if he would join me here for dinner at noon and don't bother dressing up for the occasion. After that, tell the cooks to have a meal for two sent up at three sharp and remind them that I fired the head cook at Sandomierz. You know my tastes in food.''

As she left, I said, "Satisfied?"

"With you, always, my love. You might want to dress in one of your army uniforms to remind the duke of your bond with him and the fact that you head the Order of the Radiant Warriors.''

"As you will.'' It takes so little to keep her happy sometimes.

I spent part of the morning with Baron Wiktor, getting things organized in Cracow, and then saw a delegation of the city fathers.

They wanted me to redesign the lower city for them, since it had mostly been burned to the ground. Yet at the same time, they wanted to start rebuilding immediately, without waiting to install sewers and water mains. And once we got into it, they didn't want a new street layout, either, since that would mean that all the existing building plots would change, and who would know who owned what? Somehow they wanted me to bless it and make it all better, but not to change anything!

My own private thought was that it would be easier to simply build a new city. As for the old one, well, there had been a half yard of organic fertilizer on the ground there for centuries. If they would put a plow to it, they'd have the richest farmland in the world! But I couldn't tell them that, so I told them to think over what they really wanted and promised to meet with them later.

I knew that in the end what we would do was come up with some new building codes, requiring fireproof materials for the walls at least, and plan to put in the utilities later in a piecemeal fashion, the way things are normally done. It would be more efficient to build from scratch, but there wasn't time. The people of Cracow had to have a place to live *now*. But best for them to come to that realization for themselves.

I had Natalia make a note to tell the factories to get into full production of all building materials as soon as possible. She was Baron Gregor's wife and would soon be leaving me to join him at his new post in Plock. She was trying to train one of the other girls to take her place, but she had been with me for nine years, and training a replacement to know what I wanted without being told every little thing wasn't easy.

It was a pleasant spring day, and I had lunch set up on one of the battlements that served as a balcony. I was surprised to see that the duke also wore one of our red and white army dress uniforms, probably for the same reason that I did. Francine had been right again.

"Welcome, your grace," I said. "Have a seat."

"Thank you, your grace," he said, looking pale from his recent illness. "I want to start by offering you my apology. I formulated a poor battle plan without your advice and consent. I ordered you to follow it even though you knew that it was foolish. And in anger, I have not answered your many letters and messages. For these things I ask your forgiveness."

"I accept your apology, your grace. I, too, need to apologize, since I deliberately disobeyed your direct orders. But let's just say that these unpleasant things never happened."

"Done. And since we now are both of the same rank, wouldn't equals speech be more appropriate?"

"Right you are, Henryk. Much has happened since our last meeting. It's been almost half a year." Sonya and three of the castle servants brought in our food and set the table. While it was a warm day for the season, it wasn't run-around-in-half-a-bathing-suit warm, and I could see her tiny

nipples harden up in the breeze. I waved her back into the
building with the other servants.

"True, Conrad, and that is entirely too long. Where
should we begin?"

"Well. I suppose that you have heard that Count Lambert
fell fighting the Mongols. I was there, and before he died,
he told me that I was his heir and that you had approved it.
Is this true?"

He looked down at his plate. "Oh, yes, you inherit his
lands and much more besides. Did you know that Lambert's
brother, Count Herman, also died?"

Lunch consisted of breaded chicken, deep-fried in a pressure cooker à la Colonel Sanders, with French fries and
coleslaw. And bottled beer with some fizz in it. No coffee
or Coke, alas. Henryk didn't seem to know how to handle
the chicken, so I picked up a drumstick to show him that
eating with the hands was proper for this exotic dish.

"No, I didn't, although I knew that Herman's wife was
dead."

"Count Herman died of the sickness that struck my camp
at Legnica. Now, do not tell me about your book concerning camp sanitation measures. I am well aware of it. I had
my own knights follow your suggestions to the letter, but I
was unable to control the foreign troops that well. They
insisted on doing things as they always had, and disease
spread among them the way it always does. And then, of
course, my own men caught it. As best as I can determine,
Count Herman died just a few hours before his brother did,
and the count's wife was killed a half day before that.
Therefore, Herman inherited his wife's share of their estates, and Lambert inherited them before his death. This
means that they all come down to you. You are now Count
of Cieszyn as well as Count of Okoitz!"

"Wow. I'd certainly never expected that," I said.

"It is also possible that you have inherited Lambert's

extensive Hungarian estates as well, since his daughter has not been heard from since she left, and I understand that the fighting in Hungary has been fierce. I do not think that they were hit with as many Tartars as you were, however. The number of enemy heads on pikes along your railroad tracks would be unbelievable had I not seen them with my own eyes.''

''I wish I could help the Hungarians out, but my foot soldiers would be almost helpless without the railroads, and there are none in Hungary. You know, I once tried to get King Bela to let me run a line down into his country and to put some steamboats on his rivers, but he refused me permission to do it. As to the heads you saw, well, they represent not one in twelve of the Mongols we killed. Before you go back west, we must visit the major battlefields here. Then I'll show you heads!''

''We must do that. As to King Bela, well, if he lives out the war, he will be less arrogant in dealing with you. But these are all trivial matters compared with what we really have to talk about. You know that my father spent his life trying to unite the country, and that I have done all that I can to continue his work. I now hold all of western Poland, except for the seacoast of Pomerania. You hold all of the east except for what is held by the Teutonic Order—''

''The Crossmen were sworn to my predecessor, in theory at least, and they'll damn well swear to me or leave bleeding!'' I said.

''Well put! I think together we would have little trouble getting the Pomeranians back into the fold, as well. And we must be together!''

''Indeed. I agree.''

''Good. Well, then. I came here to offer you my oath of fealty, Conrad. You will be the first king of Poland in a hundred years!''

''Hmph. And what if I don't accept your oath?''

"What? How can you say that? After all this, you mean to humiliate me further?"

"Not at all. I'm just saying that under certain conditions *I* would be willing to swear to *you*!" I said.

"Do you actually mean that? Why? You have the power now, not I! Why would you do such a thing?"

"Because I don't *want* to be a king! I'm not even very thrilled about being a duke. I'm a technical man, an engineer. I have no training in law, or politics, or sovereignty! I don't like sitting in judgment over other human beings. I don't even like sitting at the high table of a banquet! Sovereignty is a job that you have been training for all of your life, and you're welcome to it! I want to be free to get back to work at developing industry here, and I want you to take over all the other trivia for me."

"You would be a craftsman and call the crown trivia?"

"Yes, because it is! In the long run my job will be far more important than yours."

"Well, if that is truly your wish, then so be it. But a moment ago you said 'under certain conditions.' What conditions did you have in mind?"

I pulled out a list from my breast pocket.

"Well, first off, I'll stay in charge of the army. My forces will be the *only* military forces in Poland, and all other forces will be either disbanded or merged with the army over the next six years. I'll pay for the army myself, but that's the only thing I'll pay for. There will be no other taxes on me."

"Granted, although disbanding the feudal levies will be no easy feat. What else?"

"I'll have to stay Duke of Sandomierz, Little Poland, and Mazovia. Frankly, the people here wouldn't have you directly in command, and these areas will be underpopulated for some time, anyway. But I don't want the dukedoms to be hereditary. If they were, there's a good chance that your heirs and mine would come to blows, and that's best avoided now.''

"You mean that I would be your heir?"

"Yes, insofar as those parts of the duchies that are not settled by the army are concerned. You, or your heir, will inherit the fealty of those lands and peoples that remain under the conventional nobility. The army will keep its own lands and choose its own leader, although I haven't worked out how yet,'' I said.

"Then, of course, I completely agree. Next?''

"Primogeniture. This business of dividing the country up between the sons of the last king has got to stop. An equal division among the heirs of lesser titles is fine, but the country, once united, must be indivisible.''

"I had planned such a change myself. Granted. Next?''

"The lands that I have inherited border on Little Poland. I want them combined with my duchy here.''

"Very well, although bear in mind that the law in each of the duchies of Poland is different. There will be a certain reluctance to change on the part of the people living there.''

"That's another thing. I want a single, simple set of laws that is the same throughout the land. I want that law to be administered by carefully trained and very honest men, and not by the local lord of the manor. We need a system of police and judges and courts that honestly and fairly enforce the law, not the barbaric hodgepodge that we have now.''

"Now, that will be a hard thing to do. People resist changes even when they are for the better. Furthermore, it will be expensive.''

"I'll be responsible for the salaries of the people involved, if necessary, but the rest is your job. You write the laws, and you administer the system. Only check with me before you publish those laws. I don't demand veto power or anything like that, but I do want to have a chance to give you my advice.''

"I will agree to this in principle, although we both know that it will be many years in the doing. What about your army? Will these laws cover it as well?"

"If a warrior breaks a civil law, he will be punished by the civil courts. There will be military laws as well that the warriors will be subject to, but civilians won't. I'll worry about military law."

"Good. Next?"

The meal was over, and the servants cleared the table. Sonya brought in desert. Ice cream! Excellent, despite its lack of vanilla flavoring. You know, there are advantages to occasionally firing a cook!

"I'm going to be building forts all around the borders of the country. I'll pay for the land I need, but once bought, it will be army property, under army control and not taxable by anyone. Okay?"

"Very well. Anything else?"

"Well, there's Copper City. For years I've been running it and sending you the profits. The bookkeeping involved is annoying. I want it made mine entirely."

"I hereby grant you title to Copper City. Is that the last request?"

"It is."

"Good. Then the matter is settled, though we shall have to put it all in writing, of course. Since you dictated the terms, why don't you see to getting some fair copies made. Then there is the matter of your oath of fealty. We will want to do it again with all of your officers and my nobles present, but let us swear to each other now, while the sun is yet high."

And so together we raised our right hands to the sun and swore. And Poland again had a king. Or so I thought.

Chapter Twenty-one

FRANCINE HIT the roof when she found out that Henryk was to be the next king instead of me. She ranted and screamed for hours, not listening to a word I said, until I finally just left the room and went down to the Great Hall, which was the closest thing to a tavern that was immediately available. I just can't *tolerate* a screeching woman! When I came back that night to sleep, she was still at it, shouting at the top of her lungs, with her servants cowering in the corners. It seems that she had now found out that Henryk had started out by offering fealty to me and that I had turned him down. Castle servants talk too much! After another hour of this I left again, to find that Sonya had arranged another room for me at the other end of the palace. Women are so much nicer *before* you marry them!

Dammit! I never promised to make her a queen! I never promised anything except seeing to her needs, and a throne was hardly necessary for her well-being. In fact, history proves that a throne is a very dangerous possession. Too many kings—and queens—have failed to die peacefully of old age in their beds. Anyway, all this political and social aggrandizement was her idea, not mine. I mean, I'd gone along with making her a duchess, hadn't I? Wasn't that enough? What did she want to be? Empress of the known world?

The next morning Sonya told me that she had a friend who was looking for work. I interviewed the girl over breakfast, a pretty, well-built redhead who had come dressed for the job. On Sonya's suggestion, she showed up for her job interview wearing nothing but her freckles. I hired her as a second body servant. At least with servants you can fire them when they get out of line.

I never should have gotten married.

I spent the day doing administrative stuff, writing a set of building codes for the city fathers of Cracow and making a deal with them on building materials. I sold them bricks, hardware, lumber, and so on at wholesale prices and gave them three years' free credit on it. They would worry about parceling the stuff out to the citizens at retail prices and collecting payment for it. The actual construction work was up to them. I wouldn't be involved. Later, in a year or two, we'd worry about water mains and sewers, and by then, what with their profits on the building materials, they would be able to afford the utilities. A backward way to do things, but there wasn't really much choice.

A few days later Francine was calmed down enough to at least start out civil at a banquet that Henryk had insisted that I attend.

Nine years before, on the day after I had first met the then Prince Henryk, we had both joined a party hunting wild boar and bison. The regalia required for this sport included a shield, and he had been a bit offended by the motto on the bottom of my heater, which was the first line of the yet to be written Polish national anthem, "Poland is not yet dead!"

We had talked about it, and I had promised to paint it over if and when he finally got the whole country united. Our new armor was so good that a fighting man didn't

ordinarily need a shield, and I hadn't used mine in years.
Henryk had found it somewhere and had it brought into the
Great Hall, along with brushes and a collection of paint
pots. He told the story to the gathered notables and invited
me to keep my word. There was nothing for it but to put
down my knife and fork, scrape the old motto from the
shield, and publicly paint on it "Poland is alive and well!"

It was mostly a party joke, and I mugged up my part in
it to suit the occasion, the way I had to do every Christmas
for the peasants in imitation of my old liege lord, Count
Lambert.

This bit of buffoonery miffed Francine no end, since she
felt that since I was now a duke, I should be a somber ass
as well.

Later, when somebody mentioned that Henryk would be
my heir for the three eastern duchies, she got downright
livid! She flew totally off the handle again and was literally
frothing at the mouth before we got her out of the hall.

And she accuses *me* of making scenes in public! She
accused me of robbing my own children, by which she
doubtless meant *her* own children, yet to be born.

At this point I had about a dozen others by various fine
ladies, but I don't think that she figured that those kids
counted. Personally, I have always done my best to treat
them all the same. Playing favorites wouldn't have been
good for them.

To my way of thinking, saddling a kid with any sort of an
inherited lifetime job would be one of the worst possible
things you could do to him. "Well kid, here's your role in
life, written down on these here computer punch cards, ha,
ha! Live out your only earthly existence precisely in accordance with the pattern that is given you from the high mountain! Make sure that you fit the cookie cutter exactly, baby!"

Bullshit! What a horrible thing to do to a little child!

A kid deserves a good education and a lot of love, and on

top of this, I figure that all my kids started out with a pretty good set of genes. Beyond that, you owe it to him to see to it that he has a chance to grow in the directions that suit him best, and that goes double for the girls!

And damn all these Dark Ages attitudes! I had done the best thing possible for my children, for Poland, and for me!

I didn't see Francine for the rest of the week, and to hell with her. I had two new girls to take care of me. Young ones! And what they lacked in skill, they made up for with cheerfulness, obedience, and enthusiasm.

Sonya mentioned that she had another friend looking for work.

"Sonya, just why is it that you and your friends are so eager to do the dirty work around here?"

"It's not all that dirty, your grace."

"You know what I mean. Some places that I've been, the young ladies would have been insulted if you offered them work as a domestic servant."

"Then in those places the young women must all be fools, your grace."

"What do you mean? Come on, you know I'll never get angry at an honest answer."

"Well, it's a great honor to serve so high a lord, and a great pleasure to serve one who is so kind and so virile."

"The truth, Sonya."

"That is the truth! Or at least part of it, anyway. The rest is that, well, you have a *very good record*, your grace! Nine years ago Count Lambert sent you out to your new lands with five simple peasant wenches. Now, after staying with you, *every single one of them is at least a baroness*, and they're all rich besides! A poor priest's wife is now a *duchess* because of you! I've only been working for you for a few weeks, and I'm already wealthy from my share of that Mongol booty, as are both of Duchess Francine's maids and even your horses! I tell you that any woman who wouldn't

warm your bed or clean your chamber pots would be a damn
fool who wants to stay poor!''

"Hmph. You know, I've never thought of it that way,
but I suppose that a young person has to look out for herself."

"Of course, your grace. And a bright girl takes care of
her friends as well. You can never tell when you might need
a return favor. Did you want to see Kotcha?"

"Why not?"

And then there were three.

Well. Baron Wiktor was settling into his new job nicely,
and before long we had things reasonably under control.
Within a week it was time to visit Mazovia and get that
business over with.

Duke Henryk—well, he wasn't crowned yet—suggested
that he go along and that we visit the battlefields on the way.
It seemed like a good idea at the time. Francine still wasn't
speaking to me, so I left her behind.

We loaded our entourages, Big People and all, onto one
of the three steamboats I had left on the Vistula, Baron
Tadaos's *Enterprise*, and headed downriver. A few months
ago, there had been three *dozen* of them! Not one Vistula
boatman in four dozen was still alive. There were so few
river boatmen left that the boat was "manned" largely by
the baron's many wives. Training boatmen was another
thing to worry about.

Tadaos proudly demonstrated his favorite bit of war
booty, a huge leather-covered recurved Mongol bow that he
claimed was better than the English longbow he'd lost when
his old *Muddling Through* had been burned.

We stopped at each of the major killing fields on the way,
told the story of what had happened there, and watched
Henryk being properly impressed by the huge squares of
mounted human heads. The ants and carrion birds were still
having royal banquets, feasting on flesh and eyeballs. An

ugly sight, but better the Mongols should do that duty than us. Anyway, it wasn't as though we had invited the bastards here.

At the first such stop Henryk mentioned the big pile of Mongol weapons and equipment that was stacked there.

"That stuff?" I said. "That's what was left after we sorted through it. The best trophies were all taken to Three Walls to be divided out among the warriors as spoils. This pile will be taken back as scrap metal when we get around to it. If you or anybody here wants to pick through it, feel free."

The duke's pride wouldn't let him touch it, but most of his men picked up a sword and a dagger or two. Our servants all did likewise. Even Sonya got to wearing a dagger on her loincloth for a few weeks until she decided that it was silly. I passed the word that if any of the returning peasants wanted any of it for their personal use, they should feel free. It's not as though we were short of scrap iron. Weeks later, Baron Novacek, my sales manager, was angry about these gifts, and he sold much of what was left at a healthy profit.

The next day Henryk and I were standing apart from the others on the top deck of the boat as we were approaching Sandomierz. Tadaos was taking us carefully past the wreckage of yet another Mongol bridge.

"Henryk, when were you planning on having your coronation?"

"I am not sure, Conrad. In a year or so, as soon as the Pope confirms it, I suppose."

"The Pope? What does he have to do with it?"

"Well, everything! Poland is a papal state, after all."

"Poland is a *papal state*? You mean like all those little countries in Italy? I've never heard of such a thing!"

"Well, as a mere baron, you have never had to pay Peter's pence. It is no small tax, I assure you."

"But I still don't understand. You mean to tell me that

Poland is subordinate to Rome? When did that happen?" I asked.

"Why, almost at the beginning, more than two hundred years ago. At the time it was a wise political move, since we were being invaded by the Germans and it gave us a certain moral force against them that we lacked up until then. Now it has become more of a tradition than anything else, although I reaffirmed our status with Rome a few years ago for much the same reasons that my ancestors had. It gives us moral support against the Germans. In theory, Poland is a member of the Holy Roman Empire as well, though neither my father nor I have ever paid taxes to Frederick II. I suppose that he could crown me as easily as the Pope, but talking Gregory IX into it will be an easier job. It is better politically as well, what with all the troubles that Frederick has been having. I would prefer to be associated with him as little as possible, even though I married one of his nieces. He has been excommunicated more than once, you know."

"I guess I don't know. I've never paid much attention to world politics."

"By our agreement, it is all more my worry than yours, Conrad. If you really want an education in it, talk to that wife of yours."

"Whether we ever talk again remains to be seen. I never thought that she'd react to our agreement the way she has."

"And that is all more your worry than mine. But if I may make bold a suggestion about your domestic life, I would say that you should leave your wife at home, as I customarily do and as my father did before me. That way, when you do get back, you will be warmly welcomed, and when you are away, you will be unencumbered with emotional baggage that you do not need."

"I'm afraid that Francine will never make a contented housewife. She'd rather be a world power."

"Again, my friend, it is your problem, though it might

solve itself once she has a child in her arms. It often has a calming effect on them. If that does not work, I remind you that the Church allows you to beat her so long as you do not use too big a stick."

"I don't think that I could do that. The customs were a little different in my time. Back to this business of your coronation. Do you really think it's wise to let the Pope, or any other power, for that matter, crown you? If he can make you a king, can't he unmake you as well? And as to your paying this Peter's pence—that's in addition to the tithing you do, isn't it? Well, Poland has just saved all of Christendom from the greatest danger that ever threatened it! It seems to me that our military services should be taken in place of that money. We saved France and the rest of the wealthy countries to the west from total destruction. Let *them* pay Rome's bills!"

"Those are two very interesting suggestions, Conrad. I particularly like the idea of getting out from under the taxes. They would double on me, you know, since our agreement has you paying no taxes to me and someone would have to pay the Peter's pence on the eastern duchies. I think I will do it! At the worst, Gregory will scream too loudly, and I might have to back down. But it is certainly worth a try."

"If you did get off that hook, you could afford to pay for the new legal system, couldn't you?"

"I suppose I could, but first let us see if it can be done."

"And what about my other suggestion? What if *I* were to crown you?" I said.

"Now, that would require more thought, Conrad. Politically, it might be dangerous. Yet I must say I like the concept."

The boat had made the usual U-turn and was coming upstream to the landing at Sandomierz. Doing it any other way was just about impossible with a stern-wheeler.

"Well, you think on it, Henryk. For now we just have

time to visit the battlefields west of here if we are still to get to the palace for supper.''

I went with Henryk and his three guards to the battlefield, since we were the only ones on Big People. Everybody else went directly to the palace.

A city of round Mongol felt tents had sprung up on the old battlefield, housing not only the remaining sick and wounded and the troops attending them, but also the arms and property of the Christian knights who had fallen there. So far not much of it had been retrieved by the heirs of the dead.

By accident, I came across the gold-plated armor that I had once given to my former liege lord, Count Lambert. Since I was his heir, I gave orders that the armor should be sent to my jeweler for repair and then on to Baron Vladimir. Vladimir had worn that armor as my best man at my wedding a half year ago, and it had fit him well. It seemed proper that he should have it now.

Back in Sandomierz, Baron Wojciech still had everything well in hand, and Yawalda was glorying in her role as vice duchess. Watching my old lover preside made it one of the least boring banquets I'd ever attended, almost worth the time it wasted. The former peasant girl was doing her new situation up proud!

Yet the burghers of the city treated Henryk with a certain aloofness and seemed not totally pleased with my subordination to him. It wasn't as strong as it had been at Cracow, where more than one citizen had thrown garbage and dead cats at the duke, but you could tell that at best they had a wait-and-see attitude.

The next morning was spent going over the killing fields opposite of Sandomierz, and I pointed out the place where my stupidity had earned me an arrow in my right eye. But by this time the huge squares of human heads, the massive piles of rusting arms, and the vast stacks of salted-down horsehides were getting a little boring, and I was glad that our grisly tour was over.

Baron Gregor and Natalia were eager to push on to their new post in Plock, and aside from the wreckage of a few more Mongol bridges, the rest of the journey was uneventful.

The people of Plock had been warned of our coming, and they had the city decked out with flags, banners, and colored bunting. Some of Francine's annoying political posters had found their way here as well. Plock had been bypassed by the Mongols, and the city itself was entirely unharmed. Yet every fighting man in the entire duchy who could afford a horse had ridden south under the banners of young Duke Boleslaw, and most of them had died with him when he had foolishly stayed on the battlefield instead of leaving the enemy to my army, as had been planned. It was a city of women, children, and old men, and they were truly glad of our coming.

A battalion of army troops had arrived a week before, and they were cheering us, too. Judging from the color of their eyeballs, it looked as though they had spent their time and half of their back pay on drink and in the comforting of too many young widows. But I suppose that they each deserved a hero's traditional welcome. They'd certainly earned it.

I really don't like having people cheer at me, although I try to act the part. Henryk, however, seemed to be enjoying it immensely. Good. That was part of being king, and he was welcome to it. I let him make most of the speeches to the crowd, and when my turn came, I just thanked them for making me their duke and told them that Henryk would be the next king and that Baron Gregor would be my vice duke here. That seemed to make everybody happy, although in the mood they were in, that mob might have cheered if I had said that I was giving the country to the Mongols!

The palace at Plock had much in common with the others

I had in Cracow and Sandomierz. One had the feeling that
the previous dukes had competed with one another for status
symbols, and had done a lot of imitating in the process.
Natalia was delighted with her new home, and Baron Gregor seemed contented with the rewards of his faithful service to me.

I spent the usual week helping Gregor get settled in, and
Henryk was a great deal of help as well. I'd thought that he
would be treated coldly, as he had been in Cracow and
Sandomierz, but not so. Perhaps it was because the battles
had happened so far away from this city and because, since
Mazovia had never been subordinate to Henryk, he could
not possibly have ever betrayed it.

In any event, it was finally looking as though I would
soon be able to get done with this time-wasting political
stuff. I was eager to get back to my proper job at Three
Walls.

Then suddenly all bets were off.

A breathless lookout ran in and announced that the Grand
Master of the Teutonic Order was approaching the city gates
with a thousand knights and men-at-arms behind him. The
Crossmen were coming!

Chapter Twenty-two

FROM THE JOURNAL OF DUCHESS FRANCINE

So it was that because of my arrangement of the situation and Baron Wiktor's adroit handling of Duke Henryk, the duke became convinced that his only hope of survival lay in his unconditional submission to my husband. Through hard work and no small a dose of good luck, the stage was properly set for Conrad's final enlargement to King of Poland.

Oh, I knew that he would make his usual objections to this advancement, but I also knew that just as he soon found reasons of his own why he must needs remain duke, once it was thrust upon him, he would also convince himself that he must remain king. Men are really such simple beings, and so easily manipulated.

Conrad insisted on quietly conversing with Henryk at a meal alone with him, so I was not able to attend, yet I was not worried. All things had been so well managed that there could be only one possible outcome from their meeting. And better that they should think that they had done it all by themselves. It saved bruising their fragile masculine pride.

Thus, you can imagine my abject horror at finding out that they had managed to do the exact opposite of what was sensible! Despite the fact that Conrad not only held the will of the people but had vast, almost unheard of wealth and a huge, efficient army and Henryk had none of the above, somehow they had decided that Henryk should be king and Conrad but a vassal.

And my stupid dumpling of a husband was dull enough to be pleased with the arrangement!

And these two, both the bumpkin and the shyster, had sworn on it! Oh, not publicly as yet, but with too many servants present to silence them all without notice being taken of it.

Is it any wonder that I was annoyed?

Then after Conrad gleefully gave me his disastrous news, he tried to convince me of his brilliance in doing it! He kept making no sense at all until he finally lurched out of our chambers.

I then tried to get the entire story out of the servants that were present. Of course, the bare-titted hussy that he euphemistically calls a personal servant was completely useless to me. She knows how long she would last without Conrad's protection! The others were castle servants, left over from the time when Henryk ruled here. It didn't take me long to show *them* where their kasha was salted!

Thus it was that I found out that Henryk had started out by offering fealty, as was to be expected, but my stupid, doddering husband had refused it! After Conrad returned and I explained it all to him, he again left me to spend the night with his blond trollop.

I am becoming convinced that my mother was right. The pains of this world are too much for a woman to bear, and the only sensible course is to retire to a nunnery.

Why am I tortured like Tantalus, to have all that I desire but a hand's length away, only to always have it wrenched away when it is seemingly within my grasp? What great sin have I committed that I should be treated by God in so cruel a manner?

Yet still, I strived to be a peacemaker, and when I was formally invited to a banquet with Conrad and *that duke*, I decided that it would be seemly to go. Perhaps some small thing could be rescued from this debacle.

Such was not to be. At the feast Henryk taunted my husband, making him act the clown, the buffoon to him. And Conrad willingly did it! He louted before the mob and Henryk, too. Conrad, whose armies could have stomped this entire castle flat without taking their hands out of those *pocket* things of theirs!

I was mortified. And no sooner was this ugly scene over than some simpering courtier pranced up and casually mentioned that Conrad had also given away our own children's birthrights. They were to be disinherited in favor of Henryk! The child in my own womb was to be cast out before it had even had the chance to draw its first breath.

So now Conrad and Henryk have gone north to make a mess of things in Mazovia, to alienate the population and probably get themselves into a stupid, useless war with the damned Teutonic Knights!

And I sit here alone, abandoned by all save the servants, my guards, and the courtiers.

A nunnery. There must be a decent nunnery somewhere in Poland!

Chapter Twenty-three

FROM THE DIARY OF CONRAD STARGARD

Damn. I had to face yet another high-anxiety situation, and this was likely to be a big one. I had been bumping heads with the Knights of the Cross since the first day I got to this century, when one of them had bashed me on the head for not groveling properly. Later I'd caught seven of them taking a gross of children south to sell as slaves to Moslem brothels, and when we had put a stop to this molestation of children by cutting down most of the Crossmen, I had been forced to fight a Trial by Combat with their champion to stop the Crossmen from repossessing those kids.

Plus, well, I knew my history well enough to know that having those Germans on Polish soil would cause seven hundred years of misery for my country. Not only were they completely obliterating several Baltic peoples now, they would continue their bloody expansionist ways forever!

Several of the most murderous battles of the entire Middle Ages were fought against them, and once they were defrocked by the Pope and had become a secular Protestant group, they became the duchy of Prussia that was eventually to unite Germany under a military dictatorship that was one of the root causes of World War I. And World War II was started when Hitler invaded Poland to forcefully take the land bridge that separated Prussia from the rest of Germany.

Added to all this, my father and uncles had been resistance fighters in Poland during World War II. I grew up hearing firsthand about all the unspeakable atrocities committed by the Germans. I mean, the Russians are by no means pleasant, but they are sweetness and light compared to the Nazi Germans. Germans are not a lovable people!

Furthermore, while they had sworn fealty to Duke Boleslaw of Mazovia, they had failed to come to the aid of my predecessor when he had called on them to join in the defense of the country against the Mongols. All they had done was to send a puny five-hundred-man force to Henryk at Legnica, and he had been forced to bribe them to get even that!

I now had the opportunity to remove these evil people from the map of the world, and you can bet that I was going to do everything in my power to do it!

"Battle stations," I shouted. "Baron Gregor! Get the gates closed and your men and guns on the walls!"

Within moments, bugles were blowing and men were scurrying about, finding their arms and armor, readying themselves, and finding their proper positions. It wasn't as well rehearsed as most of the army's maneuvers. In fact, we had never gotten around to actually practicing it yet at all. Chaos and confusion were sucking up precious minutes.

But God was still on our side, for the Crossmen had been spotted from the cathedral tower two miles from the city and were advancing only at a walk. The troops managed to get the gates closed in time, but just barely.

I was as late as anyone, since the only armor I had with me was the damnable gold parade stuff that Francine had insisted that I wear, and it takes forever to get into it. I was panting as I joined Henryk and Gregor at the Northern Gate. Henryk was wearing the golden armor I had given him years ago, but Gregor was wearing the much more practical cloth-covered army combat armor.

The Grand Master was just coming into view, riding at the head of the miles-long column. He was easily spotted since his surcoat was more highly decorated than were those of his men, although it was done in the same drab black and white as the others. Under their garb, I noticed that they were all wearing old-fashioned chain mail, being too proud to buy better armor from my factories. Not that I would have approved the sale.

"That's not the same Grand Master I met at my Trial by Combat," I said, looking through my binoculars.

"No," Henryk replied, squinting through a telescope of the sort that all my officers carried. "Herman von Salza died peacefully two years ago, in his sleep."

"There's very little justice in this world," Baron Gregor said.

"There is even less than you think. The filthy blackguard coming toward us was sent by me to aid the Hungarians not a month ago. He could not have gone there and still be here now! It seems that he has broken yet another vow," Henryk said.

"Wonderful," I said. "Unless these bastards have changed their ways recently, none of them will be able to speak Polish. Does anybody around here speak enough German to act as a translator?"

"I do," Henryk said. When I looked at him in surprise, he added, "My mother was German, after all, and I had to learn more of the language to speak to my wife. I'll talk to them, but I think that talk is all we should do with them today. I would rather that this did not come to a battle, Conrad. If we must fight them, let us try to do it on their soil, ruining their property, not ours."

"A good thought, and the army could use a few more

months' rest after fighting the Mongols," I said. "The problem is that their property *is* my property. I *am* their liege lord, after all."

"True in theory, Conrad. In practice, I have some doubts. Well, wish me well."

The German column had stopped in front of the closed city gate, and Henryk shouted down at their leader. An exchange in German started that went on for some minutes while the rest of us on the wall waited around, wondering what was being said. All I could tell was that the words were getting louder and harsher. German seems to be a great language for being rude in.

Finally Henryk took pity on us and said, "Mostly, I've been discussing his failure to go to the aid of King Bela as promised. He wasn't expecting to find me here."

"Well, when you get around to it, tell him that I am prepared to accept his oath of unconditional fealty."

"He will love you for it," Henryk said dryly, and then started shouting in German again. The Crossman column continued to advance, crowding against the city wall and spreading to both sides of the gate. There were more than twelve hundred swivel guns on the wall, mounted in holes hastily drilled into the parapets. That much at least had been done during our week here. Every gun that could be brought to bear was pointed at the big black crosses that the Germans wore on their surcoats. Nice of them to provide us with cross hairs.

The unintelligible conversation went on for the fair part of an hour. I was beginning to wonder if I shouldn't send out for refreshments when Henryk turned to me.

"He says that he doesn't need to swear fealty to you because he is here in Poland by a perpetual written treaty with the late Duke Boleslaw's uncle, the previous Duke Conrad I of Mazovia. That man still lives, you know, but he's prematurely senile. Poor fellow, he's only fifty-four, but he can't even feed himself, let alone say a complete sentence.''

"I'd like to see that treaty," I said.

"As would I. They say they have it with them and invite us to come down and examine it. Are you minded to risk it, Conrad?''

"Don't do it, your graces!" Baron Gregor said. "Those Crossmen can't be trusted under ordinary circumstances, and just now it would be to their advantage to see both of you dead.''

"Hmph. Henryk, what say we invite a delegation of them inside the city. We can sit down with them someplace comfortable, have a meal, and try to talk out our problems.''

"A noble thought, Conrad, but it is best to meet a Crossman in the open and to be upwind of him. The rules of their order forbid all bathing, shaving, and whatnot, you know. If rumor can be believed, they don't even wipe their arses. Also, they have more strange dietary restrictions than the Jews, which they adhere to rigorously, in public at least, so it is nearly impossible to feed them without giving offense. I ate their food once, and I would not willingly repeat the experience. Enough said?''

"So there is no excuse that you could make to get a few of them inside here.''

"None that would not convince them that we were planning treachery. Dishonest people assume that all others are like them.''

"Then you figure that we should go out there and trust them?'' I said.

"Well, the first part of that, anyway. We really must see this document that they have. But their very presence here proves that they are oath breakers, so keep your sword loose in its sheath.''

"Okay. Let's do it, then. Baron Gregor, I'd like to have

six companies of troops ready at the gate to come to our rescue, and make sure that the gunners on the walls are alert!''

"Right, your grace.''

I tightened my armor, loosened my sword, and went down the steps with Henryk behind me. I ducked and went through the small door that was opened for us in the main gate, and faced my adversaries. As luck would have it, I was downwind of them, and Henryk's advice about their lack of bathing proved to be entirely too true. The small door was closed behind us, and despite the fact that we were out in the open, I felt claustrophobic. I glanced at Henryk, and he started talking to them in German. After a while they handed him a rolled-up piece of parchment, which he unrolled and studied silently for a while. Then, without a comment, he handed it to me.

"It's an obvious fraud," I said. "First off it's written in German! A Polish treaty, granting lands on Polish soil, would be in Polish, not in some foreign language. Then, there is no date on this 'document'! Anything official has to have a date. And worst of all, there is not a single signature on it. And not a single seal! It's preposterous, and I can't even read what it says.''

"Well, I can," said Henryk, "and I assure you that the content is as absurd as the format. It purports to give the Teutonic Order permission to do as they please to the inhabitants outside our borders, whether they be Christian or heathen, and grants them Polish lands equal in area to those that they conquer from our neighbors. Furthermore, it states that all such lands taken or granted become their property, subject only to the Holy See and the empire. They no longer admit to being your vassals, or the other Conrad's, either. What is your reaction to that pile of barley?''

"You can tell them that I am waiting for their abject submission to me, and barring that, that they have one year in which to leave my lands and all of Poland. After that, I will kill them all and put their heads up on pikes, as I have done with the other people who have recently invaded my land. Tell them that exactly." There was no point in prolonging the conversation, and anyway, the smell of these bastards was getting to me. At least the Mongols didn't stand upwind and breathe in your face! On the improbable chance that they *did* swear to obey me absolutely in all things, I planned to send them back to the Holy Land where they had started from and tell them to kill rag heads. I just wanted them *out*!

So I stood there while they screamed gibberish at one another for a quarter of an hour. I envied the UN people with their headsets and their real-time translations, but Henryk seemed to be doing his best, and I didn't want to break his stride.

Eventually he turned to me and said, "They don't seem to have grasped the extent of what you have done with the Mongols. What say you have some of your people give a delegation of theirs the tour that you just gave me."

"Fine, just so long as I don't have to do it myself. Their stench is overpowering me!"

After another long babbling match, with more gutturals than could have been manufactured by three dogs fighting over a dead pig, Henryk said, "Good. They will have twenty men ready to go tomorrow."

"Done," I said, though that meant that we'd have to spend days hosing their stench out of one of our only three riverboats. "I presume that you will be escorting them, your grace."

"I seem to be stuck with the task, your grace, being the only one handy who speaks German. Sovereignty is a demanding profession."

"And one that you are welcome to," I said.

That evening Henryk came to my quarters.

"You know, Conrad, fighting the Crossmen is not going to be as straightforward as beating the Mongols. The Knights of the Cross are in theory a religious order, and they have papal sanction. Certain factions in the Church are not going to be pleased with us when we kill them. Then, too, Emperor Frederick II has conferred on them an imperial charter, and he won't love us either if our plans go well."

"Are you saying that we should back off on them?" I asked.

"No. I think that we have to get rid of them or they will be a thorn in our side forever. But I think you should know that this is an issue where for the first time in a century, the Pope and the emperor will agree on something. We may well have a further war with the empire on our hands, as well as papal sanctions against us. I for one would not like to be excommunicated."

"Nor would I. Well, then, I'd say that you have your work cut out for you. You must see what you can do about gaining support for our cause in the Church and in foreign courts."

"How right you are, Conrad. And you must see to it that not all of your forces face the east. The next war may come at us from the west!"

The next morning they went away, the Crossmen and the king, and I was able to get another boat the next day, the RB47 *Millennium Falcon*. Later, as I was pulling into East Gate, I got a radio message from Henryk.

CONRAD. THE CROSSMEN ARE BOTH FRIGHTENED AND AD-AMANT THAT THEY WILL NOT LEAVE. I ASSUME THAT YOU WERE SERIOUS ABOUT GIVING THEM ONE YEAR TO GET OUT, FOR THAT IS THE ULTIMATUM THAT I HAVE GIVEN THEM. HAVE I DONE RIGHT BY YOU?—HENRYK.

After thinking about it a bit, I had them send back:

HENRYK. FINE BY ME, BUT GIVE THEM UNTIL THE FIRST
OF JUNE 1242. THAT WILL GIVE MY TROOPS TIME TO GET
THE SPRING PLANTING IN. CONRAD.

Thus, I had a year before I had to worry about any more military or political nonsense, and I was eager to get back to some simple, sensible technical problems. At the time I didn't think it would take much to throw out the Crossmen, not when I had an army that had kicked shit out of the Mongols! Of course, I screw up pretty often.

The Riverboat Assembly Building had been completed, and work was under way on the construction of four new steamboats. Two of our existing Vistula boats were doing patrol and transport duty, but the third had been fitted with a derrick and was engaged in salvaging what it could from the boats that had been lost in the war. Already, the engines, boilers, and all the major hardware needed for the boats under construction were on hand and being rebuilt, and more salvage was coming in every day. Plenty of seasoned lumber was available, and the boatwrights were sure that we could replace our war losses by late fall.

East Gate was now manned by a company of regulars, most of whom worked as boatwrights and the rest as mule skinners on the railroad.

My first inclination was to go straight to Three Walls and dive into some refreshing engineering work, but on reflection I realized that it was important that the folks at the other installations see me. Best to make as fast a tour as possible. I sent my entourage to my home by mule-drawn carriages while I went out ahead alone on Silver.

My first stop that morning was at Sir Miesko's manor. His wife, Lady Richeza, had been instrumental in starting and running the school system, and when the war had come, she had invited all the lady teachers in eastern Poland to weather the Mongol advance behind the strong walls of the manor. Most of them were still there, since commercial transportation had only recently resumed operation.

She said that her husband was in Hungary, fighting the Mongols for King Bela, and that I would know better than she where her older sons were, since they were all members of my army. I assured her that her boys were all well, and she served me a nice dinner. During the meal, she and her fellow schoolteachers proudly told me every detail concerning how the Mongols had attacked the manor and about how the ladies had shot them all down with the swivel guns that Sir Miesko had provided in such abundance.

They got quite animated in the telling of the tale, pantomiming themselves in battle with a degree of showmanship surpassed only by Baron Vladimir when he was a young man! It is surprising how much bloodthirstiness lurks in the heart of the gentlest of schoolteachers. After dinner they proudly displayed the booty that they had taken, the sacks of gold and silver as well as saddles, arms, and bloodstained armor. They had decided to keep it and divide it up among themselves, since the school system was more than well enough funded. They even had the enemy heads up on pikes in the gruesome army fashion!

It was mid afternoon before I could bid these charming, learned, and remarkably brutal elderly ladies good-bye and ride to Okoitz.

Chapter Twenty-four

OKOITZ HAD been the seat and home of my liege lord, Count Lambert, and I had built him a magnificent castle there in return for six years of output from the cloth factory that I had designed for him. Lambert had been a libertine and cocksman par excellence, though in a very friendly sort of way, and the girls "manning" his factory were remarkably loving and giving. The biggest Pink Dragon Inn I owned was at Okoitz, having been enlarged three times over the years. You see, this was where the boys came to meet the girls working at the factory. And why were so many girls eager to get work at the cloth factory? Because this was where the boys were, obviously!

The castle had room for the hundred peasant families that farmed the land in the area and worked at a part-time sugar mill in the winter. There was also room for the six hundred attractive young ladies who worked at the cloth factory and the hundred-odd servants, cooks, and repairmen who did all the work needed to feed so many people and keep the place livable.

But all these people together occupied only half the living space at Okoitz. On certain occasions Count Lambert liked to invite all the nobility in the county over for a festival, and to make this possible, there was rather posh living space here for an additional thousand people.

The count was inordinately proud of his castle, but no sooner had it been completed and furnished than he had been killed and I had inherited the place.

The problem was, What to do with it?

I toured the town, starting with the factory, looking at it with new eyes. The machinery was mostly of wood and at least eight years old. I had been pretty proud of it when I had first designed the place, but now, compared with my other installations, it was behind the times. Everything was very labor-intensive, and for a good reason. Every time I had suggested some improvement to Count Lambert, he had always found reasons why it should not be done. The truth was that he didn't give a damn about efficiency, but rather he looked at every job eliminated as one less girl he had in his fabulous harem! Eventually I had stopped trying to sell him on improvements altogether. The factory was far superior to its competition, anyway, even though there were a dozen similar operations going now in Poland alone, owned and operated by men Lambert had proudly shown through his factory.

But now, while I certainly didn't plan any reductions in the work force, there was always the need for more production, and the local herds had increased such that during the last two years the county had actually been selling raw wool to outside buyers. New factories were definitely in order—two new factories, one for linen cloth and one for wool. The old one was made of wood and lacked proper foundations, anyway. It was showing signs of rot.

Okoitz was built above the huge Upper Silesian coalfield, one of the biggest in the world, and there was already a working mine on the property. Steam-powered factories were obviously the way to go.

Of course, developing the new machinery would have to

be done here, where the problems involved with working with fibers could confront the designers directly. Designing at a distance, as the Russians usually do things, is inefficient and can lead to disaster. This meant that we would have to build a machine shop here first. Not a production shop, but a research and development shop.

So why not move the entire R&D section from Three Walls to Okoitz? Three Walls was getting overcrowded, and we were starting to run out of building space there. R&D was probably the easiest group to move, and it would give us something to do with all the extra space we had in the castle. My own household was outgrowing my old apartment at Three Walls, since everybody seemed to be sprouting body servants, and Count Lambert's vast apartment might suit me very nicely. Yes.

All this was going on in my subconscious mind as I toured the factory. My conscious mind was mostly on the hundreds of sexy young ladies who were working the machines. They were all flirtatious and tended to wear as little as the temperature permitted. Another good reason for moving R&D here was that the apprentices who made up two-thirds of the teams would surely appreciate the scenery hereabouts. I certainly did!

Mulling through my thoughts, I tried to have supper quietly in the big cafeteria, but the manager of the factory, a Florentine named Angelo Muskarini, insisted that I give a speech to those present. There was nothing for it but to oblige him.

"Thank you," I said when the girls and farmers had quit screaming at me. "As you doubtless all know, the war is over, and the good guys have won!" This brought on more cheers. When they died down, I continued. "The important fact for all of you ladies to know is that except in the river battalion, our losses were small, and that if your favorite young man has not gotten back yet, he will likely be coming here soon.'' More cheers and bouncing up and down.

"I suppose that you have all heard that my liege lord, the noble Count Lambert Piast, died honorably in the defense of his country. You also know that I was named his heir. I simply want to say that I intend to make very few changes around here, and those will all be for the better. We will be expanding our cloth-making operations, since for the last two years our shepherds have actually been selling raw, unprocessed wool to foreigners, to be spun and woven in foreign lands instead of here. To counter this trend, we will be hiring more workers and making better, more efficient machinery for you to work at. This will mean putting a new group of intelligent young men to work here to design and build the new equipment, but I expect that you fine ladies can keep these poor lads from getting too lonely!'' Again, more cheers.

"Perhaps, if you make them welcome enough, we'll move all of our research groups here. Well, we'll see. There is one other major change that I would like to make, however. Up until now you fine ladies have been working for cloth, not money. That is to say, you have been working on a barter system. What would you think about being paid in money instead? Then you could buy cloth, at special prices, if you wanted to, but you could also buy anything else you wanted as well.'' The reaction was mixed. Some cheered, but they were probably doing that out of habit. Most didn't do anything, since this was a new thought for them.

"Well, you think about it, and we'll talk it over again when I return in a few weeks. You might want to elect four or five representatives to negotiate for you. Also, what would you farmers think about my dividing Lambert's farmland up among you, thus having your own land doubled, paying taxes or a fee on it to pay for what you and your

families eat here in the cafeteria and then selling your crops
to the kitchens here for money? I'm not saying that we *have*
to do it this way, but I want you to think about it. That's
about it. I want to finish my dinner now, even if it has
gotten cold. I'll be back in a few weeks.''

Of course, a lot of the girls had all sorts of questions, and
they had no qualms about shoving the peasants aside and
putting their scantily clad young bodies out in front. After a
while I tried to get away and pleaded fatigue, but four of
them sort of invited themselves to talk further with me in
Lambert's old chambers. They were all pretty. A plain girl
wouldn't have dared to be that pushy, fearing rejection.

There is a limit to how many times a man can say no, and
I passed it. I was bleary-eyed the next morning and told
myself that I was getting too old for this sort of thing.

I met Muskarini for breakfast and told him about the rest
of my planned changes. Lambert had been running the entire factory on a barter system. Wool and flax were provided
by his vassals, and like the workers, they received a portion
of the finished cloth in return . The problem was that wool
comes in various grades, of different values. The long wool
from the sides of the animal is far more valuable than are the
short hairs that grow on the legs. And some sheep grow
much finer wool than others do. The workers had various
skill levels in different crafts, and we produced hundreds of
grades and types of cloth, again worth all different amounts.
The accounting required by all of this was so ridiculously
complicated that I doubt if anybody really knew what was
going on.

There was a very good reason why Lambert had done
things in this strange way. By the terms of his separation
with his wife, he had to send her one-half of all the money
that he took in. Not half of his net income but half of the
cash that he grossed. When he had made this agreement, it
had been reasonable enough, since most of what little

money Lambert got he received from selling his surplus agricultural products, what was left over after he and his peasants had eaten most of it. His old castle had been built for him by his people out of local materials. His smiths made many of the things that he needed. Cash money was just something with which to buy occasional luxury goods from the merchants, not something that was needed for life itself. Also, Lambert's wife had very extensive estates of her own in Hungary to support herself with, so she wasn't hurting.

But all this changed when I built him a productive factory. He could hardly pay her one-half of the gross cash worth of the products of his factory, since the cost of materials and labor was well over half the sale price. Running the clothworks with a conventional accounting system would have put him quickly out of business. Indeed, for several months, until he came up with the barter solution to his problem, he was very difficult to work with!

I was under no such liability, and I wanted to know what was happening financially, so I ordered the factory changed over to a sensible money system. We would buy our wool and flax with money, pay the workers with money, and sell all our output for money. Well, we'd offer special discounts to our workers and vendors to keep them happy, but it would now be an accountable system.

Muskarini was not at all pleased with my changes and came up with all sorts of ridiculous reasons why we couldn't convert to a cash system. This made me suspect that he had his hand in the till somehow. After two hours of arguing with the man, I told him that he would do it my way or I would send him back to the garret that I had found him in nine years before. That quieted him down some. On leaving him, I went to the inn and sent a message ordering a team of accountants and time-study men to descend on this place, ASAP!

I saddled Silver to get to my next stop, Eagle Nest, before lunch. The medieval world had no great collection of restaurants available to travelers, and you generally had to time your trips around the hours when food was served at the manors and factories if you didn't want to miss a lot of meals.

As I was leaving, one of the girls who had spent the night with me was waiting by the drawbridge. She smiled and reminded me that Eagle Nest was an all-male institution, and didn't I really want some companionship tonight? I decided that if I didn't give her a lift, she'd probably hitchhike there, putting herself into all sorts of danger. At least that was how I rationalized it to myself. I pulled her aboard and set her on the saddle bow. She was the prettiest of last night's group, with incredibly soft skin for so slender a person and the longest legs I've seen this side of a Hollywood musical. Her name was Zenya.

I found that I rather liked having a girl sitting in front of me, where we could talk easily, as opposed to having her behind, riding apillion. I resolved to have a saddle made up with a more comfortable seat for a woman up front.

The boys at Eagle Nest were always enthusiastic, bustling about wherever they went, and their mood was infectious. They had eight planes flying now, and many more were being built. Their eager-beaver attitude toward whatever they were doing was a joy to watch. It was such a pity that I was going to have to slam them down hard!

On being told that all the aircraft were brand-new, except for the engines, I said, "But there are the nine planes that were still intact after crash-landing on the battlefield at Sandomierz. They were sent here immediately after the battle. What happened to them?"

We asked around, but no one had any knowledge of them. They had received the thirteen engines that we had hauled back with the booty, but whole planes? No, sir!

What bothered me worse than losing the planes was the fact that each of those planes had been strapped to the top of a war cart that had been manned by a full platoon of warriors. Where were all those men?

I sent a dozen messages out, trying to locate them, but had no luck. A company and a half of men had simply disappeared! We never did find them, their equipment, or the airplanes, either. It remains a mystery that is told late at night around the fires, and the story grows a bit with each retelling.

Interlude Three

I HIT the STOP button and started fumbling with the keyboard, trying to call up the Historical Corps records on just what had happened to all those men and all that equipment. I wasn't that used to the system, and it took me quite a while to get what I wanted.

The naked girl at my side looked on without saying anything, so I explained to her what I was after. She just said, "Yes, sir."

She was a cuddly little thing and seemed to enjoy my light petting, but she didn't have a lot to say. I mean, she didn't actually encourage my roving hands, but she didn't object any, either.

Eventually I dug out what I was looking for.

"Those men were caught in a Mongol ambush," I told her. "They were going without a cavalry screen, and those planes on their war carts made it hard to get their weapons out. They were killed to a man. Then the Mongol commander had their armor and equipment sent straight back to the east, and the bodies hidden. If the Mongol craftsmen can figure out the guns and planes, Conrad is going to have some serious problems on his hands!"

"Yes, sir," she said.

I hit the START button.

Chapter Twenty-five

FROM THE DIARY OF CONRAD STARGARD

Since the war was over, the boys were back at their usual two shifts, going to school in either the mornings or the afternoons and working in the shops or flying on the opposite shift. I couldn't address them all until after the evening meal.

"Gentlemen. First off, I want to thank you for your dedicated service in the war that together we have just won. While a final head count is not yet in, I think that I am safe in saying that over two million Mongols were killed on the banks of the Vistula by our riverboats, and those boats could not have done half that job without your accurate scouting and reporting of enemy positions. I think that it is fair to say that a million of the enemy owe their timely deaths to your own very good work! That's more than were killed by the regulars at Sandomierz, Cracow, and Three Walls combined!

"Furthermore, the land forces were able to defeat the Mongols that got over the Vistula with relatively light losses. That would not have been true had there been another million enemy troops fighting against them. We could have been totally defeated! And had the Christian army lost, Poland would have been lost. The fifty thousand or so knights that waited with Duke Henryk at Legnica probably would not have fared any better than Duke Boleslaw's conventional knights at Sandomierz. You deserve much of the credit for saving all of Christendom!''

They spent some time cheering. I let them go on until they wore themselves out. Then I told them the other half of the story.

"On the other hand, your performance was far from perfect. First off, you totally missed the entire Mongol army that skirted the Carpathian Mountains and entered Poland by crossing the rivers where they are scarcely more than mountain streams. You got so involved with patrolling the Vistula that you didn't bother looking south of it. You not only did not find them, you made the near-fatal mistake of assuming that they could not be there!

"Worse yet, you did not sit on Count Lambert when he got the stupid idea of landing at Sandomierz to take part in the 'final' battle with the Mongols. True, he was your liege lord and you were required to follow him, but it was also your duty to give him good advice, and there you failed him completely! You failed him, and he and two dozen of your classmates died because of your failure. They died uselessly, because of one man's vanity and your pusillanimity. And then, since we had no aerial reconnaissance, Cracow was burned because of your failure! East Gate fell because of your failure! Three Walls was attacked because of your failure!''

A look of dark horror was spreading over the boys. I stopped and let my words sink in. Then I continued.

"The trained warriors of the Christian army would not have failed in this fashion. Part of the training they get clearly defines their duty to both their subordinates and their superiors. They know what courage, and honor, and duty really are. And you must learn!

"Therefore, Eagle Nest, with all who work and fly here,

is going to be absorbed into the Christian army. Starting one year from today, no one over fourteen years of age will be allowed up in a plane who has not completed the full one-year course at the Warrior's School. This means that in the next two years every one of you is going through that school, and if you want to swear fealty to me and not have to give up flying forever, you had better pass the course! That includes the instructors as well.

"The Warrior's School will be starting up again in two weeks. I will expect half of those of you who are over fourteen to be at it. In the future, no new student will be accepted here without first being a warrior. That's all that will count, besides good eyesight and physical fitness. Eagle Nest will no longer be a haven for those of noble birth. Anyone who can qualify will get in. And it will no longer be an all-male organization. Qualified young ladies will be flying within the year.

"I am Conrad, and I taught you that air is strong! Believe what I say!

"On the plus side, this means that all of you boys and men will soon be drawing a regular army salary, and your various benefits will be brought in line with theirs.

"Oh, yes. You will also be getting a share of the rather extensive booty that the army took, so if not exactly rich, you are all at least quite nicely off. I'd like to speak to the instructors tomorrow morning for about a half hour to discuss scheduling. Good night!"

I had jerked the boys around pretty severely, and I didn't want to sit in on the inevitable bull sessions that would occur while they absorbed it all. I went immediately to the small room that was always reserved for me there. Zenya was waiting for me, of course, but I firmly resolved to get at least some sleep that night.

My next stop was Coaltown, where things were booming nicely. The coal seam there was one of the most massive in the world, being fully two dozen yards thick. Once our miners had penetrated through the substantial layer of limestone above it and the layer of clay between the coal and the limestone, they had just been going in any which way. It didn't seem to matter to them, since wherever you dug, you were digging through coal.

We set up a more rational system of exploitation. Surveyors transferred a true east-west line down to the bottom of the main elevator. Then the miners cut a barrel-vaulted chamber, two dozen yards wide and a dozen yards high, through the limestone, leaving the clay on the floor. Every four dozen yards they started a cross-vault to send shafts at right angles to the main one. The limestone was sent to the cement plant.

When these miners got a gross yards east of the shaft, another group started harvesting the clay for the brick works. And this group was followed by coal miners, who could work with a stone ceiling over their heads, which, being vaulted, wasn't likely to cave in. Not only did this prove to be an efficient way to get the minerals out, it also left behind these huge, cathedral-like rooms and tunnels that sure looked to be useful for something.

The next day I went to Copper City. Here the Krakowski brothers had things well in hand, and production was going full swing. They were delighted that the city was now army property, though in fact it didn't actually change anything immediately except for some accounting procedures. In the long run, though, it meant that we didn't have to get Duke Henryk's permission to change things, and that speeded things up a bit. Mostly, I had asked for the city because I had been pretty sure that I could get it at the time. Greedy of me.

Then we raced back to Three Walls and got there on the evening of the fifth day since leaving East Gate. At last I could get down to being an engineer again!

Zenya had just sort of tagged along during the trip, and I really couldn't just leave the girl in what was to her a foreign city. Once back at Three Walls, she sort of fell in with my other three servants and proved to be outstanding at giving back rubs. A week passed before Sonya asked me if she shouldn't be put on the payroll like everybody else. By then I had gotten so used to having her around that I went along with it. Yet the whole affair nagged me. Had I hired her, or had *she hired me*?

Francine was still staying in Cracow, and that was fine by me. She could come back when she was ready, but I'd be damned if I was going to beg her to come home.

Despite my firm intentions to do technical work, my next four days were spent doing managerial stuff. There were the plans for the new standardized factories to be gone over and approved, and then the plans for the factory that would make the precast concrete structural members for the standard factories. The bills of materials had to be carefully scrutinized, since we would be putting these buildings up at the rate of one per week for the next two dozen years or so. Little mistakes can become big mistakes when you are working with those sorts of numbers.

And each of these structures was more than just a factory. Each housed a complete company of workers and their families, with a school, a church, a cafeteria, and many of the usual things that a stand-alone company needed. Well, since they would be built right next to each other, they could share facilities on certain things. They didn't each need a separate general store, for example, and inns were built only at the rate of one for every two companies, although they had to be larger, of course. Rather than having one medical officer per company, they were grouped in clinics that each served six companies, so that there were always two doctors on duty at any time of the day or night.

We were really planning a huge industrial city, and except for some land set aside for hobby gardening, there would be no agricultural work being done. But at the same time a city environment needs things that a country place can do without, and each factory had a gymnasium and a swimming pool.

The factories were to be built on both sides of the Coaltown–East Gate railway, which would be expanded to four tracks and roofed over in the course of construction. In the future, bad weather wouldn't slow down interfactory transportation.

Each company-sized factory/housing complex was to be seventy two yards long, three to six stories tall, and a half mile wide. It would be a strip with housing on the outside, then community services, and then a factory at the middle that abutted the covered railroads. All this would be under a single roof, and it would rarely be necessary to go outside in the cold Polish winter.

Building one a week, on alternate sides of the road, we would be constructing a long strip city, a mile wide and growing a mile longer every year. It would be called Katowice after my hometown in modern Poland.

A more difficult job was scheduling just what each of these factories would produce and making sure that they had the machinery and skills to produce it. There were many crowded product sections in our existing system, and much of the job would consist of moving them to Katowice and enlarging and modernizing them in the process.

After a few years, once we had at least three companies producing a given product, we would be able to use a system where the captain of each company would have almost complete control over what his group would be making and how they would make it. Functionally, it would be a free enterprise system. But free enterprise doesn't work well when there is only one producer and only one consumer, and for start-up, that would be the situation. Most of what would be produced would be needed for building these factories and for the concrete forts we would start putting up next year. We had specific requirements, and it would have to be regulated from the top. It was a massive scheduling job, but at least there wasn't much politics involved. It was such an audacious project that people got a kick out of just jumping in and doing their best.

Chapter Twenty-six

I WAS going over the truly bodacious amounts of steel re-inforcing rod that would be needed, and subconsciously worrying about how I was going to fairly divide up the booty without causing inflation, when a visitor arrived.

I wouldn't have been disturbed this way if I had still had Natalia working for me, but the new girls weren't as sharp as she was. Four people were trying hard to replace one, and they were doing a poor job at it! I didn't realize what a treasure I had until I lost her.

Anyway, this guy was standing at my drawing board, trying to get my attention while I was doing arithmetic in my head. He was covered with rings, brooches, necklaces, and other jewelry, a thing I have never liked on a man. Personally, I wore almost none at all, except for the brass on my dress uniform. And the solution hit me!

It was vitally important that each of the men get his fair share of the booty. I couldn't possibly cheat them and keep the army intact. Yet having that much spending cash dumped on the market would be equally disastrous. The answer was jewelry! Every man would get a new dress uniform with the epaulets, buttons, buckles, insignia, sheaths, dirk handle, and sword guard in solid gold. With a little creativity we could probably get three or four pounds of gold on the lowest warrior basic!

And then there would be a glorious medal for being a member of the Radiant Warriors, bigger than a man's hand, and various other medals for valor and participation in various battles. The women who manned the forts would get similar decorations, along with a nice dress uniform, which we didn't have as yet for the women, and the Big People would be decorated as well! And there should be something nice that a warrior could give to his wife, say, a necklace or a belt—or, better yet, both! They would get the booty, but not in the form of inflationary cash. Uniform doodads would stay off the market, because the men would have to come in dress uniform on certain occasions, and it would be embarrassing to show up wearing mere brass.

I was smiling insanely when I looked up at the fellow and said, "Can I help you?"

"Well, yes, your grace," he said, confused by my grin. "I am Baron Zbigniew, and I was vassal to Count Herman of Cieszyn. I have been told that you have inherited his estates. Is this true?"

Would you believe that what with all the things going on, I had completely forgotten about the city that I had inherited? I dropped my pencil and bent the lead point.

"I *knew* I forgot something! Forgive me, Baron. Yes, I now own Cieszyn and those lands that were held by both the count and his wife. There has been so much happening lately that I have not had time yet to do everything. Look, for now have one of the secretaries put you up in the noble guest quarters, and we'll discuss the matter tonight at dinner."

"Yes, your grace." The baron limped away on crutches.

When he was gone, I said to my lead architectural designer, "Do you know of anybody who would want to be my representative in Cieszyn?"

"Why not Komander Wrocek, sir? I served under him in the war. He is a member of the old nobility, so he knows the game, and he lost his leg at the fight in Cracow, so he won't be of much more use to the regular army. He should be up and around by now, I expect."

"Not a bad thought, Josep. Betty, go to records and get me Wrocek's file. Then check through the files and get me the names of all the officers, captain and above, who were permanently disabled in the fighting. Sitting at the high table and presiding might be just the job for them. There are going to be a lot of posts like this to fill once the knights get back from Hungary."

I tried to get back to what I was doing, but other things were nagging me. I sent a message to my jeweler, telling him to see me, and another to Francine:

MY DEAR WIFE, IF YOU DO NOT WISH TO JOIN ME AT THREE WALLS, WHAT WOULD YOU THINK OF BEING MY REPRESENTATIVE AT CIESZYN? CONRAD.

Francine answered back within the hour:

MY DEAR HUSBAND, YOU ROB ME OF THE CROWN OF PO- LAND, AND NOW YOU WANT TO STUFF ME INTO A BACKWA- TER PLACE LIKE CIESZYN? MAY YOUR DEAR SOUL ROT IN HELL! FRANCINE.

I deduced by this that she was still unhappy. And now every radio operator in the army would know about it. I was angry at her, but I wouldn't hire a new maid this time. I was already one up.

So I sent to Komander Wrocek, who was recovering at Wawel Castle, offering him the job at his old rank. He was delighted and promised to come within two weeks, as soon as his doctors let him free. Another message was sent telling my accountant at the Pink Dragon Inn in Cieszyn to go to the castle and see what he could do about figuring out the finances there.

By then the afternoon was over, and it was time to meet

the baron for dinner. More and more, lately, I found myself taking my dinner away from the cafeteria, and many of my breakfasts as well. Mostly it was my new servants' fault. They made eating so damn decorative! Yet I made a point of always eating lunch with the other people in the cafeteria just so I wouldn't get out of touch.

I explained the arrangements that I had made, and Baron Zbigniew was agreeable, though he looked disappointed. I decided that he probably wanted the job for himself. When I talked with him a bit, he admitted it.

"I'm sorry, Baron, but the fact is that I barely know you. I hope that you can understand that I need an old and trusted friend in such a critical position. Your services will still be needed, of course. Komander Wrocek will need all the help he can get. He lost a leg at the Battle of Cracow, you know. How did you happen to be injured, incidentally? The Mongols?"

"I only wish it had been an honorable war wound, your grace, but the sad truth is that I had no sooner gotten to Duke Henryk's camp at Legnica than my horse slipped on the ice and I went down on an iron spit that was loaded with a duck that was roasting next to a cooking fire! The damned thing went right through my leg and into my horse. It nailed us together, and after they put the poor beast down, they had to cut it — and the saddle! — in half to get the carcass off me. And all the while I had to lie there half in the snow and half in the burning coals, and me not a Radiant Warrior!"

It occurred to me that *on the average* he must have been reasonably comfortable, but I didn't say it. "Horrible!" I said.

"Yet I tell you that the pain of the wound was nothing compared to the mortification I felt while everyone stood around trying to figure out how to get us apart, and the squire who owned the duck screamed at me the whole while. The entire infamous affair took hours to resolve, and I am sure that the foreign knights were taking bets as to how it would work out. Then the damned surgeons thought that my leg would have to come off, but I wouldn't allow that. It seems to be healing well enough now, though.''

"Oh, you poor fellow! While you're here, you might want to ask one of our army doctors to have a look at it. They're better than most.''

"I'll do that, your grace, but I doubt if there's anything they can do to mend a man's broken pride! The greatest war in history, and *I missed it because of a roast duck*!''

The girls seemed to like him well enough. At least I noticed one of Cilicia's maids sneaking into his room that night. My household seemed to be developing the morals that Count Lambert's had had. Yet Lambert's dying wish had been that all the ladies would be properly loved, and I had promised him that I would do my best to see it so. It wasn't any of my business, so I pretended that I didn't see her.

The next morning I got a double-sized research crew going on light bulbs: a glassblower, a machinist, and four apprentices. They didn't have a good source of electricity yet to power it, but there were plenty of problems to be worked out first. How to blow a glass bulb around a fragile baked thread. Coming up with a metal wire that would be wetted by molten glass and have a similar coefficient of thermal expansion so that the glass wouldn't crack as the bulb heated up and cooled down. Developing decent hardware, like a screw base and a light switch. And harder yet, making a good enough vacuum pump.

An electric generator was a separate problem for a separate team. I designed what I thought would be a decent DC generator and had them get to work on building it. I knew full well that we'd go through a dozen models before we got something good enough to go into production with. Generators were one of those things that I studied in school and had seen working but had never had a chance to design. It was another one of those specialized things that a generalist like me never got involved in. It would be years.

Then there was plumbing. We were casting our pipes out of copper. This required making the walls much thicker than was necessary to carry water, but we couldn't dependably cast them any thinner. Modern copper pipes are drawn, stretched into shape by pulling the copper alternatively between outside dies of the sort used to draw wire in order to make the copper pipe longer, and inside dies in order to stretch the metal to a larger diameter with thinner walls. Simple enough machinery, in theory at least, and it seemed likely to drop the cost of pipes threefold. I got another team on it.

Yet another team was put to work on some better wire-drawing machinery.

Teams were also assigned to develop a clothes washer and a dishwasher. One group got going on a sewing machine, although privately I considered it to be a very long-term project, since it was so complicated.

I wish we could have worked on power hand tools, but that looked impossible to me. For a long time to come all powered installations would have to be permanently mounted. We didn't have any rubber or plastic with which to make an extension cord!

I thought about getting a few teams going on new weapons and developing some of the things that had been invented just before the war but too late to get into production, but I decided against it. For one thing, we had more arms and equipment of the old style than we had men to use them. New weapons would require new tactics and new training, with a lot of man-hours required. We were already so superior to anybody else in the world that making us better was simple overkill. And mostly, in twenty years, there would be as many Big People around as there were

Little People. We wouldn't be mostly infantry then; we'd be almost all cavalry. Best to wait a few years and then start working slowly on some good cavalry weapons and tactics.

A relaxing week slid pleasantly by before I got a message from my team of accountants at Okoitz. Angelo Muskarini was under arrest!

Chapter Twenty-seven

SONYA WANTED to go and visit Okoitz, so I took her along, even though taking a woman to Okoitz was on a par with hauling coke to Coaltown.

I got there to find Muskarini chained up in a storeroom. He was a mass of bruises, his teeth were loose, and both eyes were blackened shut.

"Resisting arrest?" I asked.

"No, sir," said my senior accountant. "He just made us angry."

Well, my accountants were not the mousy sorts who live on American television. They were warriors first, book-keepers second. Of course, they shouldn't have beaten the man up. I'd talked to my detectives on the importance of using the minimum possible force, but it had never occurred to me that the accountants needed the lecture as well.

After we stepped into the hall and away from the cell, I said, "You shouldn't have done that. It's not nice to beat up someone who can't hit back."

"Sorry, sir. But this dog turd was robbing his own liege lord of a fortune!"

"Can you prove it?"

"Of course, sir. I can show you the figures. Muskarini

has been stealing nine parts per gross of the entire factory output ever since the first year he got here. It was no accident. He was very consistent about it, and Count Lambert doubtless thought that it was a normal production loss."

"That must be a lot of money."

"One gross, eleven dozen, and four *thousand*, a gross, nine dozen, and three pence, sir."

I whistled. They were talking base twelve, and that came to almost a half a million, the way I was brought up. "Has this money been found?"

"Yes, sir, and then some. The figure I mentioned was just on the missing finished cloth. We think he might have been getting kickbacks on the dyes and other supplies that were bought by the count. That was what much of the beating was about. Finding the money. He was keeping it in the dye supply side shed. He had the only key to the place."

"Hmph. You know, he couldn't have stolen that much alone. He would have had to have accomplices. No one man could possibly have carried out that much cloth and not been noticed. After all, hundreds of people work around here, and many of them were Count Lambert's knights."

"We know, sir, but he won't talk about that."

I went back into Muskarini's cell. He knew I was there, even though he couldn't see me. "Well, Angelo. What do you have to say for yourself?"

"I didn't steal that money, your grace. It was mine."

"Yours? Almost half a million pence was yours? Look, I was there at the beginning, remember? You were absolutely penniless, starving to death in a garret in Cieszyn! I hired you as a gift for my liege lord. How could you have gotten such wealth? You'll have to tell a better lie than that before I believe it!"

"Count Lambert gave it to me, your grace. He did, I swear!"

"No, Angelo. The count was very generous about a lot of things, but not money. Lands, yes. Women, yes. Money, no!"

"But he did, your grace. That wasn't nine parts per gross I got. It was six percent! The count, he gave me that much as a bonus. See, I was only being paid one hundred pence a year, plus room and board. Once the factory was working well and making fabulous profits because of my knowledge and labor, I asked the count for a substantial raise, and he wouldn't give it to me. I kept on asking him, and he kept on turning me down. But he was giving cloth out easily enough. You certainly got enough of it! So I asked if I could have a share of the cloth we made, and he said that would be possible. He asked how much I wanted, and I told him six percent, figuring we would settle for some much lower figure, since he'd been so stingy with me so far. But the count said that six percent would be fine, and he went in to his latest lady. I could hardly believe my ears, but he agreed to it! I swear that this is true on the grave of my own mother!"

"Hmph. Then how did you turn that cloth into money?"

"Why, I sold it to merchants, your grace, the same way that everybody else does."

"The same way that everybody else does?"

"Yes, your grace. Many of the girls here sell cloth to the merchants. That's how they are paid, in cloth. Oh, some of the workers come here for just a season and go home with a full hope chest, but some of the ladies have been working here every year since we started. They are our skilled workers, and we couldn't possibly manage without them. Now, you can't expect a lady to save cloth for nine years and never need a penny in real money! Of course we all sold to merchants, and Count Lambert never said a thing about it. We have a regular exchange set up, with fixed prices, and a girl draws her back wages in cloth according to what a merchant wants to buy. It was our cloth, after all. We'd earned it!''

"You know, Angelo, that story is almost believable. But tell me, why did you keep your money hidden?''

"Your grace, if you had such a fabulous sum, wouldn't you worry about thieves?''

"It would have been safe enough in the count's strong room, especially what with the new locks I installed there for him.''

"Yes, your grace, but then he would have seen how much I had earned working for him. You see, I had the feeling that he didn't know how much six percent of gross was. I didn't want to remind him.''

"Hmph. And that's why you spent hardly any of the money, so the count wouldn't know that you were rich?''

"Of course, your grace. In a few more years I was going back to Florence, a wealthy man, a merchant of substance!''

"Hmph. Knowing the count as I did, I almost believe your story. Almost. The real problem is that even if every word you've told me is true, you were still robbing Count Lambert. You say that you had a verbal contract with him, and I admit that verbal contracts were the only sort that Lambert would make. But for a contract to be binding, there must be a meeting of the minds. If Lambert didn't know how much you were getting, there was no contract. You were stealing, nonetheless!''

"Your grace, you can't believe that! You wouldn't have me killed!''

"No, I probably wouldn't, but *my* contract with Duke Henryk has him worrying about all legal matters. Your life is in his hands, not mine.''

I went out and told the accountants to call in Baron Pulaski and have him hear the case. Then they would send the results to Duke Henryk for his determination.

My immediate problem was to find a replacement for Muskarini. Something that he had said gave me hope, though. There were women here who had more than six years' experience in cloth making. I went through the factory looking for them, since of course there were no personnel records. Soon I had five possible candidates for the job, and I was told of three more on the night shift, whom I sent for. Then I took them into one of the guest rooms one at a time and spent about a quarter hour talking to each them. And you know, there wasn't the slightest doubt in my mind as to who was best qualified for the job of running the whole factory.

One young lady was twenty-two. She seemed to know everything I did about cloth making and quite a bit more that I didn't. She was currently in charge of the linen-weaving operation, but she also knew what was happening everywhere else. She had taken full advantage of the educational opportunities at Okoitz and could read and write adequately as well as keep accurate books. And when I hinted about getting together for the night, she very politely turned me down. That impressed me considerably! So once I had seen all of the other candidates, I promoted her. But not at six percent of the gross.

Needless to say, the workers were happy about drawing their money in cash and not having to bother with the clumsy subterfuge of barter. The merchants were also happy, and we never had any serious problems with workers abusing their right to buy at below-wholesale prices. At least none that we found out about.

Months later Duke Henryk decided that Muskarini was defrauding Lambert even though it was likely that Lambert had agreed to the six percent bonus. Muskarini had been paid at a hundred pence a year, an absurdly low figure for a skilled worker being employed in a managerial position. Henryk decided that four thousand pence a year would have been a more honest wage and awarded Muskarini 35,000 pence in back wages. The balance of the money was rightfully Lambert's and therefore mine as Lambert's heir.

Then he banished Muskarini, saying that he wasn't the sort that was wanted in Poland. A knight was assigned to escort him over the German border, Hungary still being at war.

I'm glad that I didn't have to make that decision.

The summer passed pleasantly. Cilicia and Francine both had healthy boys, although Francine still would not come home. She spent her time visiting Cracow, Sandomierz, and Plock, playing the grand duchess and not bothering the Banki brothers too much. She was drawing money for her expenses from the Pink Dragon Inns, but not in absurd amounts. I let her be.

Baron Vladimir was getting the active reserves going and complaining that he had even less time at home than before. His biggest headache was that virtually all our men at or above the level of knight were working in the factories or in the regular battalions, and almost all the men in the active reserves were those who had come to us last fall and who had had only four months of training. He had almost no senior officers. He had a huge army of nothing but warrior basics and was forced to hand out temporary promotions to inexperienced and often illiterate men.

Baron Vladimir demanded and got back his old Big Person, Betty, so that he could cover the country properly. I suggested that he delegate most of the work to regional "barons," but he had to do things in his own fashion.

Over a thousand of my factory workers swore fealty to Vladimir, deciding to be peasants again, which was far more than I had expected. But I had given my word and gave Vladimir land enough for all of them. Anyway, very few of them were highly skilled workers. It takes all kinds. My father told me that.

As new Vistula riverboats were put into commission, officered largely by men from the Odra boats, they had plenty of business. Not cargo so much, since trade was still recovering, but passenger travel. Everybody wanted to visit the battle sites, and Baron Novacek, my sales manager, hired tour guides to tell people the stories for a price. He made an absolute killing, selling to the tourists "absolutely genuine Mongol war relics," the junk arms and armor that I thought would be melted down for scrap.

Duke Henryk made the tour five more times, impressing foreign dignitaries. I was glad that I didn't have to do more than smile and have a meal with them when he brought them around. Usually Henryk let me get away with serving them in my apartment, with my household, or even letting them serve themselves informally in the cafeteria, since he knew how I hated formal banquets. On rare occasions he felt that formality was necessary, and then we did it his way. Fair is fair. Anyway, the girls liked banquets when they didn't happen too often.

The Pruthenian children Vladimir and I had rescued from the Crossmen were all adults now, and they all spoke Polish well, but some of them still remembered their native tongue. Henryk borrowed a dozen of those who were bilingual for a diplomatic mission to the Pruthenian tribes. He also asked for and got my Mongol prisoner, why I don't know or care. I was glad enough to be rid of the smelly bastard.

Baron Piotr came up with a decent trophy-distribution program for our own troops. The stuff was sorted according to quality and put into separate warehouses according to army rank. There was a big warehouse filled with lower-quality stuff for the warriors, a smaller one with nicer things for the knights, a much smaller one for the captains, and so on. Then each man was issued a chit that let him go to Three Walls any time in the next year and take his pick. New rooms were opened up over the months so that those who came late didn't get things that were too picked over. The system assured that the higher-ranking men who had been working in the army for many years got the better gimcracks and that there were some things left for the lowest-ranking men.

Coming up with 150,000 sets of eighteen-carat military decorations was no small feat, and production lines were set up to stamp and cast it all during the summer. Many workers were shocked at the thought of working in gold instead of their usual iron or copper, and all sorts of proposals were tossed around to make sure that none of it was stolen. Aside from carefully sweeping up after each shift and making everybody dust off thoroughly before leaving the area, none of these plans were put into effect. And you know? As close as we could weigh it, not one pound of gold was stolen!

Besides an average of five and a quarter pounds of gold military jewelry, the lowest man in the army got 6,200 pence in cash. Barons got thirty-two times that amount, but then, people in the Middle Ages were well convinced that rank had its privileges. All of this was paid in our zinc coinage, of course. I kept the actual gold and silver.

Even these large amounts were arrived at only after a certain amount of mathematical chicanery. Piotr and the accountants decided that I deserved to be reimbursed for my expenses incurred because of the war. They arrived at the figure they did by taking the gross income of all my lands and factories for the last nine years, plus the value of the lands I had been granted or had inherited, and subtracting from that the value of my current nonmilitary properties. The difference between these two must be what I had spent on the war, they claimed. It came to two-thirds of the gold and silver we took!

Then they awarded shares of the booty to the conventional horsemen who had served under Duke Boleslaw at Sandomierz, in accordance with their rank. Since over half of them were knights and one in seven of these were barons, the shares were large. Since many of them had died without heirs, much of this money escheated back to me as their duke.

A generous fund was set up to take care of the dependents of the army personnel who had died in the fighting or in training. And of course these dependents also inherited their share of the booty besides.

The value of the money and jewels taken from the Christian dead at East Gate was spent on aid to refugees and war orphans, and when this proved to not be quite enough, the balance was paid by the booty fund.

All of this dubious accounting was published in the first monthly issue of *The Christian Army Magazine*, along with an invitation to object to any feature of it that was felt to be unfair. Only four letters of complaint were received, and those complaints all concerned the war trophies, not the money. I felt a little guilty about it. I mean, it looked to me like I was being paid for the Pink Dragon Inns that had been burned down, but everybody seemed to think it was fair. Maybe by medieval standards it was.

Anyway, by the time all this settled out, I had these two huge stacks of metal bricks, one of gold and one of silver. Worrying about the difficulty of guarding it and the wasted man-hours that would involve, I had each stack cast into a single massive cube, except for 150 tons of the silver, which was earmarked for silverware.

Up until now we had been using brass forks and spoons, and brass sometimes has a funny taste. I let it be known that I would be happy to hear about any good use for our precious metals, and quite a bit of it was used for things such as church vessels and medical equipment.

But most of it went to these huge solid cubes, which were put on public display at Three Walls. I felt safe, since they were too big to move without heavy machinery, and passersby would act as guards against that. People got quite a kick out of just walking up and touching them. From then on, no one ever doubted the army's credit!

And the jewels? Well, no one knew how to value them, let alone divide them fairly, so they just gave them all to me. I separated out the diamonds, which were useful industrially, and put the rest into a big, sturdy chest. Then, one day, I snuck out to the woods and buried them, very deep, with Silver as my only witness. She promised to show them to my successor after I was gone. Damned if I was going to waste good men guarding the stupid baubles!

In late summer, word came from Hungary. We had won the war! The Christian and Mongol forces had been fairly evenly matched, and they had slugged it out all summer long. Veterans returning from the south all seemed to make the trip around the battlefields in Poland, which was now running as a regular guided tour, and they were generally astounded at the number of Mongols we had encountered. Apparently, the main enemy force had been sent to Poland, and only a small one to Hungary. Bulgaria hadn't been invaded at all despite the fact that the Mongols had promised to do so. In my timeline the Bulgarians had paid tribute to the Mongols for a century.

Most of Lambert's knights came back from Hungary alive and well, including Sir Miesko and both of Sir Vladimir's brothers. They had plenty of stories to tell and occasionally even a bit of booty to back it up. Yet be that as it may, knights returning from Hungary bought an *awful* lot of Baron Novacek's absolutely genuine Mongol war relics!

Chapter Twenty-eight

CONSTRUCTION WAS the big game on campus, as usual. Double-tracked rail lines were laid north to Plock and beyond, and west to a few miles from the Holy Roman Empire. A road east from Sandomierz was sent as far as the Bug River, and another went from the Vistula to the salt mines. I seemed to own those mines now, since none of the former owners could be found, and in such cases, as in modern times, the property goes to the state. Only now I was the state. The old works manager at the mines was gone, too. A pity. He had been rude to me once, and I was looking forward to firing the man.

The Reinforced Concrete Components Factory was completed, and soon it was providing structural sections for our ambitious building plans. To a certain extent the factory built itself, since at first it was nothing but a vast field with foundations, plumbing, and concrete molds built into the ground. As these molds were completed and prestressed concrete members were cast into them, the first use of these pieces was to put up the walls, pillars, and ceilings of the building itself!

Housing for the workers went up at the same time, and within a few weeks the first additional factory was erected, a major cement plant. A continuous casting operation for steel reinforcing rods went in next, and after that it all became routine. Plumbers followed the masons, and window glaziers came next with carpenters on their heels, putting in the doors.

The new R&D machine shop at Okoitz was built of brick to match the existing castle and the inn there, although the roof was of prestressed concrete. When I had sketched the shop, I had also sketched out the additional cloth factories to be built eventually, mostly to make sure that everything would fit well and look nice. Because of some snafu, these sketches were detailed and given by mistake to the construction captain sent to build the machine shop. So while he was there, he also put up both new cloth factories. Not that we had any machinery to put in them. It hadn't even been invented yet, let alone built!

I am personally convinced that much of this happened because the construction workers *liked* being stationed at Okoitz, living in the noble guest quarters and being available to all the cloth factory's eager young ladies, and thus they did what they could to prolong their stay. Oh, I couldn't prove it, but nonetheless I gave that company all the dirty jobs for the next two years.

I suppose I shouldn't have let three months go by between visits, but a man can't be everywhere.

We wouldn't be able to start building forts along the Vistula until the next year, but the three battalions in the eastern duchies were busy preparing for it, clearing the sites and putting in foundations, wells, and septic systems. Winters were spent logging, mostly to clear the land for farming. As the saying went, a Mongol can't hide in a potato field.

The first electrical generator worked, and the third one worked very well indeed. At first we couldn't find any graphite for the brushes, but the name told us the way the oldsters had done it. Brass brushes, and I mean something that looked like what you could clean a floor with, worked just fine. We got it working one week before a merchant came up from Hungary, riding right through a war zone without even noticing, with twenty-two mule loads of graphite.

The electric light bulb team was having less luck, and the tubing team was running into problems because the copper they had to work with was too brittle. I knew that this meant that our copper was too impure, for pure copper is very ductile.

This set of circumstances naturally got us involved with electrolytic refining, where pure copper is plated out of crudely smelted bars in a copper sulfate bath. This pure copper worked well in the new tube-drawing machines, although die wear was a big problem and a lot of work was still needed to improve our lubricants.

On the bottom of the refining tanks an annoying black sludge kept building up, and I wouldn't let them throw it away because of my pollution-control rules. The team took some of the sludge over to the alchemists to see if they could find any use for it. They could. The sludge was nineteen parts per gross silver and seven parts gold. The rest of it seemed to be some metal that the alchemists had never seen before, but they promised to work on it. We didn't have a copper mine at all. We had a gold mine that also produced silver and copper!

Very quickly, we were selling electrolytically refined copper exclusively and quietly buying back our old stuff whenever possible. The silver and gold in it were worth more than the copper! Admittedly, I had a surplus of silver and gold just then, but I wanted it nonetheless.

Mass producing electrical generators made them inexpensive enough to use them for other things, besides. Putting graphite electrodes on either side of a bath of salt water generates sodium hydroxide, which is useful in making good-quality soap and is a basic chemical starting point for thousands of other things. The process also generates hydrogen and chlorine, which can be combined immediately to produce hydrochloric acid, or the hydrogen can be burned as fuel and the chlorine can be used for bleach, in papermaking, for killing bacteria in water, or for killing things in general. The same chlorine that is found in all modern city water supplies makes a very effective war gas.

It occurred to me that I could get rid of the Teutonic Order without having to get any of my own men killed at all. It struck me that there was a certain justice about killing Germans with a gas chamber.

I worked on it and other things for the war.

Our school system now covered all the lands that Henryk and I held and went quite a way beyond them, to include virtually all the Polish-speaking people in the world. In addition, there were a few schools in Germany, Hungary, and the Russias, mostly training bilingual teachers for our next phase of expansion. The plan was to educate the children of the surrounding countries to be bilingual in Polish rather than to produce schoolbooks in every single different language, a daunting task since there were five thousand different languages in the world and we had grandiose dreams. Most foreign languages weren't all that standardized, anyway.

Teacher education was still a far cry from the standards of the twentieth century, but it had come a long way in the last ten years.

The school system was completely self-supporting, since each school also had a post office and a general store that sold everything that my factories made. The schools outside the range of the railroads and riverboats lost money because of the high cost of transportation, but those within it more than made up for this deficit. In fact, it sometimes proved difficult to keep the schools from showing a profit.

The army system of weights and measures was well on its way to becoming universal, at least within Poland. We never forced anyone to adopt it, but anything bought by the army was bought in our units. If a farmer wanted to sell us food, he had to sell it in terms of our pints and pounds and tons.

Our transportation system handled things in terms of carts that were two of our yards wide, six yards long, and a yard and a half high, the same size as our war carts. They had a weight limitation of twelve of our tons. We had a standard-sized case that was a yard wide, a half yard deep, and a half yard high. Six dozen of them fit neatly into a cart and incidentally made a comfortable seat for two. Upended, they were the right height for a workbench, and our cases sometimes did double duty as furniture. If you wanted to ship something that did not fit conveniently into a cart or a case or a standard barrel, shipping charges were much higher, and most of our users soon adopted our standards.

Our glass containers were rapidly being accepted, and we made them only in certain fixed sizes. Jars were made in sixth-pint, half-pint, pint, two-pint, six-pint, and twelve-pint sizes, and that was all, except that the larger sizes also came in a small-necked version. Each had dimensions such that it fit conveniently into our cases, and if you wanted to buy from us or ship something in glass containers, you had to use our system of weights and measures. This also made it easy for consumers to compare prices.

Our construction materials—bricks, boards, concrete blocks, glass, and so on—all came only in standard sizes. If you wanted to build a comfortable and inexpensive house, you had to use our system.

There was surprisingly little resistance to this gentle coercion, and one city council after another voted to adopt the army system of weights and measures.

We had a better than average harvest in 1241, and the granary in the Bledowska desert, which had been almost emptied in the spring and summer to provide seed and food, was now half-refilled. At this point virtually all the grains grown in Poland were of the modern sort, descended from the few grains I had brought here in seed packages ten years before.

Potatoes were now a major item in the diet, as were corn, tomatoes, squashes, peppers, and many of the other vegetables that had come originally from the New World. All the old vegetables were still on the menu, of course, and many people were starting to believe me when I said that a healthy diet was a varied diet. The children were growing up bigger and stronger than their parents, and the infant mortality rates were approaching modern levels, outside of the old cities at least. Someday we'd get decent water and sewer systems in them. Someday.

On the downside, tooth decay was on the rise, especially among the children of the wealthy, and I began to regret that I had been instrumental in increasing the amount of honey and refined sugar available. Now I had to sell people on the advantages of brushing regularly and restricting the use of my own products. Dentistry. I would have to do something about dentistry.

Decent eyeglasses were being made and sold. I got into it when one of Krystyana's kids turned out to be nearsighted and I started to need reading glasses.

The never-ending work of animal breeding was still going on, and to encourage it Count Lambert had started a system of county fairs, with prizes for the best laying hen, the best milk cow, and so forth. The prizewinning animals were auctioned off, often at fabulous prices. I expanded Lambert's system of both fairs and prize herds and usually bought the best available at each county fair, often at huge prices. My buyers had fairly strict guidelines.

A sore spot was that a wealthy merchant from Gniezno, who always boasted about the quality of his table, was observed to regularly purchase prize animals to slaughter and eat just so he could brag about how good his meat was. This bastard was even slaughtering prize milk cows for their meat! I wrote him, politely explaining the purpose of the prize herds and the improvements that had been wrought because of them, but he went right on doing what he had been doing. When I had him banned from the auctions, he had his subordinates do the buying for him. So I contacted my accountants and suggested that this was a man deserving of a beating. Even then they had to work him over twice before he stopped his annoying practice.

Another example of the creative use of accounting, I suppose.

My sheep herds were expanding yearly, and for the last seven years all the males in the main herds had been culled from the prize herd. Improvements in both the quality and the quantity of the wool were manifest, but since my best sheep could produce *three times* the wool of the average sheep, there was obviously a long way to go.

The same was true of the dairy herds, except that there the best was five times better than the average. Do you begin to see why I was so annoyed at having prize animals butchered?

Our best chickens were laying five eggs a week, and some breeders were starting to ignore ducks and geese. They simply couldn't compete with the chickens in either egg or meat production. I tried to reverse this trend, but I had also shown them how to compute profits on livestock, and they knew.

Pigs were getting shorter-legged, bigger-bodied, and faster-growing. They were still hairy, though. Not only did they have to live through the winter in unheated barns, there was a big market for pig bristle, a market that is satisfied by plastics in the modern world.

My wild aurochs herd was now up to three hundred animals that had outgrown all three of the valleys that I had them in. We were feeding them a lot of grain to keep them going and culling half the bulls each year, selecting for size and meat production if not for placid temperament. Something would have to be done before too long. I needed someplace to fence in a *big* area for them. I checked with the Banki brothers, and Wiktor pointed out an area north of where Sieciechow had been that might be suitable. At least there were very few trees there and almost no people at all left. I sent a surveying team out to look at the possibility of walling it in. We had found out the hard way long ago that ordinary fences didn't impress not very domesticated aurochs much. They walked right through them! It took a thick masonry wall, built wavy in the Thomas Jefferson fashion, four yards tall to do the job. *Huge animals!*

In October another milestone was reached. From that point on our profits from our commercial services—that is to say, transporting passengers and goods as a common carrier, the mails, and Baron Novacek's mercantile enterprises—were higher than our profits from selling the output from our entire factory system. Much of the reason for this was that we didn't pay tolls, while the other merchants did when they weren't using our railroads, plus our communication system let our buyers know quickly about prices here and there.

The conventional merchant would buy goods, pay heavily to take them somewhere, and hope to be able to sell them for more than they had cost him. Since this was an inefficient way of doing things, they generally tried to make profits of from one hundred percent to five hundred percent to make up for their occasional losses.

We usually had the goods sold before we bought them, and our transportation costs were very low. Everywhere our railroads and riverboats went, people got more for what they had to sell and paid less for what they wanted to buy, and we made a whopping profit doing it. Of course, the merchants howled about it, but their shouts of anguish impressed neither Duke Henryk nor me. And we were the law. A lot of merchants gave up and came to work for us.

We moved my household and the R&D teams to Okoitz in the fall, and the researchers were soon finding uses for the large empty buildings that were scheduled to one day be cloth factories. To quote Parkinson's law, "Work naturally expands to fill the time available to do it in," I would like to add one of my own: "Building space is consumed in direct proportion to its availability, regardless of what, if anything, has to be done there."

There would be hell to pay when I threw the researchers out to make way for production machinery. I could see them kicking and screaming for days, trying to protect their precious little territories.

Nine R&D teams were set up to work on the various steps of producing cloth, and some progress was made fairly quickly. Some of the most complicated-sounding things worked right off, and some of the most trivial seemed to take forever. What worked on linen almost never worked on wool, and vice versa. You never can tell about research.

As time went on, an increasing number of researchers were foreigners, since a lot of bright kids throughout Europe were reading our magazines and wanted to get in on the action. We let them in—once they survived the Warrior's School.

Baron Piotr went to Okoitz with us both as a member of my household and as a floating member of all the R&D teams. Whenever the teams ran into math problems they couldn't handle, they took them to Piotr. He was good as a general idea man, too. He stayed head of the mapmaking group, but now he rarely went out into the field. This got the mapmakers moved to Okoitz as well, with their lithographic machines set up in the new cloth factories.

The ladies at the cloth factory gave the R&D people a warm and friendly welcome and soon got to referring to them as "the Wizards." The guys liked the title, and the name stuck.

Chapter Twenty-nine

FROM THE JOURNAL OF DUCHESS FRANCINE

Childbirth was not as bad as I had been led to fear it would be, but it was certainly painful enough. The midwife had convinced me that at thirty I was too old to be having a first child, and indeed she had me quite worried, but my son and I came through our ordeal alive and in good health.

I secured a wet nurse for him immediately so that my nipples would not become unlovely. Within a month, by fasting and exercise, I fit well into my old dresses, but more months passed before I felt myself shapely enough to keep my bargain with Friar Roman. In all, he did four nude paintings and gave two of them to me. I put them away, to look at in my old age, I suppose. Soon I could ride Anna without pain or danger, and a fast run through the country-side, often in the company of the delightful Sir Wladyclaw, became my greatest pleasure.

Conrad did not ask to come to the christening, and so I did not invite him. Baron Wojciech stood in his stead, and Duke Henryk became my son's godfather. I arranged it thus so that Henryk might be more inclined to see that my son one day got his patrimony. We named him Conrad to re-mind my husband of his duty to our child.

Yet in truth I did not not want to see my husband. My

anger at the way he treated our child was such that years must go by before the hurt was eased. Instead, I put my mind to the problem of assuring my son's future. After much thought, it occurred to me that if I could do some service to Duke Henryk, some service greater in value than the three eastern duchies, he might be prevailed upon to see to it that my son was properly enlarged, as was his birthright.

Conrad and Henryk were preparing for an utterly stupid war with the Knights of the Cross, a war that would surely get them into a further war with the entire Holy Roman Empire if Emperor Frederick II ever stopped fighting with the Church long enough to get back to Germany.

War with the Crossmen will put them in the bad graces of the Church as well, for the Teutonic Order is legally a branch of the Roman Catholic Church. Already I am sure that the real reason why the Vatican was delaying granting Henryk the crown of Poland was this planned war against the Church!

Well, the death of Pope Gregory IX and the fact that Celestine IV died after only two weeks in office haven't helped much, either. Rumors from Rome have it that the factions in the College of Cardinals are so bad that they may be years electing another Pope, and until they do, poor Henryk will have nothing to cover his head but a hat! Not that he's earned anything better.

The color change was on the trees before a suitable opportunity presented itself to ingratiate myself with Henryk. Sir Wladyclaw scouted the eastern frontiers with his men, and often they went well beyond the borders in search of our enemies. One day, he told me that Prince Daniel of both Ruthenias, our neighbors to the east, was vassal to the Mongols and not at all pleased by the situation.

It was an audacious thought, but I wondered if I could persuade this Prince Daniel to throw off the Mongol yoke and swear fealty to Duke Henryk. Surely the Mongols had learned to fear my husband, and word of his protection might be enough to keep Prince Daniel safe. If I could manage it, surely Henryk would be deeply in my debt. Perhaps enough for him to feel obligated to do right by my son. At least it was worth a try.

Sir Wladyclaw agreed to help me in this endeavor, for it was his task to protect our frontiers, and what better way to do that than to put a friend across the border in place of an enemy.

I left my baby with his wet nurse and one of my maids at Wawel Castle and rode out in the early dawn. I was accompanied by Sir Wladyclaw and a dozen of his men, three of whom spoke Ruthenian, and we rode secretly to the city of Halicz and the court of Prince Daniel.

It was a journey of two days, even for our Big People, for we dared not ride along the railroad tracks for fear that word of our mission would get back to Conrad. We had to travel by slow and winding forest trails where our mounts could not make their best speed. And once we got into Ruthenia, the trails were even worse than those in Poland.

Indeed, just before we stopped at Przemysl for the night, the trail was covered with a black grease that was at once sticky and slippery. The point man and his mount slipped in it and went down in a dreadful heap, though fortunately they were unhurt save for the grease and dirt. We all wondered at what this strange liquid was and who had dumped it there. It certainly made a mess by splashing on my dress and Anna's barding, and the knights accompanying me were spotted with it as well.

But of course, with their camouflaged armor and barding, a few spots made little difference.

I was delighted to find that there was a Pink Dragon Inn in Przemysl, and the innkeeper there, once he was made acquainted with who I was, was most helpful. He was easily sworn to secrecy, he made us most comfortable, and he was even able to show my maid the way of removing the spots, using lighter fluid. He said that everyone using that trail was afflicted with the greasy mud, for it had always been there.

We reached the court of Prince Daniel the next evening and were given by him a warm welcome. Sir Wladyclaw and I were placed next to the prince at the high table, and I was delighted to find that he spoke excellent Polish, as did many of his subjects.

Prince Daniel was a robust and fascinating man of about my husband's age, full of vigor yet with a sharp wit and a good sense of humor. He told us of many of his hunting experiences and of some of his adventures fighting the Mongols. Sir Wladyclaw was able to equal or even top a number of his tales, and I told of the Mongol attack on Three Walls, of how I manned a swivel gun, and of how Conrad's army slaughtered the Tartar horde at our feet.

"I've heard of these guns of yours, but of course I've never seen one," Prince Daniel said. I knew that he had been forced to send men with the Mongols against Poland but that he had not gone himself. Yet it was not politic for either of us to mention this unfortunate fact.

"Then you must come to Poland, my lord. My husband's factories make them by the thousand," I said.

"Now, that might be difficult, your grace, for you see, I am vassal to the khan and thus unfortunately an enemy to your people, at least in theory."

"How sad. I would much rather have you for a friend," I said, and smiled.

He smiled back and said, "You understand, of course, that things are not always what one would wish." He looked about, afraid that he might have said too much in public. "But we must talk more of this later. For tonight, we must be soon abed, for we wake early tomorrow for a stag hunt. I am very proud of my kennels here. My huntsmen and I

would be delighted if you and your fine gentlemen would
join us.''

"We would be honored, my lord."

That night I cautioned Sir Wladyclaw and his men to not
take first honors in the hunt by getting to the kill first, as
they could easily do riding on Big People. Some huntsmen
are easily offended in this way.

Hunting with dogs is rarely done on my husband's lands,
for neither he nor Count Lambert before him liked the sport.
A pity, for it is exciting to chase the dogs across the fields,
to race to the kill, and then to share the roast venison in the
evening. Conrad is such a bore about some things.

One does not hunt deer in armor, as one does with wild
boar or bison. Fortunately, Sir Wladyclaw and his men had
their dress uniforms with them, and they made a bold show
in their new red and white garb, so covered with gold. They
were proud to tell how all their decorations had been made
from booty taken from their enemies, and many Ruthenians
looked on them with envy, for these people had to pay gold
to the Mongols, whereas we had gotten it from them!

The hunt was beautiful, and the dogs tore the throats from
two stags by dinnertime. After a light lunch brought out by
the stewards, I found myself separated from the others and
in the company of the prince. This was not at all by accident, for we had both been trying to arrange it so all morning.

"You ride so beautifully, your grace. Never before has a
woman kept so close to me in the hunt. Why, I almost think
that you could have beaten me to that last kill if you had
really tried."

"I could only follow your example, my lord. But surely
you have more interesting things to talk of than my poor
horsemanship."

"Indeed I do, my lady. You spoke truth last night when

you said that I should see your country. I would dearly like to do so, but I fear both spies in my court and the fact that I could be arrested in your land as a spy myself. Yet I have heard many wondrous things about what your great husband accomplished this spring on the battlefield and the wondrous machines that he has on the rivers and even in the air. It is true, isn't it? He can really fly?"

"He has men who can pilot machines that can fly, my lord, though he does not do it himself. He says that he's too old, though his last liege lord, Count Lambert, was older than Conrad and flew a great deal."

"I would like to see these things for myself. Can you think of a way that it could be arranged?"

"You must be of a size with one of the knights that accompanied me here, my lord. If you and my party and, say, four of your men were to ride out to one of your other estates, no one would think it strange. We could even let them think that we would be lovers if you thought that wise."

"That would be a delightful thing, my lady, did I not fear the fact that your husband is called the fiercest fighting man in all the world. And in truth, my wife is no simpering lily, either! I think it would be best if we kept our pleasant relationship platonic."

"I quite agree, my lord, with much the same regrets as yours," I said with a sad smile. "Well, then, once our party is out of sight and in some secluded place, you and your men could trade horses and costumes with five of mine. In the armor of a Radiant Warrior, no one would recognize you. Indeed, you could keep your visor down if you wished. In addition, these mounts we ride are very special. They can go like the wind, and no one in Poland would question a man who rode one. We could go there and be back in a week, my lord."

"You seem to have this well planned out, your grace."

"Indeed, I have thought long on it."

But then we had to join the others, for the master hunts-man rode up carrying the droppings of a large stag in his hunting horn for the prince to examine.

And so it was that Prince Daniel got the grand tour of the battlefields, saw our aircraft, and rode on a steamboat. He was astounded almost as much by the Big People. I was able to show him some of my husband's factories, with their huge moving machines and white-hot spraying steel. We toured East Gate, and he found that starting the next spring, Conrad would be building a fortress like it every week. Yet what impressed him most was the three million Mongol heads he saw up on pikes.

"These are not all the Tartars we killed, you know," I said. "About half a million more were drowned in the Vis-tula when they tried to swim across, and they were so weighted down that most of them never did float up. There's still a fortune in booty lying for the taking on the bottom of the river."

"My God!"

So over a week passed before we were again in Ruthenia. Prince Daniel wanted to talk to his nobles and councilors, but I knew that he would throw off the Mongols and swear fealty to Duke Henryk could he but work out a suitable treaty with us.

He invited me back in a month, and of course I would be there. While back in Cracow, I sounded out Henryk, and he approved in principle of what I had done.

More importantly, I got his solemn written word, in his own hand and sealed, that if I was able to arrange a suitable treaty, my son would be given his rightful inheritance, or one even more valuable. Also, Henryk agreed that it would be best if Conrad did not know about my role in these affairs or about our agreement as well.

Again we went to Ruthenia, and again we brought back

Prince Daniel incognito, but this time to meet with Duke Henryk. I introduced the two leaders, and they soon were engaged in animated conversation. I wisely remained silent, for men do not like women to intrude on what they consider "man's talk," even when it is we women who make all the arrangements, set the stage, and even determine what is to be said.

A formal treaty was eventually signed by all interested parties, including my husband, and my son had regained his birthright!

In the winter, when all had been finalized and troops had been sent to Ruthenia to aid in its defense, I met again with Duke Henryk, who gave me a privy letter that confirmed our original agreement.

"Francine, that was a fine job you did with Prince Daniel. Because of you, an enemy has been turned into a friend, Poland now has a buffer state between herself and the Tartars, and I have gained a doubling of my territory, if not my income. It is going to take us a few years to absorb all of this, but in a year or two I am minded to send you north to talk to Prince Swientopelk so that you can talk him into giving us his duchies of East and West Pomerania!"

Chapter Thirty

FROM THE DIARY OF CONRAD STARGARD

My own personal life remained pleasantly tranquil, even though, or perhaps because of the fact that, Francine stayed away. I hadn't even seen my son by her, but I was not about to force her into coming home just so she could make me miserable. She stayed in the east, and I spent most of my time in the south. When I went to Cracow to see my confessor, Bishop Ignacy, she was always elsewhere. Twice I went to Sandomierz and Plock to check on things, but she wasn't there at the time. Even when Duke Henryk and I hit twelve cities, one on each day of the twelve days of Christmas, she managed to be somewhere else. All that I could figure was that she had an efficient spy system.

Cilicia, on the other hand, remained all sweetness and light. She continued teaching dancing, mostly as a hobby, I think, and continued to manage her string of dance studios at a considerable profit, though God knows we didn't need the money. But her real interest was now in our four children and in the other three dozen or so kids in the household.

These weren't all mine, not by any means. At least a dozen of them were orphans left over from the Mongol invasion. There were some where we knew the mother and nobody was exactly sure about the father, but nobody much cared. When in doubt, I was always happy to confess to just about anything at a baptism. I'd never let a kid be hurt over a little thing like pride, even when the mother wasn't up to my usual standards.

Piotr and Krystyana were still in the household with their six kids, and others came and went as the need and the inclination required. When it came to my household, I ran a very loose ship, and I liked it that way. About my only rules were that kids had to stay out of my office and nobody could permanently enter my household without my invitation. Well, there were some kids who sort of temporarily attached themselves to us for years, but what the heck. As a general thing, a pleasantly disorganized chaos reigned, and any time I needed rejuvenation I had only to sit down on one of the couches in the living room, and there were a couple of kids on my lap and generally a pretty girl under each arm. A good life.

During our Christmas tour Henryk mentioned an offer that he'd gotten that he didn't want to refuse. The Russian principalities to our east were Volhynia and Halicz Ruthenia, and they had a combined area that was at least as large as that of Poland, if not larger, although because of the Mongols, they no longer had anything like our population. They were Russian to the extent that the people there were mostly Greek Orthodox Christians, and their political and social ties were more with the east than with the west.

"Russia" in the modern sense, with its huge uncaring bureaucracy and its brutal central control, would probably have been better called the Muscovite Empire. Politically, it is a Johnny-come-lately, not one of the ancient nations of eastern Europe. It simply didn't exist in the thirteenth century. Moscow was now a small backwater village.

To the north, there is a major city-state called the Republic of Novgorod, which is run by an oligarchy of wealthy merchants, about the way that Venice is in Italy.

In the south, there is a Russian people who would one day be called Ukrainians and who consider their capital to be Kiev, even though Kiev had been massacred by the Mongols a few years ago and still was almost absolutely empty. Before that time it had been a fairly ordinary kingdom, with nothing particularly offensive about it.

In addition to these two large states, there were a dozen or so minor duchies and principalities scattered around the east, all of whom, like their big brothers, were either paying tribute to the Mongols or had been depopulated by them, or sometimes both. Certainly there was nothing about the Russias of the thirteenth century that you could hate.

The prince of both of these principalities of Volhynia and Halicz Ruthenia was a man named Daniel, and he had come to Duke Henryk with an interesting proposal. Prince Daniel offered to swear fealty to Henryk, to become a Roman Catholic, and to encourage his people to do so as well. He would even pay what taxes he could, but in return he needed protection from the Mongols. Henryk wanted to know if we could guarantee that protection.

Well, I had been planning to fight the Mongols again anyway, and having more allies hardly ever hurt anybody. From a strictly practical standpoint, we didn't need any more land at all. We were currently seriously overextended, trying to digest what we already had. This was one giant bite more. Yet I agreed with Henryk. It was too good an opportunity to miss, although I couldn't help wishing that it had come along five or ten years later.

I said fine, I could spare Daniel three of our nine-thousand-man battalions of regulars when they graduated in the late spring, as well as my force of scouts mounted on Big People, all as a permanent force there. I could give him some air cover, and I could get an additional fifteen battalions to him in ten days if there was another invasion, but I needed some things in return from Daniel.

I needed land along the Bug and the San rivers for the construction of forts against the Mongols. A five-mile-wide strip on both sides of each river was to become army property.

I wanted some land granted to me near the town of Przemysl, because I happened to know that there was an oil field there. In my time, the first oil wells in the world had been drilled in these fields, and that told me that it couldn't have been a difficult drilling job. I needed that oil as a lubricant, for kerosene lamps, and for aircraft fuel. The wood alcohol we were using wasn't all that energetic on a per-pound basis.

In addition, I wanted the same rights to buy land in the east that I had in western Poland, and I wanted the same rights to transport goods without paying tolls. I wanted the Polish legal system, once it was organized, to be put in effect in Ruthenia the same as it was in the rest of Poland. Ruthenia was to become a permanent part of Poland, individual Ruthenians would have the right to join the Christian army, and under no circumstances was I to be taxed by anyone.

Henryk was agreeable to my demands, said he'd keep me posted, and sent an ambassador to Daniel to finalize the deal.

We kept busy working all through the winter, for although the men in the army were all wealthy now, we never slacked off on the twelve-hour workday or the six-day workweek, one of which, on the average, was always spent in military training. I had no trouble enforcing this, since good men like to work when they know that they are working on something important.

The deal with Prince Daniel didn't work out exactly as

planned. He wouldn't go along with combining the legal systems, saying that his people had different customs than ours did. Instead of getting land and drilling rights near Przemysl, I got the whole city and much of the surrounding area. It seems that this land had once been part of Poland and the people there were still ethnically Polish rather than Russian, so Daniel gave the land back to us, or rather to me as Duke of Little Poland.

The right of the Christian army to travel duty-free across the principalities, even when we were engaged in commercial pursuits, became the Right of Transit. The right of the army to do recruiting was enlarged to the traditional Polish Right of Departure. Every man, except for convicted criminals, could leave his present job or condition without anybody's permission. And the right of the army to buy land and then not pay taxes on it became the Right of Purchase.

This meant that the political body we were forming would be more of a federation than a union, but I could live with it. I signed the treaty Henryk and Daniel had formalized.

As soon as the treaty was signed, still in the winter, a volunteer battalion of active reservists with regular army officers was called up to stand guard in the new territories until late fall, mostly to demonstrate good faith to Prince Daniel. There were a lot more volunteers than places available, and the officers in charge could pick the best. Mostly, the troops spent their time putting in a rail line along the west bank of the River Bug and another up the San, but they were ready if the Mongols wanted to start trouble. In a few months three battalions of regulars who would be graduating from the Warrior's School would go east to back up the reservists and keep my word to Daniel.

I'd kept the boys at Eagle Nest posted on the need for a longer-range observation plane to patrol the borders of Ruthenia and let Daniel know that we were doing our part. Aircraft engines were now sufficiently dependable that a second one was an asset rather than a liability. They came up with a big (for us) two-engine job that could stay up for five hours and had a range of six gross miles. An interesting plane: The pilot lay prone and looked mainly downward, just what was needed for an observation plane when the enemy had nothing in the sky. This also made for a very small frontal area. It was our first plane that could take off without the aid of a catapult, and it even boasted retractable landing gear. The boys wanted to call it the *Eagle*, but I wouldn't let them do it. I said that the eagle was the person flying it, and the name stuck. From then on, our air force was known as the Eagles.

Duke Henryk sent me a copy of his proposed code of laws with a note stressing that it was only a rough draft and that he was asking for comments from many others besides myself. There was a criminal code with clearly defined penalties for various clearly defined crimes and a civil code with long sections on inheritance, land use and ownership, and contracts. I spent a few days going over it and wrote him a lengthy commentary. This was the sort of thing where getting it done right was far more important than getting it done quickly. Any errors would be very expensive for someone. In many cases it was literally a matter of life and death.

My main objection to Henryk's laws was in the field of punishments. He called for the traditional medieval corporal punishments, such as whipping, branding, and beheading. In the twentieth century, the western governments punish people with use fines and various terms of incarceration. The eastern governments have a different theory, one that I can't help but agree with. It is felt that a criminal is one who has caused damage to society and who is therefore in debt to society for the damage that he has done. This debt must be worked off, normally with a term of hard manual labor. There are several advantages to this theory. One is that the criminal is often a mentally ill person, and hard work is often very good therapy. Another is that society benefits from the work that is done rather than being harmed again in feeding and guarding the criminal, as in the western system. It took work, but I finally talked Henryk into starting a prison coal mine and using work rather than whippings.

By spring it was obvious that the killing inflation I had so feared wasn't going to happen. Most of the surplus cash either stayed in my bank drawing interest or, rather "damages," to get around the Church's strange thoughts on usury or was spent on things like buying farmland from me. Then *I* sat on the money, and things smoothed out.

As soon as the snows melted, work was started on a second Reinforced Concrete Components Factory, this one built next to the new Riverboat Assembly Building and set up to build parts for "snowflake" forts like the one at East Gate. In a little over a month we started on the first of several thousand fortified army towns.

There wasn't any problem finding the oil fields. The stuff was running out of the ground! We didn't do any drilling at all at first but simply channeled it into some storage tanks. Why it hadn't caught fire sometime in the past was beyond me.

At East Gate we started production on a new sort of riverboat. It consisted of nothing but an engine and some crew's quarters on the back of a long, low barge. Inside the thing were two gross copper oil drums, piped together to haul crude oil from the fields at Przemysl. On the way up it was designed to carry deck cargo, such as concrete structural members. And that was all. No guns, no Halmans, and no passengers. Strictly a civilian cargo vessel. An oil refinery was started at East Gate as well.

Finally, with spring planting done, it was time to clean the Teutonic Knights out of Mazovia. In my time, despite the fact that they were theoretically a branch of the Church, they had spent the winter of 1242 attacking the Christian Republic of Novgorod and had been beaten by Alexander Nevski in the famous Battle on the Ice. Well, Alex was spared both the trouble and the fame in this world. Here, the Crossmen had spent the winter recruiting more fighters and reinforcing their city-castle of Turon, which means "thorn," appropriately enough.

They had seen what we could do in a field battle but figured that they could stand siege against us. Nice. I'd been counting on that.

My people were all looking forward to the war, for the Crossmen never had worried about making themselves popular. They still made a practice of butchering entire villages and sparing only the adolescent children who brought good prices on the Moslem slave blocks. When I suggested that a single battalion would suffice to handle the Knights of the Cross, I nearly had a mutiny on my hands. Everybody wanted to go!

I didn't want to upset our production schedules, so I forbade the industrial workers to attend. They screamed, bitched, and cried, but I wouldn't back off. There were plenty of men working their farms, and the war would take place during the slack period between spring planting and the first hay harvest. Even so, there were too many volunteers, and I finally had Baron Vladimir set up a competition such that only the best fighters from each unit in the active reserves were allowed the privilege of going and risking their lives. It's strange the things some men will do for prestige.

Chapter Thirty-one

I TOOK three battalions of reservists to the war, along with three of regulars, and made Baron Vladimir hetman in charge of all of them. This was far more troops than was required, but the pressure on me to let everybody go was pretty strong. Captains and barons were coming up with the damnedest reasons why it was necessary for them to participate even after I said that any booty taken would go first to defray expenses and that the rest would be divided out among the entire army. They didn't care. They still kept calling in old favors and trying to go.

Since it wasn't really going to be much of a fight, I took my four maidservants along, with plenty of creature comforts in a big rail car. Cilicia insisted on coming, too, and brought with her a troop of over fifty dancers and a dozen musicians. She knew of Duke Henryk's plans to invite many foreign observers, and she figured that they would want entertainment.

Over her fifty-megaton protests, Krystyana was left home to take care of the kids. Piotr wasn't going, and, well, somebody had to do it.

We had riverboats enough on the Vistula to carry two battalions with their war carts, but I wasn't about to commit

more than a quarter of them to the war, not when they were
making such profits providing civil transportation! Also, the
boats were needed to transport construction materials for
our extensive building program. Anyway, if the troops
wanted to go that badly, let them walk!

And walk they did, nonstop in the army fashion, all the
way to Plock and beyond to the edge of Crossman territory,
where the railroads stopped. From there they were ferried
downstream to Turon, where we found the city packed with
German knights and the gates closed to us.

At first there was no opposition at all. A platoon of scouts
scoured the countryside and found nothing but peaceful
peasants, whom we left alone. Turon had no suburbs, being
a military installation, so we had a clear field of fire all
around the walls. We surrounded the city, dug fortifica-
tions, and set up housekeeping. Then we waited two days
for Duke Henryk to arrive.

You see, Henryk was planning to make as much political
hay out of this battle as possible, and he wanted as many
foreign observers around as he could get. On the southwest
side of the Vistula, across from Turon, we built a good-
sized tent city for them, set up a river-crossing boat, and
assigned two companies of complaining warriors to guard
the place and cook for our guests. The numbers of delegates
arriving surprised even Henryk. Poland was big in the news,
especially since our magazines were still the only newspa-
pers. Many people wanted to see what we were doing for
themselves.

Duke Henryk arrived on schedule with his two young
sons, Henryk III, a fine boy of thirteen, and Boleslaw, who
was going bald at the age of eighteen, as well as their
mother on a rare outing from her estate. But his dozens of
delegations of observers straggled in, and another week
went by before they had all gotten there.

Rather than let my warriors stand idle, I had half of our

forces out preparing the beds for railroads while we waited, and construction companies were confidently extending the railroads downstream along the Vistula while the "war" was going on.

The tent city soon became a regular international village, with six separate groups coming from various states in the Holy Roman Empire, two from various factions in Bohemia, three from Hungary, two from Pomerania, and three from the various Danish principalities. Twenty men were sent up from Tsar Ivan Asen II of the Bulgarian Empire. A group arrived from France, personal emissaries from Louis IX, and even some Castilians from Spain.

There were delegations from all the tribes of the Pruthenians: Sambians, Natanoians, Warmians, Pogesanians, Pomeranians, Bartians, Galindians, and Skalovians. The Lithuanians came, headed by Prince Mendog, and the Lusatians were there, too. There was a delegation from Novgorod, headed by none other than Alexander Nevski, who doesn't look at all like he did in the movie. Furthermore, he was a noble prince, not a stalwart yeoman, as the old Russian motion picture would have it!

We even got a Welshman, a Scotsman, and an Irishman.

Prince Daniel was there with two groups from the Ruthenias, and Prince Swientopelk of Pomerania showed up in person. This surprised certain people, because it was claimed by some that he had engineered the assassinations of two Polish dukes. Duke Boleslaw the Pious and Duke Przemysl came, both of Great Poland and subordinate to Henryk, as did Duke Casimir of Kujawy, a small, still independent Polish duchy.

The Church was well represented by Bishop Ignacy of Cracow, plus the Polish bishops of Plock, Poznan, Wroclaw, Lubusz, Wloclawek, and Kamien, and the Archbishop of Gniezno, along with hundreds of minor clerics. Ignacy had even brought a printing press with him and was running off a four-page daily newspaper. The world's first!

In short, everybody who was anybody in eastern Europe, and most of the rest of Christendom besides, was there or was represented, except for the Mongols. No, let me take that back. The handless Mongol ambassador I had given to Henryk was there as well, in a steel cage with a double door like an air lock. Henryk wasn't taking any chances with him.

There were so many delegates that we had to enlarge their camp twice, stripping tents from my troops and making the warriors double up. Four more unhappy companies were added to guard and cook for them.

The foreigners wandered around everywhere, inspecting the steamboats and the artillery, talking to the troops, and even visiting the Teutonic Knights, who were still holed up in their city.

While everyone was there for the nominal purpose of watching a battle, Henryk had countless meetings called every day, and every night was spent in feasting, drinking, and politicking. Cilicia's dancers were the big hit of the event, and two temporary Pink Dragon Inns were running on a standing-room-only basis. Baths and massage parlors were running at all hours of the day and night.

Henryk bought two dozen of my surplus aurochs bulls, and though not fully grown, they dressed out at over a ton of meat each. They took three days to roast whole over an open fire, but he served one up each day, and that was but a single item on a large menu. The beer, wine, and mead vendors were making a fortune! And this despite the fact that many delegations were providing potables free.

My troops were coming over the river to join this festival at every possible excuse, of course. It became a major headache for Hetman Vladimir to see that Turon remained properly surrounded. Yet the Crossmen never poked their heads out of their walls. At least not that we heard of, anyway.

With so many foreigners coming and going from Turon, it was likely that there were Crossman spies among us. Not that it mattered.

While all this was going on, I had the six siege cannons I'd had made hauled up from their special barges and located out of crossbow range of the city-fortress of Turon, pointing at the two main gates, where they could be seen by the delegates. They each had a bore of half a yard and were six yards long. They were low-tech muzzle-loaders, since I wasn't in any hurry about rate of fire and didn't plan to ever need them again after this battle. But they fired a round iron ball that weighed over half a ton, and I didn't imagine that any brick city wall could stand up to them for long.

Then six huge mortars arrived, each with a bore of one yard and a four-yard-long tube. They were set up in plain view of the delegate camp, as close to Turon's walls as we dared put them. A system of racks and hoists allowed them to be loaded quickly, for here I needed a high rate of fire. The men tending these monsters wore a uniform that consisted of black boots, a black pair of pants, and a black hood, which when wet could double as a gas mask. They swaggered around stripped to the waist, a bit of showmanship on my part. Mostly, I wanted the identity of these picked men to be kept a secret.

Their ammunition was placed along the river embankment and constantly guarded. If one of these rounds should leak, it was the duty of the black guards to roll it into the Vistula, for cool water can absorb large quantities of chlorine, and the river's turbulence would soon dilute the poison to a safe level.

And still the warriors waited, for Henryk wanted the conference to continue a while longer. He made a point of introducing me to everyone, of course, and I sat in on many of the meetings, but in truth, such things bore me. The only interesting thing to me was that almost all the visitors spoke

Polish, mostly from reading our magazines. My plan to make Polish a world language was working!

And with everybody important at the camp, it was inevitable for my wife to come, too, since she loves the smell of political power. She'd been there a week before I ran into her as I was on my way to yet another meeting, this one on fixing a date for the proposed All Christendom Great Hunt chaired by Sir Miesko.

"Well," I said, trying to be friendly. "There really is a Duchess Francine. Have you been well?"

"Yes, your grace." She looked at me strangely, coldly.

"And you have to speak so formally to your own husband?"

"It seemed fitting, Conrad."

"So. And my son. He too is well?" I tried to smile, but it didn't come off.

"Yes. He's in good hands in Cracow."

"I suppose that you were right in not taking him into what is, after all, a war zone. I'd like to see him someday."

"Of course, my husband. You can see him at any time."

"And you. Will I be seeing you again? Will you be coming home, as most wives do?"

"Yes, I'm sure I will, in time."

"In time. Well. When that time comes, be sure and let me know. There will always be a place for you."

"Thank you, my husband," she said stiffly.

"You must keep in closer touch, then."

"Yes, my husband."

I turned and left. She was as cold as a killing frost and just as unsympathetic. Whatever had happened to the warm, loving woman I had married? Just because I didn't want to be a king, that didn't mean that I no longer wanted to be a husband! Yet she was still a beautiful woman for all her stone-cold features and stone-rigid bearing. I felt the old urges despite the fact that I had brought my servants to the war.

Days later I went to see Bishop Ignacy, and after confession I asked, as usual, about the Church's inquisition concerning me.

"Oh, I'm afraid that there won't be anything happening on that for some time, Conrad. You see, the College of Cardinals is deadlocked on the selection of the next Pope, and nothing much will happen until such time as they resolve their differences. It could be quite a while from what I hear."

"So the whole Catholic Church stops until they get around to doing something, Father?"

"Not in the least! People are being christened and married and buried. Souls are still being saved. The only difference is that nothing new will happen. No high offices will be filled, and no changes will take place until we have a new pontiff. You know, I've never understood your anxiety to get this matter of your inquisition finished, Conrad. After all, if they decide that you are an instrument of God and a saint, well, you cannot be canonized until after your death, anyway, so why hurry? And in the unlikely event that they decide that you are an instrument of the devil and should be burned at the stake, why, isn't it better to put off that unhappy event as long as possible? Surely there is nothing of the suicide about you!"

"I'd just like to have the thing settled, to not have it hanging over my head, Father."

"Very little in this life is ever settled, my son. It's like that story you once told me about the little people. 'The road goes ever on.' One can only live life. Soon enough God will decide it is time for it to be 'settled.' "

"I suppose so, Father. To change the subject, have you been to see the Crossmen?"

"No, but many other churchmen have. After all, you have vowed to kill them all, and you have a reputation for carrying out your vows with a vengeance."

"Oh, they'll all die, all right, as soon as Henryk has milked all he can out of this conference."

"It is remarkable how well you two dukes are getting along, how well your abilities complement each other."

"He takes care of the law and the politics, and I handle the army and the factories. Neither one of us wants the other's job. It's a good partnership, Father, and I think the world will profit by it. But back to the Crossmen. I'm going to kill them, so don't try again to talk me out of it. You already know my reasons, and I've heard all of your objections. But I don't want any innocent bystanders killed with them. I still have nightmares about the Polish slave girls that we killed when we raided the Mongol camp at night, or even worse, the Polish peasants we slaughtered when they were forced to work those Mongol catapults. I want to know that there is no one in Turon except members of the Teutonic Order."

"But surely they have had plenty of time to get out."

"Well, maybe they can't get out, or maybe they think the Crossmen will win, or maybe they think this will be an ordinary battle where plenty of people survive. You've seen those big guns I've had made. Do you think that one of those half-ton balls will stop and see what uniform they're wearing before it smashes everyone before it?"

"If you wish, I will visit Turon and examine it. Mind you, I won't do any spying for you. We've talked over my opposition to this war often enough. But I will do what I can to prevent injury to the innocent."

"Good, Father, because I want you to convey an offer to the Crossmen for me. I will pay them one thousand pence in army currency, silver or gold, as they desire, for every noncombatant that comes out of the city on the day before the battle. I'll pay an additional one hundred pence to each person as they leave. I'll even pay the Crossmen one hundred pence for every domestic animal, as well, and guarantee that all these people and beasts will be fed and housed well at my own expense until the issue is settled. If you wish, I will pay the Church for their upkeep, and you can see to it that it is properly done."

"That is a generous offer, Conrad."

"I'm just trying to save my soul, Father. Those siege cannons aren't the most deadly weapons that I have. Anyway, I'll be getting most of it back as booty once I win the battle."

"Very well, Conrad, I'll see what I can do, and I'll get the archbishop involved in this as well. However, I notice that you are again calling your weapons of war 'canons.' A canon is a law of the Church, and while your strange use of the term was funny at first, the joke has gone stale. I want you to stop it."

"Yes, Father."

"On another matter, you have not been living with your wife. This is not good. You were joined together by God, after all."

"Father, she is still angry because I did not make her the Queen of Poland. I didn't do that and I won't do that, because I don't want to be the king. Henryk is far better qualified than I am, and anybody sane can see it! I've asked her to come back and told her that there will always be a place for her. What more can I do?"

"You could be a bit more vigorous in your invitation, my son."

"You're saying that I should use force?"

"The Church allows it, within reason."

"The Church allows it, but God doesn't demand it! I'm not going to beat her or shackle her to the kitchen stove. Good men didn't do that sort of thing in my time."

"Well, think on it, my son. Meanwhile, I shall see what can be done with the Teutonic Knights."

The bishop returned to me the next day with word that the Crossmen had accepted my offer and he had worked out with them a system where there wouldn't be much cheating. They also offered me their war-horses on the same terms at a thousand pence a head, with the understanding that they could get them back at any time by repaying the money should the battle prove to be protracted. I went along with that. There was no point killing dumb animals, I'd be getting the money back, and we could probably train most of those chargers to pull railroad cars. From the Crossmen's point of view, the Church would be taking care of their horses at my expense until they were needed, but let them have their dreams.

The time was dragging slowly, and the troops were getting antsy. Finally, I talked to my partner about it.

"Henryk, I don't want to rush you, but it's been more than three weeks now. Do you realize that I am paying the salaries of over fifty thousand men while many of them sit idle every day?"

"Yes, Conrad, and I well know how you hate waste. But this is not time wasted. Prince Swientopelk is starting to come around. The Baltic seacoast could be ours! What would you think of having not one but *two* seaports, one at the mouth of the Vistula and one at the Odra?"

"It would be fine, and I've often dreamed of building oceangoing steamships. We could buy and sell abroad, explore the world, and spread the faith. We could even find coffee and rubber! But we could not start doing it for years yet. We have commitments that will take us years to fulfill. We are too overextended now to even consider further expansion at this time. You know that."

"But the iron is hot now, Conrad, and it might grow cold in five years. We need not promise to do much until then.

Just some little show of support might be enough. Your reputation alone could do it. Have I ever told you that putting those Mongol heads up on pikes was a stroke of genius?''

''Not in so many words, and thank you. But what can I tell my men? When can we start the battle?''

''A week, Conrad. Can you give me another week?''

''A week. Very well, I'll hold them back until then. But a week from this morning I'm opening fire!''

Chapter Thirty-two

THE NEXT week was simultaneously hectic and boring. A few dozen people tried to put their mark on history by playing the peacemaker. They ran back and forth between me and the Crossmen and Henryk, carrying absurd peace offers. None of us took these fools seriously, but none of us wished to appear to be unreasonable warmongers, either. My best offer to them was that if the Crossmen would go back to the Holy Land, where they'd started from, and never come back, I'd call the whole thing off, let them march out with their weapons and treasure, and let them all live, besides. Their best offer to me was less polite.

Bishop Ignacy did a good job getting the noncombatants out of Turon. There were over 500 of them, servants, stable boys, and prostitutes, mostly. He also got us 1,900 horses, all of them in very good shape. It turned out that the Crossmen had sent most of their chargers away before we got there and had kept only the best, because of a lack of hay to feed all of them during a protracted siege. There were a remarkable number of dogs, cats, and caged birds that I paid for, but I drew the line at "pet" rats and mice. They figured that it had been worth a try.

At just before noon on the scheduled day we opened up

on them with our swivel guns, shooting just enough to teach them to keep under cover. Half our guns were available for targets of opportunity, but each one of the other half had its own assigned target: a window, a doorway, a space between two merlons on the wall. They were bore-sighted and packed between sandbags, and in the course of the day, by trial and error, they got their targets down pat. This was to teach the Crossmen the art of not being seen. All through the next night the sandbagged guns fired occasionally at random, teaching the same lesson at night: Stay down! The few slit windows in the outer walls were soon plugged up tight with timbers by the defenders, nicely sealing the entire structure, which was the purpose of the exercise. This stopped the bullets, because this year we were firing cartridges with far less gunpowder than last year's. Six inches of pine could stop our rounds cold. I didn't want to put holes in anything. Quite the opposite.

The random firing continued the next day, except when the gunners actually had a target, an increasingly rare event. Around noon we took a few trial shots with the mortars, using dummy rounds loaded with sand. They did very little damage, but they let us know that our aim was good enough. Small-arms fire continued into the second night, and I was sure that by then the garrison was very low on sleep. An hour before midnight the small-arms fire slackened off.

It was a sultry night and almost completely calm. It would work tonight if it was going to work at all. I had the small-arms fire stop completely and allowed the Crossmen a quarter hour to get to sleep.

Then we opened up with the mortars, firing as fast as their crews could load them, one round a minute each. This continued for only twelve minutes and then stopped. They were out of ammunition, which relieved me. Having that stuff sit around for weeks in the sun and in public made me nervous.

The mortar rounds were a yard in diameter and two yards high. They were made of a thin iron shell with a blown-in glass lining. When the shell struck, the glass broke and the pressurized liquid chlorine inside was released. If the lining broke in the course of being fired, it didn't matter, for the metal shell kept it together long enough to get the poison into the sleeping city.

The delegates were encouraged to watch the shelling, and when it was over, I told them that I thought that we had just won the battle. When they asked me how that was possible, I told them that wars were ugly things and it was best to get them over as soon as possible. Then I suggested that they all go to sleep. Nothing else should happen until morning.

The army troops couldn't sleep, however. At first they stood to their guns with slow flares lit in front of them in case the Crossmen came pouring out of the city. Then they were all standing on top of their war carts in case something far more deadly than enemy troops came pouring out. More of the deadly gas might have leaked out than I had calculated. Chlorine is heavy stuff, almost three times heavier than air. I figured that it should fill the city up to the top of the walls, like soup in a bowl, and hug the ground until it was absorbed by the dew.

The warriors heard a few shouts and screams from the Crossmen, but soon the city was quiet. They had a boring night, but I hadn't told them to come.

I was still across the river, safe from the chlorine. I went back to my big railroad car to sleep. At the doorway of my car a foreign knight waited, standing in the yellow torchlight.

He was dressed in old-fashioned chain mail, though it looked to be washed with gold. There was quite a bit of solid gold on his outfit as well. And there was something very familiar about the man.

"What can I do for you?" I asked.

"I think it is time that we had a talk," he said in Polish but with a strong *American English accent*!

He was identical to the man I had seen killed on the battlefield a year ago, except he had all his hair. He had to be somehow connected to the time machine that had brought me here over ten years earlier.

"Yes," I said. "I would like that. Won't you come in?"

"Thank you," he said, entering and nodding to my servants. "Perhaps it would be best if you dismissed your people."

"Very well." I motioned them all out, and they obeyed.

"Good. I think *here* would be best." He went to my stand-up clothes closet, opened the door, and walked through. The closet was standing along the wall of the car, and there was nothing on the other side of it. In fact, I had just walked past that wall, and I *knew* that nothing had been set up on the other side of it. Yet when I looked into the closet, there was a modern living room in there! It had wall-to-wall carpeting, electric lights, and comfortable-looking leather furniture. There was even a cheerful fire going in a fieldstone fireplace. This was impossible!

I went to the side of the closet, moved it away from the wall, and looked behind it. The back of the closet was solid, and the railroad car didn't have a hole in it. Yet from the front, you could see ten yards into it!

But I wanted to get some answers out of this man, and I dared not turn coward now. I took a deep breath and stepped in. The door closed behind me with a solid click.

"Have a seat, cousin," he said in English. "Surely you recognize me. I'm your rich American relative, Tom Kolczykrenski. I put you through college, remember?"

I sat. "Yes, I remember now, but what are you doing here? And what is *here* doing here?" I said in my rusty English.

"This room, you mean? Well, you must understand that

when you control time, you control space as well. They're really all part of the same thing, you know.''

"No, I don't know."

"Then you will soon," he said. A very beautiful young woman came into the room completely naked, carrying a tray with drinks on it. "Have a martini. I'll bet it's been years since you had an olive."

"Thank you." For ten years a thousand questions had been racking my brain, but at the moment I couldn't think of a single one. "What can I do for you, Tom?"

"Well, it's not what you can do for me but what I can do for you that matters here. You see, in a way it's partly my fault that you were dumped into this barbaric century, and now finally I can do something about it."

The girl left the room, and my eyes followed her.

"Yes, Conrad, my tastes are pretty much like your own. But she's not what we should be talking about. Do you want to ask questions, or should I just tell you about what happened?"

"How about if you talk, and I'll ask questions as they come up."

"Good enough. More years ago than I like to think about, working with two partners, I invented a time machine. That's how we got rich in the first place, you know, playing the stock market with next week's *Wall Street Journal* in our hands. After a while, subjectively, we all grew up a bit, and we each started working on our own projects. I spent my time building a fine, rational civilization in the distant past, where it wouldn't upset our present at all, and Jim did something similar, but with a different slant on things, being a psychologist.

"But Ian's main interest was history, and he runs something called the Historical Corps, which is writing the definitive history of mankind. The Red Gate Inn that you got drunk in so many years ago was one of Ian's installations.

He usually places inns over his time transporters, since strangers aren't much noticed around one. It was some of his people that screwed up, with your drunken help. Instead of finding the rest room, you managed to go down one flight of steps too many and fell asleep in a time transporter. You went through a series of open doors that never should have been open, and even if they had been, the site director should have noticed it on his readouts. But screwups happen, and nobody noticed you at all. More snafu happened at the thirteenth-century end of the line, and you weren't seen sneaking out of the inn."

"What happened to the people who screwed up and sent me here?"

"Oh, they were punished, never fear. Punished more than they deserved, actually. We seem to have lost them a few million years ago in Africa. The search goes on, though."

"So it was all an accident? But if you have time travel, why couldn't you go back to the time I came out of the inn and put me back into the time machine?"

"Because of causality. You were not noticed until I went to observe the Polish defeat at the Battle of Chmielnick. I didn't see you until you had been in this century for almost ten years! I saw you with what was, for this time, advanced technology. That was a fact, and you can't change established facts, or so we thought at the time, anyway."

"At the time?"

"Standard English is not well suited to talking about time travel. We use a few extra tenses to cover it all properly, but there isn't any point in teaching you a new language right now. Suffice it to say that we had been operating for eight hundred subjective years on certain principles that always worked. That's eight hundred years of my own life, as I lived it. Our medical people are quite advanced, you see. Anyway, we *knew* that you couldn't change the time stream.

We *knew* that time was a single, linear continuum and that nothing we could do could possibly change it. Furthermore, from the very beginning, we were very careful not to change things. We didn't want to play God, after all. My partners and I are pretty staunch individualists, but we're not *crazy*! We never tried to see what would happen if we killed off our grandfathers, for example. We're not murderers, after all. Anyway, my grandfathers are both very fine gentlemen, and I wouldn't dream of hurting them.''

"So you're saying that you knew that you couldn't change the past, so you never tried to?" I said. "That's ridiculous!"

"Is it? Tell me, what would happen to an engineer at your old Katowice Machinery Works if he started spending all of his time and the company's money working on a perpetual-motion machine?"

"Why, they'd send him to a mental institution if they didn't fire him first."

"Right. And what if the boss of the outfit started working on the same project?"

"The same thing, I suppose, although they might take more time doing it. Everybody knows that perpetual-motion machines are impossible. They violate the second law of thermodynamics!"

"True. And what if, say, the U.S. government started a major research effort to develop perpetual motion?"

"This is a stupid line of questions. No government would ever do anything like that! The second law is absolutely correct. We've been using it for a hundred years, and it's always right!" I shouted.

"Fine. Then what if I told you that it was possible to build a machine that took in tap water and produced electricity and ice cubes?"

"I'd say that you were lying."

"You'd be wrong. Such a type two perpetual-motion

machine is quite possible, and in fact this 'apartment' that
we're in right now is powered by one. After all, we're in a
temporal loop here, so there's no place we could possibly
put a radiator. Without our 'impossible' power source, it
would get pretty warm in here after a while. What I'm
trying to tell you is that cultures all develop blind spots,
things that they don't even think about because they *know*
the truth about them. Your blind belief in the absurd second
law is a case in point. Something similar on a bigger scale
stopped the ancient Romans from developing science at all,
but that's another story. Suffice it to say that for a time we
fell into the same mental trap, until you shook us out of it."

"It was all my doing?" I asked.

"Correct. You came along and threw all our theories
right out of the window! Do you realize that you have
created an entirely new world here? That you have not only
duplicated most of the eastern hemisphere but that in some
places you have shredded it? Made dozens of worlds? And
that the shredding in some cases went back for thousands of
years?"

"Huh. I think I follow you except for these 'shreds'
going backward in time," I said.

"They can do that if you are taking information, arti-
facts, and people from several parallel timelines back down
to what had been a single line. When that happens, you
shred the past, and oscillations can be set up."

"Oh. Okay. So then the other thirteenth century, the one
in my own past, still exists? I was worried about that," I
said.

"You should have been. You have caused us no end of
trouble and damage. I managed to give you sufficient wealth
for you to survive comfortably until we could pick you up.
You didn't have to tear a hole in the whole universe!"

"Tom, all I did was try to survive. If I've hurt you, well,
I never asked to come here. The fault is yours, not mine."

"You're mostly right. But you could have just left for France and lived a pleasant life. Western Europe was fairly peaceful in this century. You never had to build factories and steamboats!"

"You're saying that I should have abandoned my country to the Mongols? That I should have stood by and watched half the babies born die because of a lack of simple sanitation? What kind of a man do you think I am?"

"I know *exactly* what kind of man you are, Conrad. You're a hero, and you do the things that heroes do. Anyway, we're getting a handle on the time-shredding problem, and things are starting to settle out."

"I still don't understand this multiple shredding that you're talking about. What did I do to start things coming apart?"

"We don't understand it all that well ourselves, and the math is such that even *I* have trouble following it. You see, the world we know isn't just one single world. It's a finite but astronomically large number of worlds, lying close to one another like the pages of a book. These worlds interact with one another and tend to keep one another identical. Philosophically, they are normally one single world with slight variations. As a crude analogy, think of a book that has been left out in the rain and then dried. The pages are wrinkled and dimpled, but they still fit into one another fairly well. That is to say, to a certain extent they interact with one another. What you did was to make two pages pop apart from each other and get some different dimples, to be slightly different from each other. Going down the page, in the direction of the normal direction of time, they continued to separate and become more different. It isn't just one page, though. You seem to have taken half the book with you! In some places, especially around the battlefields, several pages came apart, although they are starting to converge now."

"Somehow, this smacks of the Heisenberg uncertainty principle."

"Uh, sort of, as a theory, although most people misunderstand Heisenberg. He was not saying that a thing can be and not be at the same time. He was only saying that there are limits to what we can know. One of the philosophical stupidities of the twentieth century was the confusion of what we think we know with what actually is, but that's not what we should be talking about now. Yes, there is a divergence principle. Small changes happen all the time between the pages of that ruined book I was talking about. A coin comes up heads or tails, a seed is eaten by a bug or grows into a tree, and so on. It even happens all the time in our own human experience. Have you ever been *sure* that you had your keys in your pocket, only to find out that they were still on your dresser? Well, some of the time you really did *both* put them in your pocket *and* leave them behind.

"You see, there is also a convergence principle operating here, analogous to the force that is trying to force the pages of the ruined book into the same shape. The vast majority of differences are soon smoothed out. In the end, the small changes settle out and make no difference at all. The time line is not so much a monolithic pillar as a rope made of millions of fibers that are all going in the same general direction.

"*Except where you are concerned.* There's something about you, cousin, that makes you different. We don't know what it is, but with you, things don't settle out. The first split that you caused happened a month after you got to this century, when you had to decide whether to abandon a child in a snowy woods or try to save her, even though it looked impossible. Well, you did *both*. And that's the point where you split the world in half!"

"I remember that. I didn't know if it was a boy or a girl, and I christened her Ignacy," I said.

"Right. Now, before we go any further, there's something I need to know. Conrad, I can take you home now. If you want, you can be back at your desk at the Katowice Machinery Works tomorrow morning. Do you want to go?"

Now, that was a kick in the head! Did I want to leave this brutal world and go back to my safe little home? I had to think about it, and Tom was silent while I thought. The serving girl refilled our glasses and left in silence. There was my mother there. How would she take my loss? Yet there were so many people here that needed me, people that I loved. And while I really don't care much about material things, could I go back to standing in lines at the government stores after my loyal troops had slaughtered millions of the enemy? Could I give up my wife and servants, my world-shaping plans, and go back to designing nothing but machine tool controls? Did I really want to become unimportant again? No, by God, I did not!

"I think that I have a better life here, Tom. I'll stay. But try and do something for my mother, okay?"

"I'll do better than that. I'll give her back her son. You see, when you split the world in that snowy woods, you split yourself, too. Your mundane, less heroic self, the one who obeyed his employer and abandoned a child to freeze to death, did not make out as well as you did. I found him in poor straits in Legnica, and he was most eager to go home to his mother. He can warm your chair at the factory and tell himself that it was all some crazy dream."

"Well, that's settled, then. But look, Tom, I have a battle to conduct soon, and the morning is not far away."

"We have all the time we want. It's my stock-in-trade, after all. When you go out that door, not a minute will have gone by in the world outside. Why don't you stick around for a while longer. There's more to discuss, and I'd like you to have a medical checkup while I'm here. If you're tired, there's a spare bedroom with a modern bed, and the wench will get you anything you need.''

"Can I have a cup of coffee in the morning? You can't imagine how many times I've dreamed of a cup of coffee."

"We stock the best."

"Then I'll stay, cousin."

I was deadly tired, and in my years in the Middle Ages I had never gotten around to making a really decent box spring mattress. The girl came out a poor third in my priorities, but then, I really hadn't been offered her.

Chapter Thirty-three

TOM WAS gone the next morning, but he'd left me a note saying that he would be away for a while. The girl served a gorgeous breakfast with maple syrup and real Jamaican Blue Mountain coffee. After that, there were books to read that I hadn't written myself, a good stereo system, and a fine videotape library. Heaven after so many years in the wilds.

I tried repeatedly to strike up a conversation with the serving girl, but no luck, aside from getting her name, which was Maude. She was always smiling, but it was the fixed, artificial sort of smile that you see on a salesman or waitress, not a show of genuine pleasure. At first I thought it odd that Tom should choose such a strange person for a companion. Eventually I realized that she was not a companion in the ordinary sense but just another accessory in this place. She was certainly pretty and very useful, but she seemed to have about the personality of a tape deck. Still, I tried hard to be nice to her, even if she did seem to be emotionally handicapped. As the days went on, I discovered that she responded best when I treated her like Anna, my old mount, with lots of compliments and friendly banter. In time I even tried scratching her behind the ear the way Anna liked, and she smiled with a sort of twinkle in her eye that told me that she was really happy. Although she stayed naked, even of pubic hair, she never made any overt sexual advances, and while I thought that she would not reject mine, I felt it best simply to keep it friendly.

I spent seven days with her in the strange, windowless sealed-off apartment, reading up on all the bits of technology that I had needed and had forgotten or had never learned, listening to good music, and watching all the movies I had missed. It was a marvelously restful vacation, and it gave me time to think.

I got to considering the events of the past ten years, and it slowly sank into me how incredibly successful I had been in modernizing medieval Poland. I had started a primitive country on the way to industrialization and had done it without coercion, without fanaticism, and almost without pain. Looking back, I think we all had a good time doing it.

Compared to the bloodshed and suffering that Russia or almost any other country went through in turning a nation of peasants into a modern society, what I had done had been astoundingly easy and painless. I had gotten us going in ten years, not the fifty or seventy-five years that all the other nations had needed in trying to modernize. And I had done it without any outside help but a pocketful of seeds and the little knowledge that I had in my own head.

I had formulated no dogma, told no one of my long-term plans, and made as few speeches as possible. That is to say, I had made no promises. I had just gone ahead and done the best I could, and that had made all the difference.

When other people tried to change the world, Lenin and his crowd, for example, they started by publishing grandiose promises, outlining their program and claiming that all sorts of wondrous things would come of it if everybody went along in lockstep. They claimed that soon everyone would work only a few hours a week, because these silly academicians thought that work is something that nobody would want to do. Yet with their program, everybody would have free food, free medical help, free vacations, and so forth. They would move mountains, though nobody seems to have asked why a mountain should want to be someplace else.

Well, people are smart enough to notice after a while that magic doesn't happen. If you want more things, you have to make and distribute more things, and that means that at least for the first few generations you have to work harder and more efficiently.

I just offered people a low-paying job with long hours and hard work and did what I could to make that work seem meaningful to them. Once a good man or woman sees that what he is doing is good and important, work becomes a pleasure, one far more enjoyable than any silly game or amusement. The only promise I made was that we would all eat the same, and I didn't really even promise that. I just did it, and enough people responded to get the job done.

I never tried to get everybody into the program. I just took on those who wanted to help and never wasted any energy on the rest. In so doing, I made very few enemies, and I never had to set up a huge, expensive, and hated police force to coerce those who didn't want to take part. The guilds, the nobility, and the Church all went their own ways with my blessings, except for those few occasions when they got in my way. My father told me that it takes all kinds, and I've always believed that.

I never published a vast scheme of things, so I was never blamed for anything when things didn't go right. I made a lot of mistakes, but very few people noticed them, while my successes were fairly obvious.

I am convinced that the reason why things have gone so well is not so much the things that I have done but rather the things that I haven't done.

I've just been an engineer, a simple man with a job to do.

Tom returned one day in time for supper, which was a pile of fresh Maine lobsters with all the trimmings. The apartment had a time locker that was used as a sort of refrigerator. It not only kept things fresh, it could keep them alive. The girl was an amazing cook, even if she couldn't carry on a conversation.

"Where have you been, Tom?"

"Nowhere. I just went into stasis for a few days to give you a small vacation in a bit of the modern world."

"Thank you. I've really enjoyed it, but it's time to talk some more. A few days ago you said that you couldn't come to get me until after the time you saw me at the Battle of Chmielnick. Well, I wasn't at the Battle of Chmielnick. There wasn't any Battle of Chmielnick! I was at the Battle of Sandomierz, and when I was there, I saw you get killed. There was a Mongol spear that went right through your eye and out the back of your helmet. You weren't breathing, and you didn't have a pulse. Do you want to explain these things?"

"It's like I said, the shredding around the battlefields was the worst. Yes, that really was me, and I really did die. It was a me from some other subjective timeline, I hope, although it could possibly be a me from my own subjective future, so I avoid that time slot. As to whether the Mongols were killed at Sandomierz or Chmielnick, well, in a thousand years it won't make any difference. Maybe the historians will argue about it, maybe not."

"Isn't it confusing with a lot of you running around?" I said.

"No more than it is for you. There was one of *you* at Chmielnick, after all. And none of this shredding was ever noticed until you came along."

"Is that why you waited a year after the battle before talking to me? To wait for the shredding to settle down?"

"Yes, of course," he said.

"Then why do you come now on the eve of another battle? Won't that cause problems?"

"This thing with the Crossmen isn't a battle, it's an execution, and they were all dead before you got back to your trailer. But now, if you are through with that chocolate éclair, we'll give you a medical checkup."

In a side room that had been locked before there was a thing that looked like Spock's coffin, with an attached keyboard. In it was a frightening number of mostly concealed tubes, needles, and little knives.

"Are you sure that you know how to work this thing?" I said.

"Relax. It happens that among other thing, I'm a doctor of medicine. In nine hundred years you become a lot of things. Get in."

I didn't love the idea, but I'm supposed to be a hero, so I got in. The lid came down on me, and it got dark, and then the lid came up, and I got out.

"There, that wasn't so bad, was it?" Tom said.

The first thing I noticed was my eyesight. I could see as well as I could when I was a teenager. I put a hand over my left eye, and I could see out of my right. I wasn't half-blind anymore!

"It turned out to be easier to regrow a whole new right eye rather than trying to repair the severed optic nerve. And from there it was only a matter of hitting another button to regrow them both," Tom said. "Your arthritis is gone, along with your hemorrhoids, and so is a small cancer that you didn't know about. Your immunizations have been updated, and I've done a general rejuvenation treatment on you. You look the same, but your ladies will be able to tell the difference."

"Wow. I feel great! You did all that in a few seconds?"

"No, it took me three hours to set it up, and inside the machine's time field you spent four months on the program, or your body did. There wasn't any point in boring your mind with the procedure, so I shut that down for the duration.''

"Huh. Well, thanks, Tom."

"No charge. All part of the service. You've been a pain in the ass, but the trouble you've caused has been the first decent challenge we've seen in centuries. What's more, what you have done is very important. Think about it. A whole new world! A whole doubling of the human experience! As time goes on, this branch will develop its own arts, its own sciences, and its own technologies. What new music will they play, what new insights will they have, what new things will they build? I tell you that there are glorious possibilities here, and we intend to explore them! Maybe we'll even try to split one off for ourselves.''

"Well, don't rush it, Tom."

"We never have to hurry. Well, now, do you feel ready to go back to the world you've created?''

Maude left the room, and I said, "In a minute. Just a few more questions. What is it with this servant of yours? She's one of the strangest women I've ever met.''

"Well, that's why! She's not a woman. She's a bioengineered creation, just like that neohorse I gave you. They were designed in the same studio and have much in common chemically. She's not a modified human if that's what you're worried about. I'd never allow anything like that. Her equivalent of DNA was built up entirely out of simple chemicals, and she was designed to be attractive, industrious, and completely contented with her lot. Human servants are naturally resentful, doing a demeaning job. Wenches work out much better.''

"She has a lot of Anna's traits? Racial memory and all that?''

"Oh yes, along with multiple births and a similar sensory apparatus. She doesn't need a neohorse's remarkable digestive system, though, being designed for a civilized environment, and she can talk, of course, whereas if a horse talked to one of our field researchers, it could get him into trouble. But basically, the two designs are similar except for outward appearance."

"Interesting. I suspected something like that. Another thing. Once my life was saved by some golden arrows coming down out of the sky. Was that your doing?"

"Who else?"

"Who? God, of course."

"Don't be absurd. There's no such thing."

"You're so sure of that? Maybe that's why you can't change the time stream. Have you ever thought of praying?"

"I'm not even going to answer that one, Conrad."

"Huh. One last question. The afternoon before I rode your time machine, I met a girl at a seed store, a redhead. She was supposed to meet me that night, but she didn't. What happened to her?"

"Somehow I knew you'd ask that. She wanted to come, but her installation director got word of a surprise inspection the next day by the assistant secretary for agricultural research. Her whole outfit spent the night cleaning the place and waxing the floors."

"Huh. I'd forgotten what bureaucracies were like."

"If you say so. Don't you know that they do the same thing at your factories before you show up?"

"Perish the thought! I'll put an end to that! Oh, yes. You've been telling me what a wonderful person I am. Could this wonderful person have a present or two to take back with him?"

"Like what? You want the wench?"

"No, I've got plenty of those, and mine are real. Anyway, I doubt if you have one who can speak Polish."

"True."

Maude came back and was waiting attentively.

"Then I imagine that she'd be pretty lonely in Poland. But how about some of that coffee?"

"Fine, I'll have her get all you can carry."

"Thank you. And how about some reference texts, an encyclopedia, for example? And I'd give a lot for a *Handbook of Chemistry and Physics*."

"Are you sure that it would be wise, Conrad? You've made remarkable progress here, mostly because your people have had to think out and solve their own problems. This has put practical working people in charge of things. But when one culture tries to learn from another one, the sort of people who succeed and take control are the academic, unworldly sort, and history has repeatedly proved that it is easier and quicker to invent it all for yourself. I mean it! The United States developed a world-class technology in the fifty years between the Civil War and World War I. It took Japan, Russia, and a dozen other places seventy-five years to do the same thing by copying them, and they had a much harder time doing it. You are progressing just fine on your own."

"If you say so. How about some modern farm animals? Or even just some prize sperm?"

"Same thing. You'll do it better on your own!"

It was a polite no but a no just the same. Well, I tried. Maude came in casually, lightly carrying two huge leather suitcases, almost trunks. I peeked inside one of them, and it was full of freeze-dried instant in vacuum cans. Yet when I picked up the suitcases, it was a strain. That little girllike thing was incredibly strong!

"Well, good-bye, Tom, and thank you again. Keep in better touch from now on."

"Good-bye for a while. I'll be keeping an eye on you, don't worry."

And so I stepped back through the looking glass, or at least my closet. My last view was of the wench smiling at me with that special twinkle in her eye. I closed the door, and when I opened it again, there was nothing there but my clothes.

I called my servants in and went to bed. And yes, the girls could tell the difference in my rejuvenated self! All of them. Several times.

In the morning the weather was still dead calm. I had Sonya bring me a cup of boiling water to show her how to make instant coffee. But packed between two big cans inside the second suitcase was a copy of *The Handbook of Chemistry and Physics*. Maude certainly had a lot in common with Anna and was not the automaton that Tom thought she was. Nice kid!

After enjoying my coffee, I crossed the river. We waited until the sun was fully up, and then I had the siege guns blow down both of the main gates. It took only one round from each of the guns. It wouldn't have taken even that, but the other gunners weren't about to go through the battle without firing a single shot.

The delegates watched all this through the telescopes that Boris Novacek had provided them with—at strictly retail prices, at my insistence and over his earnest objections. Boris figured that we could get away with charging double.

A greenish-yellow gas flowed stickily through the shattered gates, and the gunners ran for high ground as they had been taught. It flowed down the road, through a gutter, and was eventually absorbed into the cool waters of the Vistula.

We waited until the middle of the afternoon, and then Baron Vladimir sent in a few volunteers. They came out saying that the place stank but that the Crossmen were all dead.

They weren't quite right.

After we entered, a group of Teutonic Knights in chain mail and black and white surcoats started shooting crossbows at us from one of the towers. They wounded two men, though not seriously. As he was being carried away, one of them mugged, "What? True belted knights shooting crossbows? How unchivalrous!"

We all laughed.

Then we just fell back and called in the artillery. The gunners had fun knocking down the tower. They were taking bets as to which crew would hit it first. Number six got it on the second round. They still weren't much on accuracy, but what they hit stayed hit.

Then we looted the place. It stank with chlorine but also with the stench of ten thousand unwashed bodies. I decided that the city-fort wasn't worth keeping.

Once we secured the Crossmen treasury, including the money that I'd recently paid them, we allowed the delegates in to look around. They all acted suitably impressed.

After that it was a matter of hauling out the enemy bodies for burial. The churchmen present wouldn't hear of us beheading the Crossmen and putting their heads up on pikes, so we helped them give the bastards a Christian burial. It wasn't the huge cleanup job that we had had to do after the Mongols. After all, we now outnumbered the enemy by almost five to one. There were almost enough of us to act as pallbearers. By dusk the job was completed.

All of this got me an unbelievable amount of flak.

The high churchmen were horrified not so much by the fact that we had killed them but at how easily their feared military monks had been slaughtered. I said that I'd planned it that way and that I was happy that I hadn't lost a single one of my own men.

The military men among the delegates said that this massacre of good knights was an offense against military honor.

I said that there wasn't any such thing as military honor. War is just organized killing, and while a butcher is not necessarily evil, he's no great pillar of mercy, either. Warfare as a sport was out.

And my own troops were the angriest of all. At least they acted that way, knowing me well enough to know that I wouldn't have them shot for speaking up. They had marched all the way to Turon and then had done nothing but wait around. There hadn't even been a fight. I told them that "they also serve who only stand and wait" and furthermore, I'd only wanted to take a single battalion here. They'd invited themselves along, and if they didn't like the party, tough!

But as a sop to them, I told them that I didn't plan to haul all the siege gun ammunition back, and if they wanted to try shooting down the Crossman fort at dawn, after the sunrise services, they were welcome. This got a betting pool going immediately.

The delegates were all still there in the morning, and they watched the target practice. The fort was gone before the ammunition was.

Brick walls are cannonball-degradable.

Eleven thousand four hundred and three Crossmen were killed, and that's in decimal. The accountants figured it out that way because most of the delegates weren't up on the new math.

The treasure taken didn't cover the costs of the war, so we didn't have to worry about dividing it up. We so outnumbered the enemy that you had to be a knight or better to rate a Crossman sword to take home, and many of the men got nothing but a surcoat or a bit of chain mail. But I got the Grand Master's sword and armor to set up in my living room, and his battle flag for my wall.

The delegates monopolized the riverboats for a few days,

going home, and again the army had to wait. Before the boats were free, the construction people got the railroad built down to where Turon had been, and I told the troops to march home. Single file, because there was other traffic on the road.

One battalion of regulars under Baron Josep was left to take command of the former Crossman territories, and they were soon complaining about the lack of adequate housing. That summer they actually had to rebuild Turon out of used brick.

Dammit, I can't be expected to think of everything.

As things were closing down, Francine came to me. She wasn't as icy as she'd been before.

"Conrad, this is a wondrous thing that you have done here, to kill off a great power so casually. All of these great men from so many places, they all respect you and love you and fear you all at the same time! Even Henryk feels that same confused way. They have the honors and the titles, but it is *you* that truly have the power!"

"I'm still only a man trying to do my job, Francine."

"You are far more than that. *You* are the master builder! *You* are the great mover and shaker of all of Christendom! It is *you* that really control and command all things!"

"If you say so. I take it that you are ready to come home now?"

"Of course, my love!"

Within six months Duke Henryk had treaties with Pomerania, Kujawy, nine separate pagan Pruthenian tribes, the kingdom of Hungary, and the Bulgarian Empire, the terms of which were essentially identical to those in our treaty with Prince Daniel of the Ruthenians. Even the pagans said they were willing to become Christians just so long as I didn't get mad at them.

And three months after that, since the Church still didn't

have a Pope, King Bela of Hungary, Tsar Ivan Asen of Bulgaria, and I got together and crowned Henryk King of Central Christendom.

And after that I had an *awful* lot of steamboats and railroad tracks to build.

Interlude Four

THE TAPE wound to a stop. I looked at the wench at my side and wondered just what I had been doing. Enjoying myself with a woman? Making love with an alien? Petting a dog? Whatever it was, I felt uneasy about it. I peeled myself away from her.

"Picking up another bad habit, son?" I looked up, and Tom was there.

"Why didn't you tell me about these servants, Tom?"

"Why didn't you ask me? There are all sorts of things going on around here. For your future reference, all entertainers are human, all servants are constructs, and when in doubt, ask them. If you're worried about offending her, don't. Wenches don't get offended. If you really want to, you can use her sexually. She's physically capable of it, and she'll enjoy it as much as she can enjoy anything. They're not very emotional, you know."

"So she's more of a machine than an animal or a person?"

"If you want her to be. She doesn't really fit into any of the usual categories. She's a chemical construct, self-replicating, servant, household. I supose she's an animal, but a conventional biochemist wouldn't recognize any of

293

the things she's made of. She's simply a perfect personal servant, to be used and ignored. That's not why I'm here.''

"So why are you here, and where have you been?" I said.

"Actually, I've been gone for over a hundred years, subjective, getting a handle on what Cousin Conrad has done. I gave him the garden-variety explanation, and I let you get it off the tape to save time. At nine hundred, I might not have all that much time to waste.''

"You're as healthy as one of your biocritters, and I have a better academic background than Conrad," I said.

"You'll still have to go back to school to pick up on it. For starters, we used to think that the universe had eleven dimensions. Lately, they've proved the existence of four more.''

"Damn. And here I thought I was ready for management.''

"Don't worry about it. In another ten or twenty years you will be, son.''

"Wonderful. Anyway, I'm glad that Conrad worked out so well. It was quite a story.''

"True. But stories never really end, you know. Not when you have a time machine.''

EPILOGUE

ON TOP of a windy cliff in Africa, at about two and a half million B.C., two long-lost members of the Anthropological Corps were sitting and chewing on dried meat as well as their few remaining teeth would allow.

"My eyesight is getting a lot worse," he said.

"Yeah, but my periods have finally stopped," she answered, turning her back to him.

"Then it's finally too late to do the sensible thing."

"The cowardly thing," she said.

"Stuff it," he said, turning his back to her.

"Yeah, stuff it."

There was a shimmer in the air in front of him, high above the valley floor, but his eyesight was so bad that he hardly noticed it. Only when the shimmer resolved itself into a tall, athletic young man and that man started to walk toward him on the clear air did he finally take notice.

"Look," he said.

"Look yourself," she said, unmoving.

"No. I really mean turn around and look."

"What?"

"Turn around, dammit! I think they've finally found us! Can you see him, too?"

She turned and stared at the blond young man who was smiling as he walked through the clean air without visible means of support. There was a lot of gold trim on his well-fitted red and white dress uniform, an outfit that would have looked more at home at a fancy costume ball than high above the ancient African plain.

"He's there," she said, "but he's not one of ours."

"Who cares, just so long as you see him, too, and I'm not crazy! I mean, who cares who saves us or how he does it, just so long as we're saved!"

"Sorry we took so long," the smiling young apparition said, his polished black boots resting on nothing, a few feet from the edge of the cliff.

"You're not one of us," the woman said.

"No, I'm from one of the alternate branches. I'm here on loan, lending a hand. Shall we go? I can have you home in a few moments." He reached out to them.

Fearfully, hesitantly, they reached out and took his hands.

ABOUT THE AUTHOR

Leo Frankowski was born on February 13, 1943 in Detroit. He wandered through seven schools getting to the seventh grade, and he's been wandering ever since. By the time he was forty-five, he had held more than a hundred different positions, ranging from "scientist" in an electro-optical research lab to gardener to airman to chief engineer to company president. Much of his work was in chemical and optical instrumentation and earned him a number of U.S. patents.

His writing has earned him nominations for a Hugo, the John W. Campbell award, and a Nebula, but he didn't win anything.

He still owns Sterling Manufacturing and Design but got tired of design work several years ago and now spends much of his time writing and pursuing his various hobbies; i.e. reading, making mead, drinking mead, dancing girls, and cooking.

A lifelong bachelor, he lives in the wilds of Sterling Heights, Michigan.